Zoey's Place

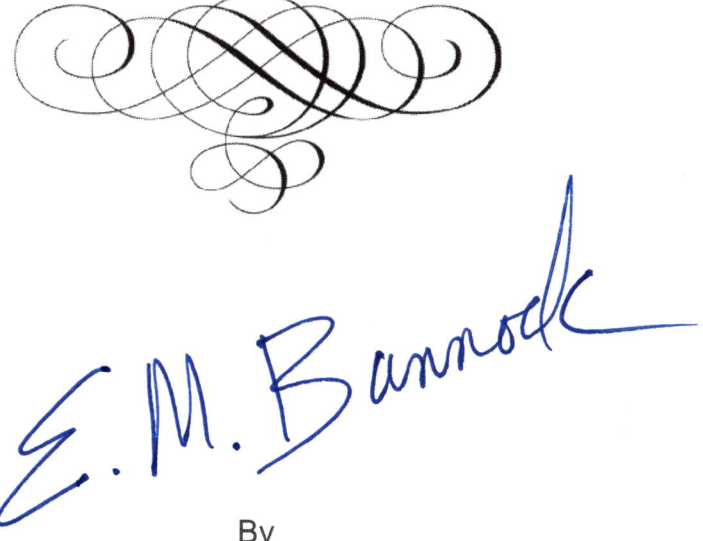

By

E.M. Bannock

ZOEY'S PLACE. E.M. Bannock

Copyright © 2019 E.M. Bannock
All rights reserved.

ISBN: 9781729791738

Cover art by E.M. Bannock
Formatted by Enterprise Book Services, LLC

Cover art formatted by Karen Ronan: www.coversbykaren@gmail.com

This is a fictional work. The names, characters, incidents, and locations are solely the concepts and products of the author's imagination or are used to create a fictitious story and should not be construed as real.

www.embannock.com

No part of this book may be used or reproduced in any manner whatsoever without written permission, except in the case of brief quotations, reviews, and articles. For any other permission please contact E.M. Bannock at embannock@yahoo.com.

First Edition 2019

TO

Keith, Damian,
Sam, and Max

Acknowledgments

I'd like to thank my sister, Annette, who allowed me to use her name for a character who expresses her intelligence and kindness. She was a beta reader and my main cover consultant. Her support and opinions mean more than she knows.

I'd also like to give my thanks to my dear friend, Ande, who did my first edits, made suggestions, read, and reread this book. With her help I was able to turn my thoughts into words.

Thank you to my cousin, Carol, who was my very first book sale. I created the Carol character for you.

Acknowledgements to all of my friends and family whose names I used in this book. You know who you are.

I want to give a shout-out to my fellow Clark, Wyoming Zumba Warriors, especially our fearless leader, Zumba Mama, for letting me bounce ideas off them while we danced.

Most of all I'd like to thank my husband, Keith, for his constant support both emotionally and financially. Thank you for the encouragement to pursue my dream.

PART ONE: LOVE

Chapter 1

It was early evening. A scarlet sunset had faded into muted grey tones. The shimmering reflection of the moon danced on the surface of the lake as the lovers emerged naked, hand in hand. They'd worked all afternoon in the sizzling sun, cutting the overgrown weeds that choked out the yard and beach of the lake house, and their bodies were hot, sweaty, and dirty. It seemed natural to strip off their clothes and cool off with a quick dip.

The week-long summer vacation was well deserved. Zoey and Mickey DeLucca were both hard-working, successful attorneys. He was a corporate lawyer who'd just landed a high paying job with a large oil development company. She specialized in family law and preferred representing men. Fathers rarely got a fair shake in divorce court. It was tough breaking the tradition of the courts that defaulted child custody to the mother without considering the best interest of the child. Although she had only been in practice a few years she had already seen her fair share of unfit mothers and was proud of her track record. It was a challenging job, but she was good and thrived on it.

Their friends were set to arrive later that night with food and drink. Zoey and Mickey's contribution was to arrive at the lake house early and get it ready for the week-long festivities. The cabin was cleaned from top to bottom. Windows were opened to replace the stale air of winter with the fresh, fragrant air of early Michigan summer. Crisp, clean sheets were put on all the beds. Bathrooms were cleaned and fresh towels laid out. Cutting down the weeds was the last labor of the day.

An afternoon of sexual teasing had added an element of excitement to the chore. She'd let the strap of her tank top fall to the side, exposing the top of her breast more than once to see if he noticed, only to pull it up quickly when he did. She'd also purposely bent over in front of him, her apple-bottomed ass protruding below her way-too-short cut-off jeans. Sometimes he'd get behind her as she was bending over, grab her bottom with both hands, and pull her to him. She could feel his hot, hard cock rubbing against her through his jeans. Their sexual anticipation mounted as the work got done but they kept on-task, letting the heat of passion rise in them like the blistering sun that beat down as they toiled.

The sweat streamed down their bodies in rivulets, making their clothes stick to their skin. His well-muscled chest and arms glistened with perspiration on his dark Mediterranean skin as he worked, giving proof to his fitness commitment. The firmness and strength of his body was undeniable. She hungered for the feel of it next to her as she watched him wield the machete, cutting down the tall thick weeds, blushing when he'd catch her staring. He'd act annoyed and tell her to get back to work but she'd seen him smiling with pride when she looked.

The coolness of the water cleansed and refreshed their bodies, but did nothing for the sexual heat that burned from inside. They lay down on the blanket spread out on the sand as they dripped with water. Facing each other, their bodies touched. His fingers tenderly traced the outline of her face, sending waves of sexual electricity down her spine.

They embraced tenderly. She reached up and held his face in her hands, his dark hair falling in front of his eyes, his brown eyes piercing her very soul. They kissed. Gently at first, but their passion rose. Their kisses became intense, tongues teasing, exploring each other's bodies with curious hands, breaking apart only long enough to catch their breath.

Pushing her back onto the blanket, he positioned himself between her thighs. Leaning forward, he grabbed her wrists with one hand and held them over her head. With his other he guided himself into her, kissing her lightly as he did.

The aromatic bouquet of freshly cut weeds and the earthy smell of the lake intoxicated their senses and added to the musk of their lovemaking. They were serenaded by a choir of crickets, night-flying birds, and the melodic tempo of waves crashing on the shore.

Darkness set in by the time they were satisfied. In the afterglow they lay side by side, staring up at the stars. In an instant, the sky lit up like a torch as a meteor blazed its way across. He said, "Make a wish." She closed her eyes and wished that the happiness of the moment would never end.

"What did you wish for?" he asked as she opened her eyes.

"I wished that we could be like this forever, like we

feel in this place, right now," she replied. "We are in a good place right now aren't we, Mickey?"

"The best, babe," he confirmed. "Zoey's place."

They turned to each other and kissed once more.

They lay there holding each other, basking in the joy of love and treasuring the moment. Suddenly the bushes that edged the driveway lit up as the headlights of an approaching car appeared, winding around the long driveway.

"Oh, my God! They're here!" she exclaimed, and they scrambled for their clothes.

Mickey stood up, laughing as he pulled up his shorts. "I'll head 'em off. You grab the blanket and take it to the house," he said as he pulled up his zipper.

The car made the final turn and illuminated the cabin as it approached. Their friends Joanne, Lenny, Carol, and Dave were laughing as they exited the vehicle.

"Did we catch you with your pants down again?" Lenny yelled out. The others were laughing as they grabbed bags and personal items from the car.

"You guys still fuck like a couple of high-schoolers," Dave added.

Mickey stood proudly with his hands on his hips. "Nothing wrong with that," he yelled back, grinning from ear to ear.

"You've been married for over three years. You're not on your honeymoon anymore," Lenny replied.

"Yeah, you make the rest of us look bad," Dave added.

"I think it's romantic, Mickey," Carol chimed in. Joanne nodded in agreement.

"Now that you've got your dick back in your pants, come and help us get this stuff to the cabin," Lenny said.

The women headed inside with bags of groceries, leaving the men to empty the rest of car. Zoey greeted them at the door with hugs and kisses.

She'd been a freshman at the University of Michigan when she was introduced to the five sophomores. She had met Joanne's brother, Jonathan, in her English Composition class. He invited her to come to a club with him, where she met Joanne, Lenny, Carol, and Dave, who were already couples, and their friend, Mickey.

As the introductions were made, she was told that Dave, Lenny, and Mickey grew up together in suburban Detroit and were best friends. They seemed nice, and friendly enough. Then she was introduced to their friend, Mickey. When their eyes met it, was all over.

The celestial spark of their love had been lit. From the start it felt like they had known each other forever. It was a strange, powerful feeling for both. The attraction was magnetic and undeniable; bad news for Jonathan, but good news for Mickey. There were no hard feelings. Jonathan and Zoey weren't really on a formal date, and although they liked each other as friends it was obvious from the start that the chemistry wasn't there for anything more than friendship.

After a few romantic dates, Zoey and Mickey became a couple. The three couples became a group. They did everything together—study, go to concerts, clubs, restaurants, movies, and take road trips. They enjoyed each other's company and formed a family-like bond.

But lately the demands of their busy lives kept them from socializing as much as they did in college, so the vacation at the lake house had become an annual tradition. Its seclusion gave them all a welcome respite from their jobs, and gave them a chance to catch up and tighten the friendships.

Within an hour everyone was unpacked and dinner was served. After a meal of chicken casserole and a variety of salads the girls had made for the late-night meal, the six friends sat around the large wooden table in the dining area, drinking wine, beer, and other beverages.

"Congrats on the new job, Mickey," Lenny said, raising his beer to toast.

"Thanks," Mickey said, blushing as he tapped his beer bottle to Lenny's.

"Now that you'll be making the big bucks, will you have time for us lowly peons?" Dave asked sarcastically. He had gone into medicine and was doing his residency at a small family clinic where Carol was the assistant office manager. Lenny had majored in Business Administration and was a manager at a large chain store. Joanne had become a teacher.

"Don't worry," Mickey said. "How could I forget my childhood pals and college brothers whose backs I stepped on to get to the top?" Everyone laughed.

"So, Zoey, are you going to quit your job and go globe-trotting with your hubby?" Carol asked.

Zoey looked at Mickey, who looked back with a serious expression. "He wants me to, but I just can't. There are too many men out there getting screwed over by their exes, and too many kids who might end up with the wrong parent," she replied. "And besides, he's going to be traveling to places where women have to wear burkas or hijabs. Can you just imagine me taking a submissive role or covering my head?"

Everyone laughed and shook their heads. "She thinks it's her civic duty," Mickey added.

"Well, we admire your commitment," Joanne said. "We're all proud of you, both of you. But when will you have time to raise a family?"

Zoey and Mickey looked at each other for a long while as their friends waited in anticipation. Mickey spoke up. "We've decided we don't want kids."

Their friends let out a sigh of disbelief. "But you'd be perfect parents—caring and loving," Carol said.

Zoey broke in. "We don't need kids to be a happy couple and live a fulfilling life. Besides, with Mickey's new job he'll be traveling, and I'm so busy with my case load. We don't even have time for a pet, let alone children. I've seen what happens when parents don't have enough time for kids. It ain't pretty. I'll live vicariously through you guys. Between the four of you there will be enough kids to go around."

Lenny and Joanne looked at each other and smiled. Zoey noticed and asked, "Okay, what's up you two? Is it starting already?"

"You got us," Joanne said with excitement in her eyes. "I'm pregnant."

The women squealed with excitement and gathered around Joanne, hugging her and patting her belly.

"Way to go!" Dave exclaimed as he raised his beer in Lenny's direction.

"Good job, my man," Mickey added, raising his beer as well.

"See," Zoey said. "I rest my case."

"Do you realize this is the last year that it will just be the six of us here?" Joanne said somberly.

"Wow, that's right," Zoey said.

"How long have we been doing this?" Lenny asked.

"Well, let's see," Mickey said as he scratched his head in thought. "I inherited this place after my dad passed away in '81 in our junior year at University of

Michigan. That was the year Zoey and I got married." He paused in pleasant contemplation for just a moment before continuing. "We started coming up here the year after that. So, since it's now 1987, that makes it six years."

"The end of an era," Lenny said sadly.

"And the beginning of a new one," Carol added as she gave Joanne another hug.

The women moved into the kitchen area and started chatting about baby showers and other baby-related topics like names and nursery décor.

The guys grabbed their beers and walked out to the porch. "Did you guys see *Untouchables* yet?" Dave asked. "I saw it playing at the movie theater in town. I've been dying to see it."

"I saw that, too. I've heard Kevin Costner is pretty good in it," Lenny added. "Don't know if the girls would like that kind of stuff, though. I think they might go for the *Witches of Eastwick*. I saw that playing there, too."

"Maybe we'll ask the girls and see if they're up for it. I'd really like to see *Untouchables* myself. I saw a preview. Looked really cool," Mickey said. "Zoey might go for it. Maybe they'll just want to gab all night. You know them. They haven't been together for a while. And now with the news of Joanne being pregnant I'll bet they could go on all night." The guys shared a laugh.

"It's probably out for tonight," Mickey said. "We've got the whole week, though, so who knows."

"So, Mickey," Lenny said. "What are you gonna be doing in your new job?"

"Well, negotiating contracts mostly, and a lot of PR," he replied. "The company I work for is working with OPEC countries. There's a big push for global economics. We don't want another oil embargo to happen and catch us with our pants down again."

"Yeah, that was hell," Lenny said.

"Isn't it dangerous there? I mean, they still don't trust the U.S.," Dave pointed out.

"I'll have hired protection while I'm there," Mickey said. "I'll spend most of my time here in the U.S. I'll just have to go there for meetings and certain political and social events," he assured them.

"Well, watch your ass, man," Lenny added. "I don't trust them."

"Don't worry," Mickey said. "They're just as addicted to our money as we are to their oil."

Chapter 2

Zoey's childhood had been tumultuous and lonely. She was born in 1960, in San Francisco, to Sally and Lyle Findley. She didn't remember much about her earlier years. But she did remember the huge fight her parents had when she was about eight, which resulted in her mother and her moving out. It was the beginning of the hippie movement and Sally, a free-spirited woman, wanted to join a commune that some of her friends were starting. Lyle was more traditional and didn't think that it was a good environment to raise his daughter in. A defiant Sally moved into the commune, and filed for divorce and custody of Zoey. Lyle fought hard to keep his daughter. He spent every dollar he had on attorneys, but in those days custody was always awarded to the mother.

Zoey saw her father twice a month on weekends and two weeks in the summer. She had always been a daddy's girl. He called her his little princess—made her feel special and loved. The separation was very hard for her. She adored her father, and couldn't understand why she couldn't live with him all the time. After her visitations she would cry and cling to him, beg him not to make her go back to the commune. She hated it there. All the women wanted her to call them "Mommy". They insisted that she obey them as she would her own mother, and Zoey didn't like that. She missed her daddy and the family life that had been taken from her. Zoey always had the feeling that her mother resented her because of Lyle's attentiveness to her, and as a result Sally never seemed loving, as a mother should be.

One day Zoey asked her mother why she didn't act like she loved her. Her mother said of course she loved her, but explained that it wouldn't be right if she showed Zoey special favoritism over the other kids. They were all one family. She had lots of brothers and sisters now.

Zoey didn't like the answer. She'd never asked for brothers or sisters and, because she was the oldest, when anything went wrong she was always blamed. Zoey felt abandoned, and withdrew. Trying to stay out of sight whenever she could.

The worst part was all the creepy men who lived in the house, a constantly changing cast of characters. The commune members believed in free love, and seeing her mother kiss the other men just seemed wrong. She never knew which 'daddy' she was going to see coming out of her mother's room in the morning. It should have been her daddy and no other. Zoey came to have hard feelings about her mother, and their already strained relationship became non-existent.

It wasn't until she was fourteen that she was finally able to live with Lyle full time, and that was only because she had starting to mature into a young woman and some of the men in the commune began to express sexual interest in her. One day one of her 'daddies' cornered her in a back storage room, kissed her on the lips, and fondled her budding breasts. She managed to wriggle out of his grasp and run out of the room. When she told her mother about it she was called a liar.

As soon as she could she told her father about it, and he was outraged. At the end of his next weekend visitation he called Sally and told her that Zoey wouldn't be coming back. Further, Lyle informed Sally, she was damn lucky he didn't call the cops and have her pervert boyfriend arrested. He also told her he had a good mind to come over there and beat the shit out of him, and if she ever tried to contact Zoey, he would make good on his threats. Happily, Zoey never saw her mother again.

Determined to start a new family life together, Lyle took Zoey to Michigan. They lived in a small apartment in Detroit close to where Lyle got an assembly line job at the Ford Motor Company. Life was hard, but he did the best he could to provide a decent life and a happy late childhood for his daughter.

Zoey had never made friends in school because she was embarrassed about her life. She didn't want to tell anyone about her mother. Then, one month before she was set to graduate from high school, Lyle was killed in an accident at work. She felt cheated, only having had a few years with her father. Zoey had already been accepted at the University of Michigan, and intended to study law after she got her undergraduate degree in social work. She wanted to help men get custody of their children if it was in the better interest of the child, and fight to change the current trend. Lyle was very proud of her.

When she tried to contact her mother to tell her of Lyle's passing, she found out that her mother had died a year earlier from pneumonia. Zoey felt nothing at this news, and remembered how horrible it was when her parents were divorcing and her father's futile battle to keep her. His death was a hard blow but she pulled herself up, accepted this hard knock, and did what her father would have wanted her to do: go to college and become a lawyer to change the world in a way she knew mattered. She wanted to make a difference to honor the memory of her father and the difference he'd made in her life.

For years, a small part of every paycheck Lyle received had gone to a separate bank account set aside for Zoey's college education. She was planning on taking out student loans to cover the rest of the expenses, but Lyle had named Zoey his beneficiary on his life insurance policy, and after his accidental death she had more than enough for college.

The experience of her childhood left a bitter taste in her mouth and made her determined not to have kids. She had no real example of what a good mother should be, and she didn't want to risk falling in love with the wrong man and having to put her kids through what she went through. She didn't even think she would ever fall in love, let alone get married, but that part at least changed the night she met Mickey.

*****

Mickey grew up in an upper middle class family in suburban Detroit. His parents, Ida and Nicolai DeLucca, were first-generation Italian immigrants. The little family lived a very comfortable happy life.

Mickey enjoyed being an only child. He always had the latest toys, the nicest clothes, and more Christmas presents than his friends with siblings. They always had share toys, wear hand-me-down clothes, and never seemed to go on the kind of luxurious vacations Mickey's parents had taken him on. Like trips to Disneyland as a child, and when he was older, a dude ranch in Wyoming, vacations in Niagara Falls, Yellowstone, and Glacier National Parks, a week at the beach in Hawaii, a Caribbean cruise, even a trip to England, France, and Italy.

Mickey's parents were older when he was born. They had never planned to have children and always called him their mid-life surprise. But they loved him dearly, and he them. As he got older he realized the carefree, lavish lifestyle they gave up to raise him. He had decided early that he wanted to live like they did when he got older; before they had him, of course. He didn't think he would make a good father, and really had no desire to try. He enjoyed life and the finer things it could provide. He knew that he would have to get a good education and a good job. That meant long hours and dedication. He really didn't think it would be fair to a child to have an absentee father. He just wasn't cut out to be a dad.

His parents were also nudists. They were unashamed of their bodies and instilled that philosophy in their son. Mickey was taught that the naked body is a thing of beauty. He learned the proper names of body parts. Men have a penis. Women have a vagina and breasts. Everyone has an anus. Mickey's parents frequently walked around nude, and so did he when he was growing up. Every summer they visited the local nudist colony. It was no big deal. So, when he reached puberty, the female body was not such a mystery.

When Mickey saw Zoey's slender, 5'6" frame sashay into the bar that night, he took notice. He was mesmerized by her shoulder-length auburn hair.

When he was introduced to her and looked into her sparkling hazel eyes he was hooked. She had smooth alabaster skin and full, pouty lips. He leaned in to shake her hand and was intoxicated by her subtle perfume. Her touch was electrifying. He knew she was the one. He was in love, and had to have her.

As they got to know each other that night they found that they shared very similar philosophies, even though they had come to the common conclusions via very different circumstances. This included the decision to not have children. They began to date.

It wasn't long after they started having sex that they discovered they had an insatiable craving for it. Neither was a virgin when they met but had only had casual sexual relations before, never feeling comfortable enough with their partners to go beyond the norm in the bedroom. In fact, Zoey had always held back before Mickey, never able to completely trust a partner after her first sexual experience in the commune. Zoey and Mickey hungered for each other's bodies. They felt free and uninhibited with each other. Mickey teased that they fit together like pieces of a jigsaw puzzle. Sex was enjoyable and it felt natural to experiment with various positions, sexual aides, and role-playing. It became almost a hobby. Whenever they traveled they would always check to see if there was a local sex shop. They loved going to the stores together to buy objects for their ever-growing collection.

After two years of dating they married. Shortly after that, Zoey had her tubes tied. It seemed like the logical thing to do.

Chapter 3

Zoey sat at her desk and picked up the folder in front of her. She reviewed the forms inside that her staff had prepared, making sure everything was correct before they were filed at the courthouse. Setting it down, she put her hands over her face and rubbed her tired eyes. She reflected briefly how her chosen lifestyle was so perfect for her long work hours and Mickey's travel schedule, both as demanding of time as raising a child.

Through the years, as Mickey climbed the corporate ladder, his job duties took him away from home more often, sometimes six weeks at a time. The pay had increased exponentially but, in her eyes, it was small compensation for being separated from her beloved husband. This trip had Mickey gone for almost a month already, and she missed him. She tolerated the long periods away by immersing herself in her work. However, she couldn't help but miss his touch on her body, their lovemaking, his manly musk, his embrace. This was one of those times. He would be home in one week. The anticipation was almost more than she could bear.

Both had excelled in their selected field and were enjoying the fruits of their labor. They still lived in Michigan but moved from their small suburban home in Ann Arbor to a spacious home in Birmingham, an upscale suburb of Detroit. Their first home in Ann Arbor served its purpose. It was close to the U of M campus and was a convenient location while attending college. It was the hangout for their friends who lived in dorms or on campus during their college days. After graduation everyone seemed to gravitate towards the suburban Detroit areas. That's where the jobs were. Since both Zoey and Mickey were only children of only children parents and both sets of parents had already passed on, their friends were their family, and they wanted to stay close to them. So it seemed natural to move where they did.

It was easy to like Birmingham. It had an abundance of culture. To unwind, Zoey went to the Robert Kidd Gallery. Its founders, Robert Louis Kidd and Ray Frost Fleming, had both graduated from local Cranbrook Academy of Art. She enjoyed seeing the work of the young aspiring artists on display there and Cranbrook was close, just a stone's throw from Birmingham in neighboring Bloomfield Hills. It also provided her with a quiet place to view fine art. And if she really felt like seeing art, she was close enough to the Detroit Institute of Art downtown, where she could see the works of the masters.

She often thought that if she hadn't been an attorney, she would have been an artist. There were times at U of M when she debated whether she should major in art or to further her goal of family law. She loved her law work, but wondered if she would have been an even better artist. She appreciated all forms of art and sometimes, when stressed out, she unwound by wandering the galleries for hours on end.

She looked at the group picture of her friends framed on her desk. It was the last summer vacation at the lake house with their best friends before life got complicated. Mickey started his new job and her friends started having babies in rapid succession. Joanne and Lenny had two boys: Francis, who liked to be called Franky, and their younger son, Sam, who was born two years later. Carol and Dave quit after having the twins Mary and Betty, born a year after Sam. Mickey and Zoey felt honored to be referred to as Aunt Zoey and Uncle Mickey by their friends' kids. They had fun watching them grow up. It was the perfect relationship, and they felt privileged to be part of it. They could spoil the kids all they wanted and return them to their respective parents when done.

Zoey attended every birthday party, school play, and awards ceremony of the kids, and if Mickey was home he went, too. Christmas was always a shared joy. Shopping for them was so much fun. Every year Zoey took all the kids shopping for gifts for their parents. It was a crazy day full of commotion and confusion. She picked up the tab, of course. Joanne and Carol told her she was insane for taking all the kids at the same time, but Zoey loved it. It was fun but only because it was one day a year. The thought of adding the 24-hour responsibility of being a parent to her hectic schedule gave her shivers. The chaos and disorder of the day only reaffirmed that her decision to remain childless was the right one as she dropped them off at home and retreated to her calm, quiet house.

After the kids got old enough, during the summer when Mickey was traveling, Zoey would have sleepovers with Mary and Betty. She would treat them to a trip to the beauty salon for haircuts, manicures, and pedicures. The night would end with both girls snuggled in bed with her, eating ice cream while they watched the latest princess movie checked out from the video store.

For Franky and Sam, the sleepovers included a trip to the toy store and an afternoon at the park, bowling, or whatever they wanted to do. Usually Mickey was home and he would toss a ball around with the boys and grill hot dogs or burgers for dinner. Their selected rental movie was always some horror flick or one with an action hero. They ate their share of ice cream as well. The boys slept in the guest bedroom, but Zoey noticed that they always made sure the night light was on.

It was rare that all the friends could manage one dinner a year together now. The annual summer week at the lake house was just a memory. The old family cottage had been in constant need of repair as it aged, so they sold it. Now they had a vacation home in Incline Village on the Nevada side of Lake Tahoe. They called it the cabin but it was really a 3,400-square-foot, three-bedroom, three-bath home; actually quite small by Incline Village standards. The 'cabin' wasn't right on the lake but it could be seen easily from the living room window, and enjoyed in all forms of weather from inside.

Mickey and Zoey could ski in the winter and golf or swim in the summer. They enjoyed doing all three, as well as hiking in the wooded mountains. Sometimes they rented a boat just to be alone and make love out on the vast, open expanse of Lake Tahoe.

Mickey did a lot of business with foreign customers in Las Vegas, which was just a short plane ride away. It constantly amazed Zoey that so many of the clients loved to go to Vegas. She figured it was the fast-paced gambling, half-naked women running around, and the party lifestyle that was forbidden and so different from the lives they had in Saudi Arabia or whatever Middle Eastern country they were from.

Most of the time she stayed at the cabin when Mickey went to Vegas with his clients. It was peaceful and quiet, and as beautiful in summer as it was in winter. It served as their own little hideaway, and she loved it there. The house was set back off the road and was accessed by a winding drive. The two-acre lot was thickly wooded, which gave them total privacy. This suited Mickey just fine, as he liked to walk around the back patio naked. It was their personal Shangri-La, the one thing in their lives that was just theirs. Mickey called it Zoey's Place because she was always so happy and at peace there. They never brought company to their hideaway.

Life in Birmingham was different in so many ways from the simple life they had led in Ann Arbor. It was much better now. They could afford to shop at the expensive stores. They hired people to do the landscaping. No more thrifty old Hondas and VWs to be cobbled together until they died to save a penny. Now Mickey and Zoey bought the cars they had always wanted: a BMW convertible for Mickey and a Mercedes sedan for Zoey. They also had a Land Rover and another Mercedes in Incline Village.

Zoey always hated housework and now had a housekeeper named Stella, a patient, hard-working woman with three kids of her own, do it for her. Stella's husband had a good job working for the Ford Motor Company, and her job with Zoey was just to have extra cash. She came in to clean twice a week and do the laundry.

When Zoey was home alone it seemed like a waste

of money, but when Mickey was there Zoey felt like she should pay Stella double. He never did learn to pick up his clothes or put things away and, although he thought of himself as somewhat of a gourmet chef and loved to surprise her with homemade dinners, by the time he was through it looked like the kitchen had been hit by a tornado. Stella never complained. When they entertained it was always catered, with Stella in charge. The arrangement took a lot of pressure off Zoey, and Stella enjoyed it.

Most of the time Zoey and Mickey had dinner out. She loved the selection of specialty restaurants close by. That was one of the reasons they chose Birmingham. The restaurants accommodated them at all hours of the day or night, and they were on a first-name basis with most of the owners and chefs. Funny what money could do. They never had to wait for a table, and most of the chefs were in competition to come up with new and exciting dishes for them.

They traveled extensively, thanks to Mickey's job. In the last twenty years Zoey had been to Spain, Italy, France, England, Ireland, Scotland, Norway, Russia, Australia, and a quaint little island country called Malta in the Mediterranean, not to mention all the destinations in the U.S. When Mickey was in town, they spent New Year's Eve skiing at the Incline Village house. It was always a great time, and the winter landscape there was breathtaking.

Mickey had been to many more countries than Zoey. Some of them just didn't hold any interest for her. She didn't care for the Middle Eastern countries and didn't like going there. She did venture to Saudi Arabia once and a few other Middle Eastern countries a handful of times. She hated the way they treated women and how she had to cover her head with a hijab whenever she was in the presence of men, even though it wasn't law. Mickey's company said it showed respect. She was told that a Muslim man could not look at a woman unless he was married to her, and that shaking hands with one was unheard of. Being unseen and not heard was not Zoey's style at all. She was used to being part of the conversation and having her opinions respected.

She thought it was so hypocritical because, when the men visited the U.S., Mickey was always expected to get them hookers. Most of the time it meant that he had to fly them to Nevada where prostitution is legal. Technically it was not legal in the city of Las Vegas, but with Mickey's connections he always found suitable 'escorts'. Zoey was always suspect as to their actual thoughts when the men were so polite to her face in the States, knowing the social mores back home. More hypocrisy, she felt.

She used to wonder if Mickey ever had an 'escort' as well, and asked him once. To answer her he grabbed her ass, squeezed it hard, and kissed her passionately as he pulled her close. "How could anything be better than what I've got at home? Don't worry, baby. This," he said as he grabbed her hand and pressed it against his hard penis, "is only for you. I promise." He had never lied to her before, and she had no reason to doubt him then. With that, he picked her up and carried her into the bedroom to show her just how much he loved her.

Zoey was getting wet just thinking about that time. It had been almost a month since she and Mickey had had sex, and she was horny with excitement over their planned reunion. It seemed that those were the most passionate times. Sometimes they would spend all day in the bedroom, only coming out long enough to answer the door when food was delivered. The couple had been married over twenty years but their lovemaking was still fresh, hot, and exciting.

That was the hardest part about being away from him. They spoke on the phone a couple of times a week. Hearing his voice was a comfort, but she missed the touch, feel, and smell of him, and especially the physical closeness of sex.

Through the years of marriage they always kept the spark of excitement alive in the bedroom. Both were still adventurous and, between the two of them, it was just about anything goes. If they liked it, they added it to their repertoire. If they didn't, it was a one-time deal. They had tried almost all the positions of the Kama Sutra. Some they passed on because it seemed that only contortionist could get into the twisted positions. They experimented with toys of all kinds, a little SMDS, role-playing, and porn.

They weren't afraid to masturbate in front of each other. In fact, Zoey found that particularly erotic. She loved watching Mickey's muscular arm pump as he slid his hand up and down on his erect shaft. She loved seeing the pleasure on his face when his eyes closed, concentrating on his gratification. Perspiration beading up on his forehead as he bit his lower lip and exploded in orgasmic bliss.

Her sexual recollection was interrupted by the buzz of the intercom on her desk. She picked up her phone. "What is it, Annette?" she asked.

Annette Barrand was her personal assistant and office manager. She had applied for the position right after graduating from Oakland Community College with an Associate degree in Business Administration. She was born and raised in the general vicinity, and had a feel for the people who lived there.

Annette was plain-looking by most standards, with

wavy, dirty blonde hair that swished around her face like a gentle breeze. It was never really quite styled, it just hung there. It brushed past her shoulders and fell wherever it pleased. It suited her. She had sparkling blue eyes that made you feel you could trust her. She dressed modestly, but with no particular flair for style or femininity. She usually wore slacks. Although meticulous in her looks, she was not pretentious. She didn't wear makeup, just a little lipstick to give her face color. She was rather tall, at least 5'9". Annette spent a great deal of time at the gym and was in prime shape. She could take care of herself.

Annette lived in Berkley and had worked part time at the construction company Zoey hired to do the renovations on the building she had just leased for her office. Annette was looking for a full time job, something the construction company decided they couldn't give her. It was a thriving business, and it puzzled Zoey when they refused to hire Annette full time after graduation. After she got to know the situation, she had a sneaking suspicion the only reason they didn't hire Annette was because she'd announced to the world that she was a lesbian. Annette took a chance and asked Zoey for the job. The two women hit it off right away and Zoey hired her.

She found Annette to be competent, trustworthy, and loyal. She had good people skills and made Zoey's clients feel at ease and important. Zoey always knew the office was in good hands when she was traveling or was otherwise away. Annette managed the two legal clerks who also worked in the office. Zoey paid Annette well, but she earned it.

Annette was able to start working for Zoey the day she put out her shingle. Zoey opened her modest office in Berkley, a peaceful, middle-class city close to

Birmingham, because she felt it would be less intimidating for clients to come there rather than Birmingham. Her hourly rate was half of what most divorce attorneys charged. She felt the process of divorce was traumatic enough without adding to the devastation with an outrageous bill for legal services. And Mickey made enough money for them both. She really didn't have to work, but she wanted to.

This allowed her to be selective in the clients she chose to represent. She was aware that there were plenty of good mothers and an abundance of deadbeat and unfit dads out there, and if she truly felt shared custody was in the best interest of the child, she negotiated for it. Although she never represented women, she also didn't represent men she considered unqualified as a parent. Annette had a nickname for this type of man, referring to them as 'dick-heads'. They were never welcome in the law office.

"Joanne Morgan is on line one. She said she needs to speak with you."

That was strange. Joanne never called her at work. It had been several months since the two women spoke. She hoped it wasn't bad news. "I'll take it, Annette. Thank you." She pressed the blinking light that connected her to line one. "Joanne, good to hear from you. Why are you calling on my business line? Is everything all right?"

"Oh, Zoey, I'm so glad you're in. No, everything isn't all right. It's Jonathan. His marriage just fell apart and we need you." Joanne began sobbing uncontrollably.

Sadness filled Zoey's heart. Jonathan had married late in life, barely two years prior. Mickey had flown in so that they could attend the wedding.

Jonathan had become a good friend. He was a handsome, smart guy with a great job at GM. He married a girl he met in Florida on vacation with friends just six months before. Her name was Rhonda Kruger. All Zoey knew about her was what Joanne told her at the wedding. Ronnie, as she liked to be called, came from a dysfunctional family in Pasco County, Florida. Her mother was an alcoholic and her father was always running around on his wife. Ronnie told Joanne that her father used to sleep with the single mothers of her high school friends, and a few married ones, too. The first time Zoey saw her was at the wedding, and she remembered the strange vibe she got from her. There was something about her eyes, shifty or sneaky, something that made Zoey feel uneasy. She didn't trust her. She only saw her a handful of times since then, holidays and Jonathan's and her son's baptism, and every time Zoey got the same vibe.

Rhonda was cold and impersonal and made no attempt to befriend Zoey, even though she knew that Zoey and Mickey were long time family friends. Joanne had always blamed it on Rhonda's upbringing. "She's had a rough life," she would defend. "She doesn't know what family is all about. Give her time. She'll warm up to us." This told Zoey she still hadn't 'warmed up' to Joanne and Lenny.

Planned or not, Rhonda was two months pregnant when she married Jonathan. She worked as a bartender at a dive bar in Livonia, close to Joanne and Lenny's house, and didn't stop working until the baby was born. She went back to work three weeks later. Joanne didn't like the fact that Rhonda smoked cigarettes, and even though she told Joanne she quit she was still exposed to second-hand smoke at the bar. Joanne was equally upset by Rhonda's drinking.

She swore she quit drinking, too, but considering she drank to excess at her wedding, knowing she was pregnant, Joanne doubted that she could be sober working as a bartender. Whenever Joanne brought up the subject of the baby's health to Jonathan, he would get defensive and tell her to butt out.

Now it appeared as though the whole thing had come to a head. Joanne stopped crying long enough to blow her nose. Zoey tried to comfort her friend. "Joanne, sweetie, take it easy. Of course I'll help. Now calm down and tell me what happened."

"It's horrible," Joanne said, half-weeping. "Two days ago Jonathan caught Ronnie in bed with his best friend, Jacob. They had a big blowout and she left him. She left the baby, too."

Zoey broke in. "What do you mean she left the baby, too?"

"Well, I didn't know about what happened, and Ronnie dropped little Jon off here yesterday at noon like she always did, but she never came back for him. When Jonathan came home from work last night, he was frantic. He called me and I told him I had the baby. Then he told me what happened. He told me about finding her in bed with Jacob the day before and the fight. He said they'd agreed to try to work things out, but when he came home he found a note on the counter. All it said was, 'I hate you. Good-bye.' He thought she'd taken the baby, too. I assured him that little Jon was safe with me. What kind of mother leaves a one-year-old child?"

"Not a very good one, hon." Zoey tried to calm her friend. In reality, Zoey saw this many, many times in her years of practice. "Listen, Joanne, we can talk about the details later. It's very important that Jonathan be the first one to file for divorce. He also needs to get an Emergency Temporary Custody Order. Tell him to be in my office at 8 o'clock tomorrow morning and I'll have the paperwork ready. And tell him under no circumstances is he to talk to her or give her the baby."

"Thank you, Zoey. I didn't know who else to call. I couldn't sleep last night. I'm a mess." Joanne sounded relieved but worn out.

"You did the right thing. I handle this kind of case all the time," Zoey said reassuringly. "I'll take good care of Jonathan. I'll do everything I can. Do you still have the baby?"

"No, Jonathan has him," Joanne answered. "He's understandably upset and couldn't go to work today. They're coming over tonight after Lenny gets home from work."

"Good," Zoey said. "You need to rest up today. Jonathan is going to need you to help care for that baby until this is over. It's going to be a rough road, but I'll help you every step of the way."

"I don't know how to thank you," Joanne said. Zoey could tell she was on the verge of crying again.

"You don't have to. I'm happy to help. I'm your friend."

She hung up the phone and buzzed for Annette. "Annette, clear my calendar for tomorrow and schedule an 8 AM appointment with Jonathan Baker. Please prepare an Emergency Ex Parte Order naming Jonathan Baker as the plaintiff against Rhonda Baker, defendant. The two have one child, Jonathan Baker, Jr. I want to ask the Court to give Rhonda two-hour supervised visitations on the first and third Tuesdays of every month, with CASA in charge." CASA was the acronym for Court Appointed Special Advocate. Other attorneys liked to use CIS, Crisis Intervention Services, but Zoey felt that most of that organization's local staff seemed to consist of women who had gone through nasty divorces and had a reputation of being man-haters. She even saw one CIS worker lie in court to protect a woman who had no business getting custody of her children. At best, the local chapter was less then impartial. The women at CASA were, in general, a bit more focused on the child's legitimate needs and safety rather than revenge. "I'll get the birth date details and anything else we need tomorrow," she added as a final note.

"I'm on it," replied the voice on the intercom. Zoey hung up the phone and looked at the clock. It was almost twelve. She decided to have a quick lunch and finish up any other business in the afternoon. She wanted to be able to concentrate on Jonathan's case exclusively the next day. She knew other women like Rhonda, and this was going to be a tough case. A challenge. They lie on the stand and work the system to their advantage. But this was Joanne's brother and her friend, and Zoey wasn't going to let him down.

Chapter 4

It was a hectic week. Jonathan's divorce took up most of Zoey's time. She filed the divorce papers claiming infidelity, desertion, and irreconcilable differences. The Emergency Temporary Custody Order was granted by the Court and in place, giving Jonathan's estranged wife, Rhonda, the bi-weekly, two-hour supervised visitations with CASA Zoey had asked for. The supervised visits would be held at the CASA office. This way they could be video-recorded.

A GAL, Guardian Ad Litem, had been assigned at Zoey's request. This was a court-appointed attorney to represent Jonathan, Jr. and his interests. The appointed GAL, Lucy Banks, had no allegiance to either parent, making her a non-partial voice in their private battle, fighting only for the child involved. Lucy would have access to all the court files and evidence. She would hold interviews and submit opinions in court that held a lot of weight. Zoey found that in at least 80% of her cases the judge based his decree on the GAL's opinion. It was vital that the GAL be on Jonathan's side. Zoey had worked with most of the GALs and found them to be honest and fair, and Lucy certainly seemed like a conscientious and experienced advocate. Most GALs had been exposed to enough divorce cases to be able to tell who the fit parent really was. It was a good card to hold in this game.

Zoey went to the bar where Rhonda worked, a dark, dank little place called Smokey's Lounge, and came across some interesting facts about her from her very eager-to-rat-her-out co-workers. Big surprise, none of them really liked Rhonda. It seemed she was always hitting on the customers, especially if she knew they had money. Some of the women were sure she'd had sex with several of the male customers in the back of her Yukon. They told Zoey that Rhonda constantly flirted with their boyfriends. One woman was quite vocal in pointing the finger at Rhonda for her recent split with her piece-of-shit fiancé. The co-worker caught Rhonda and her now ex-fiancé having sex in the Yukon, in the parking lot no less. A few ladies told Zoey they had complained to their boss, Smokey, about her. It was suspected that Rhonda kept her job because she was having sex with him as well. No one at the bar was surprised to hear that Rhonda's marriage fell apart. Apparently, she'd made no secret of the fact that she hated being a wife and mother, claiming she'd never wanted to get pregnant. It was an accident on a drunken night, but she figured the baby would be an asset in a divorce.

Rhonda hired an attorney, Phillip Cahill, a young sleaze-ball type. Zoey saw his picture and advertisements on the back of bus stop benches. He'd only been in practice a few years, and thought of himself as a kind of ladies' man. She figured Rhonda would go for someone like that. No doubt she would pay most of her attorney's fees on her back. Zoey hadn't gone up against him before, but talked with colleagues who had.

Phillip quickly filed an answer and counter to the divorce papers, claiming mental cruelty. It stated that Jonathan made Rhonda's life so miserable it forced her into the arms of another man and, of course, she wanted full custody of little Jon, child support, and alimony. This was going to be a tough case and Zoey knew it. Phillip also had a reputation for dragging out proceedings to jack up his fees.

Zoey had dealt with Rhonda's type before. She was the kind of woman who did a disservice to all hard-working, loving mothers out there. A sudden chill ran up her spine as a memory of her own mother flashed in her mind.

In her mind's eye she saw her father and mother arguing loudly. Zoey remembered clutching her father's hand and crying for him to take her home. Then her mother was crying and begging Lyle to let Zoey stay with her. Zoey could still feel the horror as Lyle tearfully handed her off to Sally, turned, and silently walked out the door. Zoey also remembered that, as quickly as the door shut, Sally's tears would stop. Her mother's face would turn ugly and mean as she commanded Zoey to go to her room and think about what a rotten child she was for wanting to be with her father instead of her mother. Zoey shook her head to rid herself of the memory.

Zoey figured Rhonda would use her beauty to full advantage, and no doubt there would be plenty of lies and buckets of tears on the witness stand. The fact that Zoey was best friends with Jonathan's sister made it even more stressful.

Her last task for the day was to have Annette schedule a deposition for the middle of the following week so Rhonda could tell her side of the story. Zoey used this tactic to know straight away what she was up against. In her experience, she discovered that women like Rhonda got most of their lies out in deposition. This way Zoey could disprove them before they were brought up in court, saving money and time. The foolish women usually didn't realize that just because they weren't in front of a judge they were still under oath, and could be charged with perjury if the lie was serious enough. That being done, she headed for home.

By the time she got there it was seven o'clock. Zoey changed into her workout clothes and did two miles on the treadmill. Exhausted, she collapsed into the living room recliner, called her favorite deli, and ordered a sandwich and pasta salad for delivery. Her thoughts drifted to Mickey, who was supposed to be coming home in a day or two. She never knew the exact day ahead of time. In his line of business, nothing was ever scheduled. Last-minute meetings always came up. She missed him terribly. It was over three weeks since he'd been home, and they hadn't spoken in two days. She needed him now more than ever.

Zoey had just closed her eyes when the phone rang. "What now," she said out loud, perturbed at the disturbance, and picked up the phone. "Hello?" she said rather forcefully.

"Hello, gorgeous," she heard on the other end.

"Mickey," she uttered with anxious relief.

"Hey, babe," he said with concern, sensing desperation in her tone. "Is something wrong? Is something wrong in Zoey's Place?" They'd begun to use the phrase as a reference to her state of mind after she took a college meditation class. She said it was her place of calmness and inner peace, where she always strived to be, her happy place. Whenever she felt stressed out, she would sit alone with eyes closed and use the breathing and visualization techniques she'd learned in class. It wasn't a magical cure, but most times it helped her find and maintain Zoey's Place again.

"Oh, Mickey, you have no idea."

"Jonathan's divorce?" he asked.

"Yes. I've been finding out what a shit Rhonda really is," she answered.

"Don't let it get to you," he encouraged. "You've had tough cases before and won."

"But this one is special; Jonathan is a good friend," she said. "It's personal."

"I know, I know," he tried to comfort her. "But, hey, how would you feel if they hired another attorney to represent him? You know you're the best divorce attorney in town."

She pulled herself together. "You're right," she said, feeling more confident. "I can't wait 'till you come home. When *are* you coming home, by the way?" There was a long silence on the phone. She could tell bad news was coming. "What is it?"

"Well, I've got bad news and great news," he said, trying to keep things light. "The bad news is I'm not coming home for another week."

Her heart dropped. "Are you kidding me? Why? I really need you, honey." She couldn't hide her disappointment.

"I know, babe," he said apologetically. "There are some last-minute meetings that I can't get out of." Before Zoey could respond he continued. "But the great news is once I'm home I won't have to travel again until after the first of the year."

She couldn't believe her ears. "Seriously? You're not just saying that?" She was ecstatic.

"I'm as serious as a heart attack," he responded. "Corporate is paranoid about the Y2K thing and they want everyone Stateside until they know there aren't going to be any glitches."

In truth, the company wanted to make sure there were no terrorist attacks or kidnappings to mark the turn of the millennium. The U.S. State Department had sent out warnings of a terrorist organization headed by a man named Osama bin Laden. They believed he was responsible for the embassy bombings that killed 224 people in Kenya and Tanzania in August of 1998. They had been watching bin Laden and another terrorist named Aymen al-Zawahiri since they had issued a religious edict, or fatwa, in February of 1988, instructing all Muslims to kill Americans, civilian and military, "anywhere in the world where they can be found."

Camps believed to be used by bin Laden in Afghanistan and a munitions plant in Sudan were already the targets of U.S. cruise missile attacks that year and the State Department was sure bin Laden wanted revenge. The State Department wasn't specific, but had indicated to Mickey's company that they had seen an increase in activity and suspected that bin Laden was getting ready to "cause a scene". Oil, the life blood of the U.S. and the world, and specifically the old industry, was the natural target. They believed the attacks would take place in the Middle East. That was Mickey's territory, and his company took all threats seriously. Considering the stress Zoey was under, he thought it best to keep this a secret.

Zoey felt the disappointment of his delayed arrival vanish and a sudden joy filled her. "You mean you'll be home for Thanksgiving, Christmas, and New Year's? I'll have you all to myself?"

"I might have to visit corporate in Texas a few times, but only for a day or two, and you can come with me if you want. Other than that, I can work from home. Wanna go to Incline Village for New Year's and see if we can find Zoey's Place again?"

"Oh, Mickey, you bet I do," she said, relieved. Her mind was racing with excitement. "Oh, oh, can we have a Christmas party and invite Joanne and Lenny and Carol and Dave and all the kids?"

"Anything you want, babe," he answered. "The company Christmas party is in Galveston this year. I don't know the date yet."

"Mickey," she said with dismay. "You know I hate going to those parties. All those old biddies are so stuck up." She was referring to the wives of the other company execs. They seemed to resent the fact that Zoey had a life and career of her own, and they seemed so wrapped up in their husbands' lives that Zoey doubted they could do anything on their own. She always felt shunned by them at social gatherings.

"Come on, honey," he said. "You know they're just jealous because your husband is so handsome and still has the hots for you."

She laughed. "You're right," she conceded. "Most of them probably haven't had sex with their husbands in years."

"No doubt," he said. "I bet they're all horny as hell." They both laughed. "It won't be that bad. Allen and Fen will be there. You haven't seen her since the summer cruise. I'm sure the two of you will have lots to catch up on. Even if it's bitching about how much time your husband spends on the road."

Allen Webber was Mickey's closest associate at the company. He'd started a few years before Mickey and took him under his wing. They usually worked in tandem on the same jobs. Fenella, who liked to be called Fen, was Allen's wife. She came from affluence, but never flaunted it in Zoey's face like the other women. She was about ten years older than Zoey.

Fen had a great appearance. She was tall and slender, and had that regal profile that demanded respect. She always dressed crisp and stylish, and wore just enough jewelry to let everyone know she had wealth. She had a soft and melodious voice that could make even the stingiest of tightwads open their wallets and give generously.

At first Zoey was intimidated by Fen's stately appearance, as she looked just like the rest of the corporate wives. But Fen sought her out and quickly dispelled that notion. Zoey and Fen formed a bond over their principles. They usually hung out together at the company gatherings. Zoey liked her values, and always enjoyed hearing about the things she had done since they last met. They became fast friends.

In her many conversations with Fen Zoey discovered that, as much as Fen loved Allen, she had spent her married life serving his advantage. She created her own identity and career around his. Allen's job always came first. They spent their married life moving from location to location as opportunities to advance his professional position presented themselves.

Fen really didn't mind. She was proud of the way Allen worked his way up the corporate ladder. He did so without compromising his morals and integrity. That was one of his traits that she admired most. In reality, working wasn't a necessity. She was a trust fund baby and would never want for anything material. It was for her own self-worth that she pursued any type of work, whether it be volunteer or for pay. The love she received from Allen was her reward.

Fen was much more social than Zoey. She did a lot of charity work and fund- raising with various foundations, and was active on many projects with the wives of corporate upper management, which was still a man's world. No women had been able to break the glass ceiling at Taylor Resource Development. The wives of the execs were expected to look good and throw better parties. So, she did just that. She smiled and made small talk with everyone, and organized the charitable events. She liked that part. She had earned a degree in public relations, and couldn't let that go to waste.

The corporate projects were humanitarian in nature but strictly PR, carefully chosen by upper management so as not to show oil and gas in a negative light. But because they were humanitarian in nature, Fen didn't mind being part of it. It did make her feel like she was making a difference, even though the corporation always got the credit and the glory. That part wasn't important to her. She had great organizational and people skills and got things done. Heck, they needed Fen. Zoey was of the opinion that the other wives couldn't wipe their own asses based on the petty things they complained about at gatherings with regard to their maids, butlers, and other hired help.

And, of course, there was Allen. He was a great husband. He was tall, at least six inches taller than Fen's 5'9", and slim and stately like she was. He had a great head of hair; deep auburn, full and shiny. It had become greyer in the passing years, but that merely gave him a distinguished aura. They made a handsome couple, Fen and Allen. Dignified and cultured.

In the professional world Allen was a hard-ass corporate attorney, aggressive but professional. Fen got to see the other side of him, the personal side, dedicated to his family and his community. He was a decent man; sensitive, caring, loving, honest, and loyal to his wife. Fen loved him dearly.

Life with Allen was comfortable. She was independent, and Allen's frequent absence worked in her favor. It gave her time to immerse herself in her charities and be involved in family activities.

They had planned on having children, and tried to get pregnant right after their wedding. But after Fen had two miscarriages within as many years she was diagnosed with endometriosis. She had to have a hysterectomy. Fortunately, their multi-sibling families supplied them with many nieces and nephews and, like Zoey and Mickey, they experienced parenthood from the outside.

Allen and Fen took advantage of the time they were together. Fen traveled with her husband on a regular basis. She embraced foreign cultures and the experiences they brought. They lived a luxurious lifestyle. She really had no reason to complain about her life, and she didn't regret a moment of it.

Zoey rarely attended company functions or trips, but when she did decide to go to one, like the summer cruise, she'd always call Fen to see if she was attending as well. If Fen wasn't going, neither would Zoey. Allen and Fen were the only couple Mickey and Zoey had anything at all in common with, and Fen was the only company woman who didn't look down her nose at Zoey because of what she did for a living. Some of the biddies held the opinion that Zoey's career somehow reflected poorly on Mickey, as if she 'had' to work. She and Fen had shared a laugh about that.

Zoey thought about the opportunity to visit with her friend again and her mood brightened. "I know. I do like Fen. The rest of those nosy old bags can just kiss my ass."

"That's my girl," Mickey added.

"I love you, Mickey," she said. He could hear the desperation in her voice. "I miss you so much."

"I love you, too, babe," he replied. "I'm getting hard."

"I'm getting wet."

"I'm gonna fuck your brains out when I see you."

"I'm counting on it."

"I gotta go. I'm gonna jerk off and go to bed."

"I wish I could watch."

"You'll have your chance soon. But really, babe, I gotta go. I've got an early meeting tomorrow. I've got to wrap up a lot of loose ends before I leave next week. I'll call you in a day or two and tell you what day I'll be home."

"Mickey, you're the best. I love you so much." Her heart was aching for him. "Goodnight, my husband."

"Goodnight, my sweet angel. I love you, too." And with that he hung up.

She felt sadness and joy at the same time. It had been years since Mickey was home for such a long stretch of time. This would be the best Christmas ever. Carol and Dave always had Thanksgiving, so that was covered. They all usually got together on Christmas Eve as well, but it was always a small celebration, usually at a restaurant. Most of the time Mickey had to leave the day after Christmas. But this year it would be at the house and it would be the best ever. She started to make a check list in her head: call Joanne and Carol to tell them the good news and share her celebration plans, call the caterers and make sure it wasn't too late to reserve their services.

Call Stella. There was a menu to plan, gifts to buy, and a house to decorate. She could feel the Christmas spirit already.

Then reality set in: Jonathan's divorce. She had to focus. There would be plenty of time to celebrate. Actually, now she had another week to make progress. By the time Mickey got home, the deposition would be over and there would be time to catch a breather before it got hot and heavy into discovery and subpoenas.

She looked over at the end table and saw herself and Mickey in their wedding picture. Their young love glowed like a bright star. The smiles on their faces reflected the feeling they shared, the love that continued to shine to this day. She felt lucky and blessed, but also a longing in her heart and an ache between her legs. She missed Mickey and needed to feel close to him, *and* she really was getting horny.

She ran upstairs and entered their bedroom. When they moved into the Birmingham home a special hidden room was build off the master bedroom closet. She stood at the secret door, opened it, and entered the 'Play Room'. In here they kept their porn DVDs and magazines. They had shelves full of dildos, whips, floggers, blindfolds, feather ticklers, butt plugs, handcuffs, cock rings, and other assorted sex toys. There was also a collection of sexual attire. Mickey loved it when Zoey appeared at the bedroom door wearing crotchless underwear, a bustier, a cup-less bra, or some other sexual apparel that he could remove during foreplay. She also had costumes like the French Maid, Catholic school girl, farmer's daughter, nurse, librarian, warrior princess, and Vegas hooker.

Mickey also had clothes that triggered sexual fantasy for Zoey, like the lumberjack, or the horny cowboy—which consisted of a black leather vest, red bandana, and a pair of chaps worn without jeans underneath so his ass and cock were exposed for easy access. That was her favorite costume. A nostalgic standby was a pair of worn jeans Mickey wore shirtless. It reminded her of their youth. The jeans were faded and threadbare in the ass and crotch area from years of Zoey's rubbing them, and just looking at them made her hot. Mickey was a fanatic about fitness and still had a great physique.

Pressing the jeans to her cheek she closed her eyes, their softness reminding her of his tenderness. Their musky smell harkened of the many amorous nights she had pulled them off him, revealing his hard, throbbing cock. In her mind she was reliving the last time she and Mickey had sex, her desire growing to a fever pitch.

She looked around and grabbed her favorite dildo. It was red with ridges and she had nicknamed it Jondalar, after the main male character in one of her favorite books, *Valley of the Horses*, by Jean M. Auel. Rushing out of the closet she fell to the bed as she tugged off her sweatpants. She pushed Jondalar into herself and flipped the 'on' switch. She closed her eyes and fanaticized that Mickey was in control, surrendering to the pleasure. It had been a while since she had masturbated, and her orgasm came quickly. She lay there motionless for a moment as the rush of pleasure left her weak. She reached down with her other hand and quieted the still-buzzing device, savoring the full feeling of having something inside of her for just another moment before she pulled it out. She sprawled out on her bed with her eyes closed, still basking in the sexual afterglow.

Just then the doorbell rang. Her dinner had arrived.

Chapter 5

The deposition proved to be a shocking surprise. Rhonda accused Jonathan of everything from drug dealing to child abuse. Several times during the questioning Zoey held Jonathan back as the accusations flew. She told him ahead of time what to expect and to let Rhonda hang herself with her own words. She assured him it would work out for the best when they actually went to court.

Zoey couldn't believe Rhonda was talking about the Jonathan she knew. Rhonda was aware of the close relationship Zoey had with Jonathan's family, and yet her depiction of him, Joanne, and Lenny were that of total strangers. She portrayed Joanne as a demanding, controlling sister-in-law constantly meddling in her marriage, who treated her more like an overbearing mother-in-law than sister-in-law, always trying to tell her how to raise little Jon. She stated that Lenny called Jonathan ten times a day and insisted on being involved in their every decision. She complained they never had any privacy.

It appeared that Rhonda's attorney, Phillip, was suckered in by Rhonda's charm. He held her hand during the questioning, always with a tissue at the ready when the water works started, like when Rhonda described watching Jonathan toss little Jon across the room because he wouldn't stop crying.

"You liar!" Jonathan yelled back as he rose from his seat.

Zoey quickly grabbed him by the arm and sat him back down. "Remember what I told you," she reprimanded. She could tell this was hard on him. Poor guy.

"Did you tell anyone about this?" Zoey continued her questioning.

"I was afraid," she answered.

"Afraid of what?" Zoey asked.

"Of his sister and her husband. I knew they wouldn't believe me. I didn't know what they would do to me," she replied between sobs.

"Did you fear for your safety?"

"No, not really. I mean, I don't know."

Zoey saw that Rhonda was fidgeting in her chair. "Did you take little Jon to the doctor after Jonathan threw him?" she asked.

"No," was the reply.

"Oh? Why not?" Zoey calmly asked. "If it was as bad as you say it was, weren't you concerned for your son's wellbeing?"

Rhonda looked confused, as if she was trying to think of something to say. "Well-well, I didn't know who to call or what to do. I was afraid. I-I-I..." She began to stutter. Zoey knew Rhonda was making this up as she went along.

Rhonda's attorney could see that Zoey wasn't buying it and broke in. "Counselor, this subject is obviously very upsetting to my client. She is clearly shaken. Can't you see how distressing this is for her to recall the incident?"

Zoey decided to let it drop. "Fine," she said, looking at her notes, then continued.

"And what about your relationship with Jonathan's friend, Jacob? Why did you decide to sleep with your husband's best friend?"

"Spider was always there for me," Rhonda replied.

"Spider?" Zoey asked.

"Yeah," Rhonda replied. "That's what everyone calls him. You know, 'cause he's so tall and skinny." Zoey had met Jacob at the wedding, but didn't know about the nickname. He had been introduced as Jacob.

Zoey looked over at Jonathan. He nodded to confirm.

"So," Zoey continued. "When did you and Jacob start committing adultery?"

"That's putting it a bit crudely, don't you think, Mrs. DeLucca?" Phillip interjected.

Zoey looked him straight in the eye and replied coldly, "Infidelity is always crude, Counselor."

Rhonda looked at her attorney before she answered. "We're in love," she said, holding her head high. "Have been since before the baby was born."

Zoey could see the sword pierce Jonathan's heart and patted his hand to comfort him. "So," she continued, "your infidelity has been going on for over a year? Are you sure Jonathan is the father of your child?"

Rhonda looked at Jonathan then back at Zoey. "Yes," she said with confidence. "Spider and I fell in love right after I found out I was pregnant."

Zoey could see the arrows of hurt hit their mark as Jonathan buried his head in his hands and let out a painful sigh.

The rest of the afternoon was just as excruciating. Rhonda said Jonathan sold drugs at work to supplement his salary. She said he beat her if the house wasn't clean. She claimed his lovemaking was inadequate and clumsy, and he didn't appreciate her or know how to sexually satisfy her. This, she claimed, was why she fell in love with Spider. He loved her. He knew how to treat a woman and how to make love like a man.

After about five hours, Zoey had enough and put an end to the deposition. This was Rhonda's deposition, and Jonathan wasn't allowed to answer or defend himself in any way. When Zoey asked Philip if he was going to depose Jonathan, his answer was a terse, "Not necessary."

After Rhonda and her attorney left Zoey looked at Jonathan, who hadn't moved from his chair. He was deep in thought. "Jonathan," she said softly, "I know you, and I think I know the answer to this question before I even ask it, but as your attorney I've got to ask. Is there any truth to any of the accusations that Rhonda made about you?"

Jonathan looked up. His eyes were red and she could see the pain behind the tears that struggled not to flow. "No," he said, emphatically shaking his head. In a voice barely above a whisper and tinged with pain, he continued, "Not a word was true. I would never hurt my son. I never beat her. I never sold drugs."

"It's okay. I believe you," she told him, putting her hand on his shoulder. "I know this was rough on you, but now we know what angle they're going to use against you to try to get custody."

Jonathan's head cleared. "Will they win?" he asked, looking at her with red eyes.

"Not if I can help it," Zoey said confidently. "She has no witnesses. She was unfaithful. She left you and deserted her son. The odds are in your favor."

"Will I get full custody?" he asked.

"In the old days it would be joint custody, even though she's a piece of shit. Things are different now. I've been before Judge Jones before, and I know he's fair and savvy. It's our job to make him believe you and not her. I'm confident we can do it."

Jonathan managed a smile. "Thanks, Zoey." He stood up and gave her an exceptionally tight hug. It melted her heart. She could hear his sobs as she hugged him back.

She looked at her watch. It was almost five. "Time to go. It's been a long day. Tell your sister to call me. Did she tell you? Mickey's going to be home for Christmas and we're going to have a big Christmas party. You're all invited."

"Great," he said, dabbing his eyes with a tissue before putting on his coat. "What do we do next?"

"We go home and relax. I'll see you on Thanksgiving. You'll be there with little Jon, won't you?" He nodded. "Good. We'll meet again after that. I'll have Annette set up an appointment. Rhonda hasn't asked for additional visitations for Thanksgiving, so we'll keep on the current custody schedule for now. When does she see him next?"

"Next Tuesday," he answered.

"I imagine she'll want extra time with him around Christmas. Decide if you're willing to give it to her. You don't have to, but it might look better in court if you do. If not, they might try to say you're heartlessly keeping your child from his mother." Zoey thought for a moment. "How's the little guy doing? Does he ask for her?"

Jonathan shook his head. "Not at all. He's perfectly happy being with his Aunt Joanne during the day and me at night."

"That's good," she responded. "How are the

transitions before and after the two-hour visits?"

"He's a little on edge, and gets kind of weepy when I hand him off to the woman at CASA. But I get a really big hug when I pick him up."

"Poor little guy," Zoey said. "This has got to be confusing for him. I've asked for the taped recordings of the visitations. When I get them, I want you to look at them. I also want you and little Jon to start seeing Dr. Angelika. She's a therapist. She can help you both with the emotional distress. Her observations will be a big help to us in court. She works well with the GALs, and that's important. I want her to see the tapes, too. Here's her number. See her as soon as you can." Zoey opened her desk drawer and retrieved a business card. She handed it to Jonathan. "For now, just go home and be a daddy to your son. He needs you now more than ever."

Jonathan put the card in his pocket and hugged her. "Thanks again, Zoey. I don't know what I'd do without you."

Zoey gave him a kiss on his cheek. "It's okay, Jonathan. It'll be fine."

Chapter 6

Mickey traveled with protection when overseas. His 'friend' stayed with him until they made their mandatory one-day debriefing at corporate in Texas. Then he could continue home. He had arrived back in the U.S. the day before. The plane from Houston landed at Detroit Metro just minutes before Zoey arrived. Her anticipation was mounting and her body tingled with excitement. She could almost feel him approaching.

    She stood at the baggage claim with her eyes glued to the escalator. There he was, the most handsome man in the world, her one true love and soul mate. Their eyes locked as he descended. He was easy to spot. The electricity of their desire was almost visible as they met and embraced, their kiss full of heated passion, their union complete.

    "I missed you," she said, staring into his familiar eyes.

    "I missed you more, babe," he replied. Her hazel eyes were edged with tears. They were the same eyes that stole his heart the first time he looked into them. "You smell good."

"Just for you," she said, pushing her leg against the inside of his. She reached into his long overcoat, feeling the hardness growing in his pants.

"I want to take you right here, right now, in front of all these people," he said, breathing heavily.

"I want that, too," she said. Hypnotized by his dark, piercing eyes, her body grew weak from their power. It took all her strength to maintain her composure. She took a deep breath. "But I think you'll like what I've got waiting for you at home much more."

Mickey gently pushed away. Grabbing her hand, he tenderly kissed the back before letting it go. A salacious smile crept across his face. "You always know what to say to make me want you even more. I love you." She smiled. He saw his suitcase coming around the turnstile. He grabbed her hand and headed for the bag. He snatched it up without missing a step and continued to the exit, still holding her hand firmly.

On the way home the two made idle chit-chat about his flight and the upcoming holiday plans, but inside their sexual hunger was rising. Every time they looked at each other they got hotter and hotter, though neither one mentioned the growing sexual volcano ready to erupt inside.

The drive home seemed like an eternity. Finally they arrived. Mickey pulled the Mercedes into the garage and pushed the remote to close the door. He faced her. She looked beautiful in the dim light of the garage. He'd missed her terribly. The separations were the worst part of his job. Being apart from her was the one thing he still hadn't gotten used to. He cradled her soft face in his hands, pulled her close, and planted a long kiss on her hungry lips.

"Ready?" he asked.

She looked up into the dark pools of his eyes and

nodded.

"Okay, my little vixen," he said. "What room?"

"Room number three. Twenty minutes."

A large smile came across his face. "Oh, baby," he said with excitement. "Room number three. See ya." He looked at his watch and gave her a quick peck on the cheek before he popped the trunk.

By the time he got his bag out she had already disappeared into the house.

It was a little game they'd developed through the years to add an extra element of fun to their sexual play time, not that they needed any help. They'd learned long ago that it was much less distracting for them not to talk about how horny they were on the way home. This was the time to catch up, find out how the trip went, any new local news, events of the day kind of thing. That way, by the time they'd made the 45-minute trip home they'd said all that needed to be said. They could concentrate on their lusty hunger.

Every room of the house had a number. The number was associated with a sexual performance, complete with costume and an assortment of sexual aids. They didn't have enough rooms to accommodate all of the different sexual fantasies they had created, so they assigned three to four different scenarios to each room. The element of surprise still remained. He didn't know which of the possible scenes he would find tonight. Room number three meant that Zoey would be dressed as a prairie wife, a French maid, or a librarian. He knew what to expect. The common thread was that she would act shy but submissively open to almost anything. It was wild card night.

He entered the house from the garage and headed straight towards the master bedroom. On the way, he passed the bedroom they called "Room number three". He glanced inside without pausing. The room was dimly lit with candles next to the bed. He could definitely smell the aroma of sage incense coming from the room, which meant someone who was practical. *Okay,* he thought. *That narrows it down to two: prairie wife or librarian.* His anticipation grew. Maybe she wanted to get spanked tonight.

He dropped his bags by the bed in the spacious master bedroom and started to strip off his clothes. He always liked to shower as soon as he came home. It was symbolic and therapeutic to him, the shedding of the staunch and powerful business man known as Michael DeLucca and becoming the husband and lover Zoey called Mickey.

The hot, cleansing shower felt soothing on his back and he could feel the tension there lessening. For a brief moment he forgot about everything. He could feel the stress of his job and the world wash away and disappear down the drain. As he stepped out of the shower, he grabbed a towel and began drying off. In the mirror he saw her reflection in the doorway of the master bedroom. Yes! She was wearing thick, black, horn-rimmed glasses. She was the librarian, one of his favorites. His cock began to grow hard just at the thought. He caught her looking at his reflection in the mirror.

"Oh!" she squealed, and went running out of the bedroom and down the hallway.

He threw the towel down and looked at the clock next to the bed. Exactly twenty minutes had passed. It was time. He walked naked to room number three. The practical sage scent he'd smelled earlier was growing more pungent as he approached. Soft classical music was playing from somewhere in the room. The flickering light of candles invited him in.

He stood in the doorway and looked into the muted

light. It was a guest room that also served as a quiet reading room, furnished with a small desk and a few file cabinets. There were also two curio cabinets displaying various family heirlooms and souvenirs from his travels and their vacations that the French maid was responsible for keeping clean. The centerpiece of the room was the king-size sleigh bed. The bedding was extra thick, as were the pillows. On the end table next to the bed he could see a variety of sex toys laid out. His eyes moved over to the plush recliner chair and reading lamp next to the bookshelf.

There she was, stretched out on the chair reading a book, her hair pulled up into a bun at the top of her head. She was wearing a tightly fitted blouse that covered her arms. Its high collar was buttoned up to the top. He could see she was wearing a tight, dark-colored skirt that was suggestively riding up her thighs and the outline of the sleek black spike heels she was wearing. The heavy black glasses were down low on her nose. Her lips were ruby red and inviting.

He knocked three times on the door.

"I'm sorry," he heard from the other side of room. "The library is closed."

"But I've got an overdue book I need to return."

"I can't let you in," she said without looking up.

"Well, it's your job," he said firmly. "I might have to report you to your supervisor if you don't service me."

She glanced toward him as she sat up straight and undid the buttons on her blouse until her cleavage showed. She pushed the thick glasses into place with her finger, then let it drop to her pouting red lips for a moment before cupping her breasts. She began massaging them, making the nipples visibly erect. "Oh, please," she begged. "Don't do that. I don't want to get into trouble. I'll do anything you say."

He was getting excited and walked towards her.

Her eyes were locked on his perfect naked body. She admired his toned muscles reflecting the dim light. He flexed as he approached. His noble, chiseled face and thick hair never seemed to age. This was her man. She needed no other.

He stood in front of her, naked and clean-smelling from his shower. "Anything?" he asked. She could see his manhood fully erect in front of her face.

She put the book down and reached for him with one hand. She grabbed his hard cock and pressed her cheek against it. "Anything," she said, looking up at him through the thick-framed glasses.

He picked up the book. "What are you reading?" he asked. He looked at the cover. It was titled, *Sexual Positions: A Photographic Guide to Pleasure and Love*, by Glenn Wilson. They had both read it long ago. It was another clue as to what he could expect from her tonight. In short, whatever he wanted.

A smile came across his face. "So, you like getting nasty, you naughty girl. I like a naughty girl. But that still doesn't excuse you for not doing your job. I think we should start with a spanking. Follow me," he commanded. He proceeded to walk to the bed and sit on the edge, putting the book down next to him. She stood in front of him. "Now take off your blouse."

She obeyed, unfastening each button, slowly revealing a lacy, floral, strapless bra underneath. Taking off the blouse, she threw it to the floor. He reached out and unsnapped the bra's front hook. Her breasts heaved forward. Pulling from behind he removed it. Her hands went up to cover herself.

"Now take off your skirt," he ordered, ignoring her attempt at modesty. Slowly she pulled the back zipper down, let the skirt fall to the floor, and carefully stepped out of it. He admired the view before him. She still had on a white lace G-string, the spiked heels, and the glasses. "Why, Ms. Librarian, you *are* a dirty girl under that stiff collar." He looked her over like a piece of merchandise. "Mmm. That's better," he said with satisfaction. "Turn around for me."

She obeyed. Her anticipation was growing and she could see that her nipples were hard as acorns. She loved the foreplay games they played. It was part of what kept it exciting all these years. She quivered in anticipation of what he would do to her.

Once she was facing him again he stood up, reached around her back, and pulled her close to him. He kissed her with open mouth. She did the same and savored the taste of him. Their tongues danced in harmony as they pressed together, feeling each other's warmth. He pushed her away. She stood before him again.

He sat down on the edge of the bed, picked up the book, and patted his knees.

She muffled a squeal but obeyed his command. She adjusted the band of the g-string and placed herself over his knees, ready to receive her punishment.

Gently he removed her glasses and looked at the perfect round ass before him. He began to tenderly rub his palm over its curves, feeling every part. He cradled it and began squeezing the soft flesh between his fingers a little more aggressively. She sighed in anticipation.

"I'm sorry, Miss," he said, staying in character, "but you are a civic employee and are derelict in your duties. I have to do this."

"I understand, sir," she replied in a soft voice. "I noticed that your arms are extremely strong. You won't hurt me, will you?"

Patting her bottom gently with the book, he said, "That's entirely up to you, now isn't it?" With that he slapped her ass with the book. Its sharp report echoed in the room. She giggled.

"You think this is funny?" he asked. He slapped it again, this time a little harder.

She let out a squeal. "Oh, I've been much naughtier than that."

"You have, haven't you," he replied with a smirk as he brought the book down again, harder. She flinched but quickly relaxed. After a few more hard slaps he asked, "Had enough?"

"Almost," she replied.

Again he cracked the book hard on her ass, which was now a scorching red. After a few more she let out a moan. The stinging was exquisitely painful and she liked it. It heightened her sensitivity. He put the book down and grabbed the lotion that was sitting on the night stand.

"I think you've learned your lesson, young lady." He poured some lotion into his hand and began rubbing it into the red-hot skin of her ass. Its soothing coolness gave her skin relief but did nothing to quench her burning lust. He always knew just how much spanking she could take. His lotioned fingers wandered down the crack of her behind. She raised her ass to meet his touch. He felt that she was wet and hungry for him. He pushed aside the g-string and slid his fingers into her as she moaned loudly, tickling her anus with his thumb as he did. Something he learned from the very book she had just been spanked with.

Zoey was in heaven. She'd fantasized about this moment for weeks, and wasn't disappointed. She was willing to give herself to him in any way he wanted. Her heart was beating strong. She gave in to her desire and got ready to let him take his pleasure as he chose.

Flipping her off of his knees, he spread-eagled her

on the bed. He stepped back and admired the view for a moment. She lay there, writhing in pleasure, looking up at him with hungry eyes. "I'm here for you," she said, touching herself between her legs.

Reaching down, he grabbed the front of the g-string and pulled it off. He climbed on top of her and began kissing her amorously. She sucked on his tongue as his hands explored her body. Reaching down, she cupped his balls in her hand.

"You want me in you?" he asked.

She nodded and said, "More than anything."

Rolling over, he guided her head toward his cock. "You have to suck it first." He reached over to the end table and grabbed the glasses. "Put these on," he commanded. She obeyed.

She took his shaft into her mouth and began twirling her tongue around it. Then she deep-throated him over and over. Now it was his turn to moan. "Ah, that's it, baby. Just like that. You sure know how to give a good blow job. Did you learn that in one of your books?" Grabbing her head with both hands, he guided it down as her mouth performed its magic. He felt his orgasm surfacing. "I'm not gonna come now. I'm not finished with you yet," he said, and pulled out of her mouth.

She lay still in the bed next to him. He regained control and breathed heavily for a moment or two. She could see sweat beading up on his forehead and his body was glistening. She smiled.

He reached over and cupped her breasts in his hands. He kissed them. His hands found the warm, wet area between her legs and he began exploring it with his fingers. He found and rubbed her clitoris. She moaned blissfully and began pushing into his hand. As she reached over and grabbed his cock, which was still quite hard, he asked, "Now what did that book say you should do with that?"

"It said that you could put your cock in me," she replied. "It doesn't make me a dirty girl, does it?" she asked softly.

"The dirtiest," he answered. "The kind of girl I like. I think you need a proper fucking, Miss," he said. She giggled. She was hoping he would say that, and prepared for his next move.

He spread her legs. She gave him no resistance; in fact, she pushed herself into him. He could tell she was eager for it. After a minute, he could take it no longer. He pushed his dick into her, hard. Again and again he slammed into her, feeling her warmth around his cock. She moaned, arched her back and pushed right up to him, allowing him to enter her fully. The harder he pounded into her the harder she pushed him in. The two were moving as one. Their passion and lust reached its peak and they crested simultaneously, their cries of pleasure echoing through the room and the house.

He rolled off. They reached out and held hands as they caught their breath.

"Wow!" he said, breaking the silence. "That was incredible. I missed that. I love you, babe."

"I love you, too. Welcome, home, my husband."

Chapter 7

The heavenly smells of Thanksgiving permeated the house for hours as the guests talked and played video games to pass the time. The smell of roasting turkey tormented them all day. Now the wait was over. At long last Dave walked into the dining area, carrying out the beautifully roasted turkey on a silver platter. Carol followed close behind. "Time to eat, everyone!" she called out. Dave set the bird down in front of his seat at the head of the larger of two festively set tables, a smaller one for the kids and the larger one for the adults. Both were loaded with a variety of holiday favorites that could feed twice the amount of people in attendance.

"About damn time," Lenny said. He set his beer down and took his seat. When everyone was seated the room became quiet and everyone held hands.

Dave spoke, "Heavenly Father, Divine Mother, we thank you for this bountiful feast. We thank you for our friends and family. We are grateful that Mickey is able to join us this year. Keep him safe in his travels. Keep us all healthy and happy for many years to come. Bless our…"

"Come on, man," Lenny interrupted, "we're starving. Good friends, good meat, good God, let's eat!"

Everyone, including Dave, laughed and said, "Amen."

Dave got busy carving the turkey and plates were filled as the holiday food was passed around. The sound of forks on plates replaced the room full of voices as stomachs began to fill.

It had been several months since all the friends had been together. Zoey had lunch with the girls when she could. But throughout the years everyone's jobs and families kept them busy, and the monthly lunches became less and less frequent. Mickey's job kept him away so much that the only time he really had to get caught up with his friends were the rare social get-togethers.

Everyone was just about finished eating when the conversation turned to Mickey's job. "So, Mick," Lenny said as he shoveled the last of his cranberry sauce into his mouth, "what's new in the oil business? Why has the price of oil doubled since March? You got anything to do with that?" Everyone chuckled.

"Don't worry," Mickey said. "Iran just found a new oilfield in September. It's about 26 billion barrels. Biggest one they've found in about thirty years, should produce about 400 million barrels a day. I see prices going down."

"Iran, eh?" Dave chimed in. "Those people make me nervous. Their lifestyle and values are so different from ours. Are you sure you're safe over there? You know, after those protests in Tehran last July I read where 70 students disappeared. They arrested about 1,400 people. I don't think they think too highly of Americans either. You were around there then, weren't you?"

Worry swept over Zoey's face. She knew that Mickey was in danger whenever he traveled, but especially in that part of the world. Luckily his dark Italian features helped him blend in better, but he was still an American. That meant he was a target. In August, for two weeks after the protests Mickey had extra bodyguards and had to wear a bullet-proof vest whenever he left the hotel. There was always some sort of religious or territorial war going on. She thought it was ridiculous and primitive that they still had tribes who fought each other. Through the years it hadn't bothered her so much, but it seemed like this year was different. The partings were harder. The long separations became unbearable. It was worse when Mickey was in the Middle East.

She was plagued with an upset stomach more and more, and experienced what one might call panic attacks, which was something new to her. A client had described the symptoms to her when he told her about the panic attacks his mother had because of his divorce. Zoey did some research at the library in an effort to diagnose and treat herself. She thought that if she went to the doctor it would worry Mickey. Her symptoms fit the profile. She tried to meditate more, but found it harder and harder to center her thoughts and clear her mind. Zoey's Place was becoming more elusive. She thought at first that it just meant she was burned out over being an absentee wife. But her inner self told her it was more. She had an unnaturally dreadful feeling about Mickey and his safety. She was beginning to think it was a sign. The world was starting to get crazy and her beloved, her soul mate, the man she couldn't live without, was right smack dab in the middle of the turmoil most of the time. She learned to manage it in a fashion, but how long could she control her fears?

"Oh, it's not that bad," he said, trying to make light of the threat he knew was real. "I wasn't in Iran then. I was actually safe and sound in Jordan. I'm always with my bodyguard, and because I represent a U.S. oil interest I'm treated like royalty. They don't want anything to happen to me."

She felt her body tighten and her breathing grow quick. Her stomach got that queasy feeling, and suddenly the food on her plate lost its appeal. She became slightly lightheaded and could feel the blood rushing from it. She wished they wouldn't talk about it. She closed her eyes for a few moments and forced herself to take slow, silent, deep breaths. She opened her eyes and looked across the table.

As if he sensed it Mickey turned to face her, and was shocked to see how pale she was. He could tell she was thinking about the August incident and could feel her fear and panic. She was uncomfortable and he needed to do something.

"Hey, I don't really want to talk about work." He tried to quickly change the subject. "So, which game are we gonna watch: Bears and Dolphins or Lions and Cowboys? You think the Lions can win this year?"

Mickey looked over at Zoey again and she was still staring at him from across the table. He looked deep into her eyes and smiled with reassurance, as if to tell her he knew what she was going through and he loved her. They could read each other's thoughts, feel each other's emotions. She felt his love. A warm feeling spread over her and she began to relax. She smiled back, letting him know she was fine. Mickey turned and joined in on the football conversation.

"So, let's talk about Christmas," Joanne said to the table, taking Zoey's attention away from the men. "Zoey, are you sure you want everyone at your house?"

"Sure," she answered. "It'll be fun. This is the first time Mickey will be home for the whole season in years, which reminds me. You both need to give me a Christmas list for the kids. They're so old now, I just don't know what to buy for them. You guys are easy. You like what I like."

"Oh, you're such a good aunty. So, when is this soirée?" Joanne asked.

"Hold on, I'll get the calendar," Carol added. She walked into the kitchen and pulled a well-marked American Scenic calendar she got free from the bank off of the side of the refrigerator, flipped to December, and put it down in front of Zoey.

"Let's see," Zoey said as she dragged a finger across the weeks. "Christmas is on a Saturday this year, so Friday, Christmas Eve, say about three o'clock? That way we can have a nice dinner and still have plenty of time to open presents." The ladies thought for a moment before agreeing.

"Don't go overboard now, Zoey," Carol said. "I know you can afford it, but you really don't have to make it a big deal. Just do us all a favor and make sure you don't leave any of your—" she put her hand up to her mouth to shield it from the kids' table, lowered her voice, and enunciated clearly, "—dildos, ticklers, butt plugs, or other toys," she raised her voice to her normal tone, "lying around like the last time."

Joanne gave out a loud "Ha!" and almost spit out her food. It was so loud everyone stopped talking and looked at her. "Sorry," she said sheepishly. "Carry on."

Zoey tried to cover her blushing face with her hand as she shook her head. "I promise. Mickey and I will do a quick inspection before you come over to make sure there will be no embarrassing moments like the last time." A smile crept across her face. "Although I'll never forget the look on your face when Betty walked out of the bathroom, holding out my crotchless underwear, and asked how they got ripped. You've got to admit that was classic." They started laughing.

"That was hilarious," Carol said sarcastically. She thought for moment. "Hey, that was the last time we did Christmas at your house."

The women fell silent, letting their minds wander to think about each of their own lives since that time. Carol looked at her own children, now almost teenagers. Joanne thought of her kids and her brother Jonathan and his divorce. She saw him sitting at the kids' table with his son, feeding him mashed potatoes. Zoey thought of all of wonderful things she had done with Mickey. "Time flies," she added.

"You got that right," Joanne said with melancholy. "Nothing stays the same."

Zoey could tell sadness was creeping into Joanne's thoughts because of Jonathan's divorce. She reached over and squeezed her friend's hand and whispered, "It'll be all right," in her ear, adding, "I promise." Joanne smiled and nodded.

"Seriously, though, Carol's right about Christmas, Zoey," Joanne said. "Don't go overboard."

"Are you kidding?" Zoey replied with a smile. "You forget that Mickey and I don't have family. You guys are all we've got. Mickey is home and I'm in a good mood."

"Well, can we bring anything?" Carol asked.

"Nope," Zoey insisted. "I've got it all under control. You know how much Stella likes to throw parties. She's just as excited about it as I am. And now that Mickey's home, I've got a helper." The women looked at each other before they burst out laughing.

Zoey felt relaxed, even happy. She looked across

the table at Mickey. He was smiling and talking to the guys. Suddenly her anxiety came back full force. She reached out and grabbed her wine glass. She hoped Carol and Joanne didn't notice that her hand was shaking, but they did. The smiles on their faces vanished in an instant and turned to concern.

"Zoey, are you all right?" Carol asked in a low tone. "What's wrong?"

Zoey could feel her face redden. "Oh, it's nothing. I'm fine," she answered, not convincing anyone.

"You are most certainly not fine," Carol said as she got up and motioned to the kitchen. "Come on, ladies." The women flanked Zoey and ushered her into the kitchen.

"Now, what's going on?" Carol asked as Zoey leaned against the kitchen counter. "Are you and Mickey fighting?"

Zoey chuckled, "Oh, God no. It's just..." She hesitated.

Joanne put her arm around her friend. "It's okay. You can tell us. We love you."

Tears welled up in Zoey's eyes and began rolling down her cheeks. "I keep getting the feeling that Mickey's in danger, like something's going to happen to him." She began to gently sob as the women hugged her.

"Oh, sweetie," Carol said softly. "I thought you were used to his being away by now. It never bothered you like this before. Do you know something we don't?"

"No, yes, oh, I don't know," Zoey replied with confusion. "It's just a feeling I've been getting lately. I've never felt such apprehension."

"Maybe it's just the Y2K thing and all the crazy things that have happened this year," Carol said. "I know I freaked out when that kid went crazy at Columbine in April. I thought about my kids and their safety. And then when JFK Jr. died in that plane crash in July, how crazy was that? I thought about that for weeks. Everyone's emotions are high right now."

"That's right," Joanne said. "There's a weird vibe going around the world. All those kooks who think the world will end just because it's the end of the millennium... it's nuts."

Zoey regained her composure, taking comfort from her friends. "I guess you're right. I'm being silly. But I don't know what I would do if I didn't have Mickey." The thought of life without him brought another flood of tears.

Carol handed her a tissue and Zoey blotted her eyes dry. "Honey, you want to lie down for a while?" she asked. Zoey shook her head and declined the offer.

"You want some water?" Joanne asked as she reached for a glass and began to fill it. Zoey nodded and took the glass. The friends had never seen her so distraught.

Once again Zoey pulled herself together. "No, I'll be all right." She took a deep breath. "We'd better get out there or they'll think something's wrong. I don't want Mickey to know how upset I am."

"You sure you're all right?" Joanne said as she put her arm around her friend.

Zoey straightened up and smoothed back her hair. "I'm fine," she replied confidently. "Let's go out there." They all hugged.

"Grab a pie and the plates," Carol said. "They'll think we just came in to get dessert."

Carol grabbed the pumpkin pie off the stove and Joanne took the cherry. Zoey picked up the nearby plates, spoons, and a knife off of the counter and grabbed the whipped cream can out of the fridge. They walked out together. All attention was focused on the pies.

It was about ten o'clock before Zoey and Mickey got to bed that night. "You were awfully quiet on the ride home," he mentioned casually, reaching for her hand and kissing it. "Everything okay?"

"Sure. I'm fine, just tired."

"No, you're not," he said firmly. "I know you. You're not fine. Are you still worried about me?"

She hung her head before answering, "Yes."

"Babe, I told you. I've got bodyguards. I'm never alone. There have been no specific threats against our company. I'm safe."

"I know," she replied, "but I've got this bad feeling. I can't shake it."

He felt helpless. "Zoey, I'm not in danger. Trust me."

She began to doubt herself. "I guess you're right."

"Have I ever been wrong, babe?" He rolled over to his side and pulled her close. "Now, how about I do what I've wanted to do to you all day?" He planted a wet kiss on her mouth.

Felling safe and a little foolish, she relaxed completely. She was in the moment again. She kissed him back with passion and pressed her body to his. "Let's," she said. "Whatever you want, I'm all yours."

"Oh, baby," he moaned. "I'm on fire. That's why I love you."

Chapter 8

The feelings of trepidation gradually faded as the days went on, and Zoey began to enjoy the novelty of having Mickey home all the time. Well, most of the time. He took a few business trips, but they were just overnighters, and he was always home late that night or the next day before noon.

He actually was a big help in organizing the Christmas party. Although everything was subject to Zoey's final approval, he met with the caterers to choose the menu, picked out the floral arrangements, and as long as Zoey gave him a list of stores and complete descriptions, sizes, and brand names of the items to be purchased, he actually did Christmas shopping by himself while she was at work.

Dinner time with him every night was joyous. He attempted to cook a few meals, but Zoey had him so busy it was easier on them and Stella if they went out or had it brought in.

It had been a rough year for both of them. Zoey's heavy case load and Jonathan's divorce added extra stress. His case was different, however. She couldn't help but be emotionally involved.

Mickey's work became more political than legal and a lot more dangerous. World events were changing quickly and anti-American sentiment was fast becoming a big concern, especially when it came to oil. In the last two years he spent more time out of the country than in, and it didn't look like that was going to change.

There was so much he was privy to that the public didn't know. Things he couldn't even tell Zoey, which was actually better. If she knew how perilous his job had become, she would make him quit. He actually thought about it himself. The job had lost its appeal. There was a new breed of contenders who played by different rules. It was all about money and corporate greed now. He put a lot of thought into it. Just a few more years and he could quit and be set for life. He hadn't told Zoey anything about it in case things changed, but it was hard to keep it from her. They knew each other so well.

She had noticed the change in his demeanor the last few years. He was more somber. She had even asked why he didn't smile as much anymore. She thought it was something she'd done. He blamed it on complicated contracts and difficult negotiations. But he knew she would figure it out sooner or later. It was no wonder she began to have panic attacks.

Mickey was noticing how uncomfortable things became for her, and he knew she picked up on the turmoil and danger without realizing it. He really noticed what a negative effect it was having on her during Thanksgiving dinner at Dave and Carol's, and it worried him. He hated doing this to her. He planned to tell her he was going to quit at the end of the coming summer. He would work only one more year and then retire.

He hoped she would quit her legal business, too. He figured she could stop taking new clients, and within the year wrap up everything she had going on and find another attorney to refer her current clients to. He had observed that, when it came to child custody, the final divorce decree was just the beginning. It seemed like they all needed adjusting every few years due to life changes of the parents. Zoey felt personally responsible for every one of her clients. It would take time to find the right attorney for each of them.

Mickey knew they both needed to unwind, to disentangle from the outside world for a while. He took advantage of their time together and they did fun things like they used to do back when they were first married.

They spent a whole afternoon at the Detroit Institute of Art. Mickey played dumb and took pleasure in listening to Zoey explain a particular piece of sculpture that he saw no value in. He watched intently as she interpreted a modern art piece after he called it scribble. They ended the day with dinner in Greek Town. Another day, Mickey took her to the zoo.

The home time also gave them a chance do things that normal couples do. They rented a couple of movies and watched them while snuggling together on the couch, munching on popcorn or chips or nibbling on the homemade Christmas cookies Stella had given them. They actually went out for dinner and a show, just like they were on a real date. Zoey thought it was romantic.

One day Zoey played hooky from work and they took a road trip to Frankenmuth, Michigan. They had fried chicken at the famous Zehnder's restaurant. Zoey couldn't resist doing a little Christmas shopping for stocking stuffers while there.

But the topper on the cake was all the sex they were having. They had, as Mickey liked to say, fucked themselves silly in the first week. It started with a marathon two-day session the day after he came home. That turned into a couple of times a day. Within a week they'd had sex in every room of the house at least once, and gone through most of their favorite role-playing scenarios and a fair amount of their toys. By now, two weeks before Christmas, they slowed down to a quickie in the morning or real sex at night. Weekends were still a free-for-all of debauchery.

It had been years since they'd done those kinds of things together. Mickey loved to see Zoey smile and hear her lighthearted laugh. It made him feel good to see her so happy. Her sparkling eyes warmed his heart. He loved her more now than ever.

Zoey noticed the stress lines in Mickey's face ease as the days went on. He seemed more relaxed. The best part of him being home was being able to snuggle together at night and fall asleep cloaked in his love, knowing she wasn't alone. They were together. One heart, one love.

*****

It was Thursday, December 23rd. The decorations in the house made it look like a Currier and Ives Christmas card. There were presents galore under a huge, heavily- decorated tree. Zoey was on her way home. Just an hour before, Mickey picked up one of her favorite meals from her favorite restaurant. Shrimp a la Zoey, the chef called it. It was a special meal he'd created just for her many years ago. Mickey was having a rib- eye steak—his favorite. Tomorrow was the big Christmas party and he wanted to help her unwind. He knew she would be going full steam ahead all morning, preparing for the party guests.

As for tonight, everything was ready. The table was set and a sexual clue to the evening's merriment was waiting on her chair—a cowboy hat. That meant she was in for a rootin'-tootin' good time. There would be a lot of yipees and yee-haws once things got started.

It was about seven o'clock before the sound of the garage door opening woke Mickey from his cat nap in the living room recliner. He greeted Zoey with a kiss and a hug as she walked into the house. "How was your day, babe?" he asked as she hung up her coat.

"Not bad, just long," she replied. She walked through the dining room on her way to the kitchen. She noticed the table was set and saw the cowboy hat on her chair. She picked it up and looked over at Mickey.

He gave her a salacious grin. "Yippee-ki-yay, darlin'," he said in his best western drawl.

She grinned from ear to ear and set the hat back down. "How am I ever going to get through dinner knowing what dessert is?"

"Eat fast," was his reply as he followed her into the kitchen. Zoey pulled the already filled salad bowls out of the fridge and pulled off the plastic wrap. She grabbed a couple of bottles of salad dressing as well and placed it all on the table. Mickey opened the heating oven and pulled out the plated dinner he was keeping warm and followed her out. He placed the shrimp in front of Zoey.

Her eyes got wide. "Shrimp a la Zoey? Oh, you shouldn't have. Now I don't know what I'm going to enjoy most this evening—the shrimp or your dick."

"Both, I hope," he quickly added, placing another kiss on her lips. He reached for the bottle of wine from the table and poured them both a glass.

After he sat down she raised her glass to him. "I love you, Mickey," she said sincerely. "You are the best husband in the world."

He raised his glass to meet hers. "Can't argue with that," he boasted.

They chatted and laughed while they ate. Life was good. She was in Zoey's Place again and there was no place either would rather be. After they were done, he helped her clear the table.

She stood by the sink, rinsing off the plates and loading them into the dishwasher when, suddenly, she felt him behind her. She reached back and grabbed a rock-hard cock protruding from his unzipped jeans. "Is it playtime?" she asked.

He bent down and whispered in her ear, "Time to get on your pony and ride, girl. Twenty minutes, room number one." Then he backed away and disappeared out of the room.

Her heart skipped a beat with anticipation. The cowboy was her favorite. She quickly ran upstairs to shower. Room number one was their bedroom, and as she passed through she could see that Mickey was busy preparing the room. He had laid out her attire for the evening in the bathroom. It consisted of a black lace g-string, a black and red tightly fitted corset bustier that unhooked in the front and left her breasts exposed, and a dance-hall-style red satin dress that fastened with ribbons in front.

She quickly showered, dressed, and braided her hair. She was applying a coat of red lipstick when she heard Mickey fussing in the bedroom; the sound of country music twanged through the air. It was Alan Jackson singing his song 'Gone Crazy'. She looked at herself in the full-length mirror and readjusted her braid. Her breasts were flowing out of the low-cut dress. She dabbed some Chanel No. 5 on the back of her neck, each wrist, and down her cleavage. She was ready. She waited until she heard Mickey give the signal.

"Whose pussy does a guy have to eat to get a whiskey around here?" It was on.

She pushed opened the door. It took a moment for her eyes to adjust to the glowing red lighted room. She looked over at the bed and saw him sitting on the edge. He was wearing his cowboy hat and was looking down at the empty glass in his hand. He glanced up at her and tipped his hat. "Howdy, ma'am," he said, speaking in a thick western drawl as he stood up. "You own this joint?"

He looked delicious. He was wearing a black leather vest over his bare chest. A red bandana was tied around his neck. She could see the cowboy boots poking out from the bottom of the fringed leather chaps. He wasn't wearing pants underneath so his genitals were exposed. "I'm the owner," she said in her best dance hall gal voice.

"Got any whiskey?" he asked.

She sauntered over to the dresser by the window and grabbed the bottle of Maker's Mark from the dresser. "Will this do, stranger?"

"That'll do fine," he said, still in character. "You all alone?" he asked.

"Sure am," she answered. She walked over to him and poured him a drink.

"You smell good, pretty lady. I don't like to drink alone. Why don't you join me?" he said as he picked up another glass from the nightstand and held it out to her as he sipped his drink.

"Don't mind if I do," she replied seductively as she held out the bottle and filled the empty glass. She set the bottle down, took the glass from Mickey, and gulped down the whiskey. It burned the back of her throat as it went down and took her breath away. "You know, I've been alone for a long time," she said. "A woman has needs." She looked him straight in the eye. "Do you know what a woman needs?" she asked.

"No, ma'am," he answered. "But I'm willing to find out. Why don't you tell me what your needs are and I'd be happy to oblige."

She smiled. In this scenario she called the shots. It was all about pleasing her. She gave the orders and he obeyed. She looked at the toys he had arranged on the cedar chest at the foot of the bed: lubricant, g-spot vibrator, a feather tickler, a vibrating dildo, a small pleasure whip, and a cock ring. She loved the cock ring. It slowed the flow of blood from his erection to make his cock hard for a much longer period of time. She grabbed the whip and slapped it against her hand a few times before she spoke.

"Okay, cowboy, let's see how you do taking orders from a woman. Stand up in front of me," she commanded. He obeyed.

She reached out and cradled his penis in her free hand. "Nice," she said as she manipulated his hardening manhood. She let it drop. "Now turn around."

He obeyed. The chaps left his backside exposed. She found herself inches from the most beautiful man butt she had ever seen. Reaching out, she ran her hand over each cheek before slapping it with the whip. The stinging took him by surprise and he flinched. Zoey laughed. "Scare ya?" she asked.

"Just a little," he replied.

"Good," she said as she stood up. "Now I want you to undress me."

He turned to her and pulled the satin ribbons that lined the front of her dress. He gently pushed the dress off of her shoulders and let it fall to the floor. He could feel his hardness growing as he gazed up and let his hungry eyes take in the view and smell of her standing in front of him, naked except for the corset and g-string. Her breasts were heaving as she breathed, inviting him to touch. He reached out but felt the sting of the whip on his ass.

"I didn't say you could do that," she reprimanded.

He bowed his head and said, "Sorry, I couldn't help myself."

She stretched out on the bed and spread her legs wide. "Now I want you to go down on my muffin and keep at it until I tell you to stop. Got it?"

"Whatever you say, ma'am; you're the boss."

She smiled. "That's a good cowboy."

He positioned himself between her legs and obeyed her command. Years of experience had taught him exactly what she liked. His tongue performed its magic as it worked its way into her female folds and coddled her secret places. She wriggled with pleasure as she felt her passion rising. He could tell she was close to climaxing and performed his task with more intensity. She let out an orgasmic moan and pulled him closer with her hands as she scissor-gripped him with her legs, riding the waves of pleasure coursing through her body.

She loosened her legs' grip and pushed his head away, motionless until her heart stopped racing. "Did I do good?" he asked sheepishly.

"You did fine, cowboy. Now pour me another drink, and one for yourself, too. You've earned it."

He smiled. "Thank you, ma'am."

She drained the second drink in one gulp. She closed her eyes and felt the burn as it went down, heating her from the inside out like hot iron. She was starting to feel the effects of the first shot and this one should intensify the sensation.

"Cowboy!" she commanded. He stood at attention. "Get buck naked but leave your hat on." He quickly stripped down. She reached over to the end of the bed and grabbed the cock ring. She looked over at him and could see he was smiling. The cock ring prolonged the love session and intensified his orgasm. This was going to be fun. She threw the ring at him and said, "Put this on."

Two hours had passed before she had her fill of him and he of her. It was a rip- roaring, down and dirty sexual rodeo. The last event ended with Zoey in cowgirl position, wearing the cowboy hat. The events of the evening left the two naked and spent on the bed. The blankets and sheets lay on the floor in a jumbled pile. The Maker's Mark was nearly drained and the toys Mickey brought out were scattered around the room.

She looked over at her husband with blurry eyes. "Mickey, do you think other people have as much fun with sex as we do?"

"Some, probably," he replied as he sat up on his elbows and pushed his dark hair back in place. "But not enough, or else the world wouldn't be as fucked up and filled with so many assholes."

"Their loss," she said. "I can't imagine not having sex. Maybe it's because they're not as good at it as you are." She rolled to her side to face him. He lay back down and looked into her eyes. They embraced and he kissed her gently on the forehead.

"Well, you don't have to worry about that because I plan on making love to you every chance I get," he said tenderly.

"Oh, goodie," she squeaked, and then yawned. "But I'm afraid it will have to wait until tomorrow. I've been rode hard tonight. I'm plum tuckered out, cowboy. Goodnight, my love." And with that she curled into the fetal position, closed her eyes, and dozed off.

He looked down at her, his sleeping angel. He picked up the bed covers from the floor and swathed his exhausted lover, now sound asleep, tucking the blankets in around her. He walked around the room, blowing out the candles. He turned off the red light and the stereo, crawled into bed, and spooned his wife before falling asleep.

Chapter 9

It was Christmas Eve at last. Party guests would soon arrive. As promised, Zoey and Mickey did a quick walk through the house, making sure there was no obvious evidence of their many anything-goes love sessions lying around. Good thing, too, because behind the recliner in the living room he found the red g-string he had flung over his shoulder the last time they played Naughty Nun.

"Hey," he called out to her in the next room. "Look what I found." She came rushing to the sound of his voice in time to see him hold the lingerie up to his nose and take a sniff. "Ah! That's my girl." She couldn't help but laugh. He motioned to pocket the underwear.

"Give me those," she demanded as she made a reach for the panties, but he was too quick. He balled them up and shoved them deep into his front jean pocket before she reached him.

"No," he insisted as he turned away from her. "We have to be on our best behavior tonight and I want to be able to pull these out and remind myself of what else I could be doing."

"You are such a pervert," she replied with a smile, shaking her head. "I appreciate the sentiment, but if I know you you'll pull those out when Dave and Lenny are around and rub it in their faces that we have so much sex."

"Rub it in their faces," he laughed. "I love that."

Zoey got flustered. "Oh, you know what I mean."

"So what, babe," he said. "I want the world to know we have the best sex this side of the Mississippi, maybe beyond, and lots of it. We were both blessed with high libidos."

She hugged him around the waist and breathed in the clean, crisp scent of his aftershave. It was his unique musk and it filled her with comfort and safety. She missed that when he was gone. Sometimes she would keep one of his shirts from being laundered just so she could 'smell' him when she was lonely. Looking up into his dark eyes, she said, "You are the best," and kissed him. She could feel him getting hard as he pressed himself against her and kissed her back with open mouth.

"Oh, baby," he said. "Do we have time to knock one off before they get here? How about right here?"

"Mickey!" she admonished. "Much as I would love it, darling, no, we don't. Besides, Stella is in the kitchen. Give me that g-string. It's dangerous in your hands."

He looked sad and rejected. "How 'bout a rain check?" he asked sheepishly.

"How can I resist," she said sympathetically. "Of course, lover. Now hand them over."

Reluctantly, he relinquished the prize.

*****

The house was aglow inside and out with hundreds

of Christmas lights, and plenty of sparkle and shine. It had snowed a couple of inches the night before, which just added to the holiday atmosphere. Zoey checked in with Stella to make sure the food was ready. Mickey decided to watch some TV until the guests arrived. They were ready for the festivities to begin.

Right on time, both families arrived with armfuls of gifts and suddenly the house became a flurry of activity and sounds. Christmas music was heard throughout the house on the built-in sound system. Eggnog was flowing. Everyone helped themselves to the appetizers and plates of Christmas cookies Stella placed throughout the house.

Dinner went off without a hitch and no one brought up Mickey's job. Everyone opened their presents during dessert. Zoey outdid herself and, to the chagrin of her two women friends, she bought several items from the Christmas lists and more, from trendy clothes to the latest, most popular video games. She even bought a new laptop for each child. She figured they seemed to be becoming a must for every student. She knew her friends couldn't afford them so, what the heck.

Little Jon was outfitted for the next year in the latest baby couture and got a dozen or more new toys to keep him busy.

For her friends, the gifts ran the gamut. There were movie and restaurant gift certificates, Kitchenaide mixers, golf balls, silk scarves, and leather driving gloves. She topped that off with small baskets full of bath products and large baskets filled with gourmet food.

Their friends returned the favor with a bottle of aged single malt Scotch and two bottles of Zoey's favorite wine. Zoey and Mickey also were given new driving gloves, gift certificates for massages, sweaters, and crystal wine glasses. Carol included four 'Carol Coupons', which entitled the bearer to a homemade treat of choice from desserts to main dishes. She was a terrific cook, and Zoey and Mickey looked forward to cashing them in.

The guys were in the garage, smoking the Cuban cigars Mickey procured with his connections. Smoking was one thing Zoey did not allow in her house, especially cigars, Cuban or not.

The kids were all busy with their gifts and the women began to clean up. "What are you guys doing for New Year's?" Carol asked. "Going to Zoey's Place again?" The Incline Village cabin was often referred to as that because just the mention of the place never failed to bring a smile to Zoey's face.

"Yes," she replied, grinning from ear to ear. "It's become a tradition with us. I hope there's lots of snow. I want to go skiing."

"Yeah, right," Joanne joked. "You guys don't do anything but have sex when you're there. We've all heard the stories." The friends shared a laugh.

"Must be nice," Carol bemoaned. "We're so busy all the time and the kids are always involved with so many things. We could never get away like that."

"Us, too," Joanne chimed in. She looked at Zoey and sneered, "I hate you."

Zoey pouted. "Well, if it makes you feel any better, we won't exactly be alone this year." The women looked puzzled. "A group of Saudis are coming to the States. They want to spend New Year's Eve in Vegas." She hesitated for a moment and added, "with hookers." The women moaned. "Mickey's got it all set up so he won't have to babysit them, but he might have to spend a day with them."

"Boo-hoo," Joanne said sarcastically. "Not New

Year's Eve, I hope."

"No," Zoey answered. "I've got Mickey all to myself on New Year's Eve." She closed her eyes and twisted back and forth as she hugged herself, smiling.

"Good," Carol said. "I envy you. Not that I would give up my kids for all the tea in China, but it must be nice to be on a perpetual honeymoon like you and Mickey are."

Zoey nodded. "We've been lucky."

"And blessed with enormous sex drives," Joanne added.

Mickey and Zoey said goodnight to Stella shortly after dinner clean-up and thanked her for helping out. She would be back the day after Christmas to clean the house. They handed her an envelope which contained her Christmas bonus. It was a check for $2,000. Stella was grateful and gave them both a hug. They watched her get into her car and waved goodbye as she drove off.

By the end of the evening, after the last guests departed, all that remained of the night's festivities were scattered scraps of wrapping paper, plates littered with crumbs, and partially-filled glasses. Mickey and Zoey looked at the living room then looked at each other. Mickey spoke first. "Well, we can be good and stay up and clean before we go to bed or we can be bad and just go to bed, and you can let me ravage you like I've wanted to do since I found your panties this morning."

She looked around. Then she looked at him and his silly grin. His eyes were wide and his expression was one of wanting. He reminded her of a kid with his face pressed against the candy counter glass. "Bah humbug. I'm a bad, bad girl. I'll race ya to the bedroom," she said as she sprinted to the stairs.

Chapter 10

For two days after the Christmas party, Zoey and Mickey didn't leave their home. Meals were delivered. Any business there was had been conducted by phone. Stella had been in once to clean the downstairs, but knew better than to venture to the top floor in situations like this. The rest of their time consisted of torrid and intense lovemaking, ever mindful that all good things must come to an end.

Too soon, it was the day of the corporate Christmas dinner party. They had to once again become part of the world and play the game of life.

Zoey and Mickey took their seats in the private jet that had been sent for them. As they fastened their seatbelts, the flight attendant approached. She was a pretty blond in her early 20s, with long slim legs and wearing spiked black heels. She was sharply dressed in a tailored black jacket and short skirt. A green and black silk scarf patterned with the corporate logo was tied pertly around her neck. Green and black were the company colors. Mickey told Zoey that the green represented nature and black represented authority and power. It was the corporation's way of stating it had power over nature by making her give up her treasure—the oil. Zoey always teased Mickey, saying the colors represented money and oil, the real symbols of Taylor Resource Development Corporation.

"Good evening, Mr. and Mrs. De Lucca," the attendant said as she nodded respectfully, first at Mickey then at Zoey. "My name is Allison and I'll be your flight attendant today. I believe we're ready for take-off. May I get you a drink once we're airborne?"

"Dewar's on the rocks," Mickey said.

She turned to Zoey. "I'll have Bailey's if you have it, please, no rocks."

"Of course," the attendant replied. "And might I add you look lovely today, Mrs. DeLucca."

"Thank you," Zoey replied modestly. The attendant retreated to the front of the plane and strapped herself in.

The plane taxied to the runway.

Mickey grabbed Zoey's hand and squeezed tightly. She looked up at him and gazed into the dark pools of his eyes. "She's right, you know," he said, smiling.

She looked puzzled. "You mean about the Bailey's?"

"No, about you, gorgeous," he whispered. "You look more than lovely. You look scrumptious." He smiled seductively. "I wish I could eat you right here, right now, and so does she."

Zoey's mouth dropped open. He smiled and nodded. "How do you know?" she whispered.

He leaned over and whispered in her ear, "Last year, on a flight from Houston to New York, I saw her making out with another flight attendant in the galley when they thought no one was watching, full tongue."

Although Zoey wasn't attracted to women, the

thought of one wanting her sexually was quite exciting, and actually made her quiver.

Mickey noticed as she squirmed in her seat. He could feel himself get aroused and placed her hand on his growing hardness. At that moment the plane tilted up as it left the ground. The gravitational pressure pressed her hand down harder and she curled it around him. She continued to hold on as the plane climbed and then leveled off.

"Your drink, ma'am," the attendant said as she held out a brandy snifter of Bailey's towards Zoey. She looked up into Allison's sparkling blue eyes and blushed. After what seemed like an unusually long pause, Allison turned her attention to Mickey. "And your Dewar's, sir." She handed the drink to him and returned to the galley.

"She did that on purpose, you know," he said. "She saw your hand on my dick and she was jealous."

"Stop it, Mickey," she teased, and sipped her Bailey's. "You're making that up."

"Seriously, I heard that corporate was only hiring lesbians now because there was too much sex between the execs and the flight attendants. The wives were complaining."

"Well, that's one way to stop it," she contemplated. "Now they just have to worry about the wives getting hit on."

A limo was waiting for them when they arrived in Houston and took them to the Bay Oaks Country Club. The private club was reserved by corporate for the evening and closed to the public. As they approached the door, Mickey grabbed Zoey's hand and kissed it. "You ready for this, babe?" he asked.

She took a deep breath. "Ready as I'll ever be."

The banquet room was decorated like a scene from

a classic Christmas movie. Huge Christmas trees adorned with lavish, old-style decorations and trim were found in every corner. Holly and twinkle lights were strung across the ceiling of the main banquet room. A string quartet was playing Christmas music in one end of the room, and several buffet tables full of foods and desserts of all kinds were set up in another. They spotted Allen and Fen Webber sitting alone at a table and headed in that direction. On the way they were intercepted by Randolph Taylor, one of the company founders, and his wife, Mitzi.

"Mickey, Zoey, nice to see you. Merry Christmas. Glad you could make it," Randolph said, clasping Mickey's hand and giving it a quick shake. Then he and Zoey exchanged a quick, stiff embrace. Mitzi offered a forced smile but not her hand or a greeting. They quickly moved on to the next arriving couple.

Zoey looked at Mickey. "Is it just me or was that weird?"

Mickey gave her a forced smile, grabbed her by the elbow, and directed her towards the table Fen and Allen were sitting at. "Let it go," he said through his teeth. "Be nice."

Fen and Allen stood as the couple approached. Fen looked exquisite in a full-length, deep red velvet dress that draped in just the right places to show off her slim and elegant body. She was adorned with matching ruby earrings, necklace, and bracelet that reflected the twinkling Christmas lights of the room. Her long dark hair had been pinned up and held in place with a diamond and feather comb that complemented her long regal neck. Zoey felt far less extravagant in her midnight blue satin dress and pearls.

The men shook hands and turned to face the women. "Merry Christmas, Zoey," Allen said sincerely, and gave her a warm hug. Mickey greeted Fen in similar fashion.

"You look lovely, Zoey," Fen said as she turned to her and gave her an enormous bear hug, taking Zoey by surprise.

"Merry Christmas, Fen," Zoey said. "You look beautiful and elegant, as always."

"This is the most boring Christmas party ever," Fen said. "Can you believe that band? I feel like I'm at a funeral."

Zoey smiled as she took a seat and quickly scanned the room. "Well, by the looks on the faces around the room, it looks like it won't be long before that's the case." She knew she didn't need to filter her thoughts around Fen. The women shared a laugh.

"You got that right," Fen responded. "You need a drink." She grabbed Zoey's hand and headed towards the bar. "It's good to see you. You look stunning. What have you been up to, Counselor?" she asked.

Fen's friendliness made Zoey feel at ease, and she was grateful to have a friend in this unfamiliar environment. She quickly filled her in about her current cases without going into too much detail. She sometimes felt that her work was unimpressive in value compared to the vast amount of charity work Fen was always involved in and the millions of dollars she generated for good causes. She purposely left out the personal aspects of Jonathan's case. To be honest, she felt that Rhonda's actions gave the case a trashy aspect she didn't want to be associated with.

"Enough about my boring life," Zoey concluded. "What charities have benefitted by your involvement since I saw you last?" she asked, hoping to shift the attention away from herself.

"Oh, same old ones I've always been involved with; nothing new," Fen said modestly, without offering any more.

Zoey grabbed the glass of wine the bartender placed in front of her and the two headed back towards the table. The men had gone and were standing a ways off with a group of colleagues. By the look on their faces and the tone of their voices, they were obviously discussing serious business matters.

Fen noticed the concerned look on Zoey's face. "They're always on the clock, aren't they?" she commented.

Zoey turned to face her. "Yes," she said with disdain. "I've been worried about Mickey's safety lately when he's travelling. Things are getting crazy over there."

Fen grabbed her hand. "Don't worry, honey. Our golden boys are treated like sacred cows over there. Nothing's going to happen to them."

"If only I could be sure," Zoey said. "I've had some serious anxiety about it and now I'm having bad dreams."

"Sweetie, you need to stop that," Fen said. "Corporate wants Mickey and Allen safe more than you do. Hey, I've got some good gossip for you. Want to hear it?"

Zoey forced herself to let it go. Allen had worked for the company longer than Mickey, and she trusted Fen to give good advice. "I guess you're right," she replied, trying to empty her head of all negative thoughts. "I'd love to hear the gossip. You always have the good stuff."

"Good," Fen said happily. Her eyes narrowed as she scanned the room. "See that heavy-set woman over there in the dark green chiffon dress?" She discreetly lifted her hand, pretending to wave away an invisible fly, and pointed towards an elderly woman sitting at a table with three other women of the same stature.

"You mean the other Mrs. Taylor?" Zoey asked.

"So, you know who she is?" Fen asked.

"Yes," Zoey replied. "I met her a few years back at one of the summer parties. You were out of town for that one. She's Ronald's wife, isn't she?"

Ronald and Randolph Taylor were brothers, and founders of Taylor Resource Development. Ronald was rarely in the public spotlight and almost never attended social events. Even rarer was the appearance of his wife, Elizabeth. Zoey had only met her the one time before.

"Did you ever wonder why Lizzy never comes to these social events?" Fen asked.

Zoey gave it some thought. "I just figured she didn't like them."

Fen grinned. "Not even close. You know it was Lizzy who supplied the seed money to begin the company in the first place, don't you? Her family is loaded. *Was* loaded," she corrected. "They're dead now. She's like you, only child. When her parents died, she got it all."

"No, I didn't know." Zoey was intrigued.

"Well, it's true. Both her parents got pneumonia at the same time and died within days of each other. She met Ronald about six months before that. They got married as soon as the funeral was over. Without her, Taylor Resource Development wouldn't exist. She really wears the pants in the family. She has no mind for business, so she doesn't get involved in the mechanics of the operations, but that's also why Ronald puts up with her shenanigans."

Zoey laughed. "Shenanigans. That's a word I haven't heard in a while. What does she do? And what does that have to do with her not coming to the parties?"

"Be patient. It's a long story," Fen said as she settled back in her chair. "I can't believe Mickey never told you the story."

Zoey shook her head and took a sip of her wine. "Mickey rarely talks about the company."

Fen nodded in acknowledgement. "Probably a good thing," she agreed, and continued without missing a beat. "Bottom line is she's got a real craving for young men."

"You're kidding!" Zoey exclaimed with surprise, almost choking on her wine. "That old biddy?"

"Unbelievable, isn't it?" Fen continued. "Many rumors abound, and only she and Ronald know the real truth. But," she hesitated, "rumor has it that she was kind of a party girl in her time. And let me put it this way… she always had a party to go to."

Both women giggled. Fen went on. "She met Ronald at one of these parties and, for whatever reason, he became a keeper. Well, I guess she missed the good old days after the company became successful and Ronald was spending more time away on business. It started as slight indiscretions when he was gone. There's also a rumor that, because of some kind of accident, Ronald is sexually disfigured in some way and it made him impotent."

Zoey chortled out loud but caught herself, and forced her laugh into her cocktail napkin.

"*Shh!*" Fen admonished, trying to act nonchalant and not burst into laughter herself before continuing. "So, one thing led to another and yada-yada-yada, now she has sex parties with groups of men when Ronny is out of town."

Zoey looked at her in disbelief. "Wait just a minute," she said. "That visual is going to stay with me for the rest of my life. Thank you. And you still haven't told me why she doesn't come to the company parties."

"Oh, yeah. I forgot," Fen replied apologetically. "Well, like I said, it was all kept quiet and never discussed, until about twenty years ago when she started coming to the company parties and began making sexual demands of the new, young employees. She would tell them she was in charge and it was one of the conditions of employment. She also told them if they told anyone, they would be fired. You're lucky Mickey wasn't in the high position he's in now back then."

Zoey cringed.

"Well, you know how that goes. Someone told Randolph, who told Ronald, and a deal was made. She could still have her boy toys and parties, but discreetly, and employees were off limits. So, to avoid new rumors, and because she really doesn't give a shit about the goings on of the business, she doesn't come to many company social gatherings. I can't believe you didn't know that before."

"I know," Zoey said. "But in all fairness, this is the first time she's ever been at a party that both you and I have attended. And who else would volunteer that kind of information?"

Fen agreed modestly and nodded her head.

Zoey thought of her own sexual appetite and suddenly felt a pang of sympathy for the old woman. "Actually, I kind of feel sorry for her and admire her at the same time. Some women have the need for a lot of sex, and she found a way to keep having it."

"I guess you're right," Fen conceded. "You know, if men want more sex they go to Nevada and no one bats an eye or judges them. But what is there for women? Nothing, right?"

"Yeah," Zoey agreed. "And if a woman acts on her desires she's considered a whore, ostracized for unacceptable behavior. It's not fair."

"No, it's not," Fen concurred. "You know, through the years I've heard all kinds of stories about, let me see..." She put her hand to her chin, squinted her eyes, and surveyed the room before continuing, "Oh, maybe half the wives in this room. They've all had young men on the side at one time or another. Can't say as I blame them, since their husbands are hardly ever home. And besides, look at them. Who would want to have sex with those guys?"

Zoey laughed. But inside she contemplated what she would do if Mickey couldn't satisfy her sexually. Her thoughts were pleasantly interrupted when she felt the gentle, warm touch of his soft lips on the back of her neck. The men had returned. Mickey sat down beside her.

"So, what have you girls been talking about?" he asked. "We could see you laughing from across the room. Must be pretty funny."

Allen had also sat down and looked interested as well. The women exchanged glances of embarrassment at having been caught.

"Oh, you know," Fen said calmly, "just girl talk and rumors. Nothing you execs would find interesting."

Mickey looked at Zoey with puzzlement on his face. She looked at him and discreetly whispered, "Later."

The party was over by eleven o'clock. A line of limos carried couples to the airport where private jets whisked them off to their respective homes.

On the flight home Zoey was surprised to find that Mickey already knew the stories about Ronald and Lizzy Taylor. He said he'd never told her about it because he didn't think she was interested in his corporate world. She decided to keep the information about the other wives' indiscretions to herself.

Once safely back at home, Zoey and Mickey resumed their sex-fest. They went through their entire sexual scenario menu and invented a few new ones. The erotically blissful days blended together and time seemed to stand still. Zoey could imagine no better Christmas.

Chapter 11

Christmas was over and "Happy New Year" became the greeting of the season. Zoey was excited to get to Incline Village. At the airport, Mickey decided to wait at the bar closest to their departing gate while Zoey went to the ladies room.

Her task completed, she walked back to the bar and saw Mickey sitting at a table in the back sipping a cocktail, most likely a Dewar's on the rocks. For a moment she stood there and enjoyed the sight of the man. Despite his age, his features made him strikingly handsome. He carried himself with confidence that exuded refinement and style. He was perfect. She knew other women looked at him with lust in their eyes, and today was no exception. She smiled as she walked through the bar, knowing he belonged to her and her alone. Joining him at the table, she scooted close to him in the booth and kissed him on the cheek. She dug into her travel bag, pulled out a book, and set it on the table.

She needed a book to read in-flight and at Incline Village for the time Mickey was in Vegas with his client. She had just finished *Angela's Ashes* by Frank

McCourt. It was a great book, but so sad it brought her to tears. It left her depressed and she vowed never to read a book like that again. She'd made a quick trip to the library the day before and decided to go with *Memoirs of a Geisha,* by Arthur Golden. She thought it apropos since they were going to a land where women provided sex for money. She didn't know much about geishas really, only that they were virgins who were sold to the highest bidder. She thought it would be insightful if nothing else.

Mickey greeted her with a short but loving kiss. A glass of wine was waiting for her. She took a sip.

"What're you reading?" he asked as he picked up the book and examined the cover.

"*Memoirs of a Geisha,*" she replied with a smile.

"Why?" he quizzed. "Is there something you don't already know about sex? 'Cause listen, babe, I'm not complaining." He pulled her closer.

"Good," she said laughing. "I just thought it would be interesting to get into the head of someone who has sex without love, kind of like the hookers in Vegas. I could never figure that out. How do they handle it?"

"Wouldn't know. Never had sex with one," he said casually, sipping his drink and looking straight ahead.

"I know that. But you hire them for your clients. Don't you ever talk to them?"

"First of all, I don't talk to them. I talk to their pimp or the madam. Second, it's all very formal. I tell them what kind of hookers I want, and where and when I want them, and they send 'em."

"Seems kind of cold, almost like ordering a pizza."

"It is kind of, I guess, when you think about it like that. It's a business, babe."

The subject had piqued her curiosity. "What kinds of things do you ask for?"

"You mean the pizza toppings?" he teased.

"Yeah," she laughed.

"Well, let me see." He accessed his mental data base, recalling the many calls made on behalf of the corporate clients. "The biggest request I get is for blondes. Some like Asian girls. I've got a few guys who like to have multiple women."

"So, it's mostly physical appearance requests? Nothing sexual?"

"Well, it's none of my business what these guys do with the hookers, but there's an understanding that the women will do whatever they're asked to do. They're professionals. It's their job."

"I don't know. I just can't imagine having to pay for sex, or for that matter having sex for money."

He turned to her with a surprised look on his face. "Are you sure?" he asked with a sinister smile. "Because I could have sworn that two nights ago I shoved a $100 bill deep into a sexy black g-string worn by a hot chick who looked just like you in the game room of our own house. She did a killer lap dance to Limp Bizkit's 'Nookie'. And then she let me do all kinds of nasty things to her while she was bent over the pool table. Oh, baby, I'm getting hard just thinking about it now." He closed his eyes and threw his head back, savoring the memory.

She smiled, shook her head, and pushed lovingly on his arm. "It's not the same thing, darling. It was *Stripper at the Pool Hall* night and it wasn't for the money. And we love each other. I couldn't have sex without love." She leaned over and kissed him gently on the lips.

Just then a scratchy voice announced to all in the terminal that United Flight 5700 to Denver was ready for boarding. Mickey sat up straight and said, "That's us. Let's go." He downed the rest of his drink and picked up their bags. Together they headed for the gate.

The flight from Detroit to Denver was long but uneventful. Flying first class made the trip bearable. They had just under an hour layover in Denver and grabbed a quick sandwich before boarding the plane to Vegas.

A driver with a sign was waiting for them when they arrived at the Las Vegas airport. It was just after noon when the Mercedes limo dropped them off at the front of the MGM Grand Hotel. The client wouldn't arrive for several hours yet. Mickey always came in before to ensure all the preparations had been completed.

Today's client was a very rich sheikh from Dubai. He would be arriving by private jet in the late afternoon or early evening. Zoey had met him once about five years before. She remembered that he was very young and very attractive. He didn't seem like the kind of guy who would need to buy sex. Mickey explained that this was strictly recreation for him. A stress release, so to speak. The sheikh had a couple of wives in Dubai, but he enjoyed the fact that he could do things in Vegas anonymously, mostly sexual things, without the religious and political scrutiny he would be under if he did the same at home. He revealed that the sheikh had confided to him that it would not be honorable to ask the mothers of his children to do what he asks the hookers to do. Zoey didn't understand that aspect. She thought it was morally confusing and dishonest, and really had no respect for the man.

The sheikh also liked to gamble. Sometimes he won big. But it wasn't uncommon for him to lose several million in a night without breaking a sweat.

That's why the MGM always comp'd him with a stay at one of The Mansion estates. They were a palatial collection of one- to four-bedroom villas reserved for only the "Big Whales" as they were called. In Vegas, a whale was a high roller like the sheikh, who didn't bat an eyelash at a multi-million-dollar loss or gain.

The Mansion rooms were spacious and lavishly furnished. Zoey always enjoyed walking through them as Mickey verified preparations. She loved the bedrooms with their giant beds, the regal furniture and fireplaces, everything trimmed in gold. The bathrooms were all imported marbled with enormous tubs, jetted showers, and steam rooms. Each suite was equipped with a formal dining room, full kitchen, meeting room, and living room. There were massive archways and huge crystal chandeliers in almost every room. The architecture was meant to resemble an 18th-century Tuscan villa, and it succeeded. There was a private game room, pool, and lush patios available only to Mansion guests.

The Mansion estates could be accessed by a gated entry driveway. This was usually how the hookers made their discreet arrivals and departures.

"Everything is set," Mickey announced. "I'll call the front desk and tell him you're ready to go to the airport. The Mercedes will be waiting for you when get to Reno. Are you sure you don't want me to have a drive service take you to the cabin?"

Zoey could see that he was all business now. He was good at making arrangements and getting things done. Taking charge came naturally to him. That's why he was so successful at his job.

"I'll be fine driving, Mickey. It's not that far. Besides, I want to get something to eat and go grocery shopping before I go home."

Mickey nodded. "Call me when you get to the

house. Even if I don't answer, leave a message. I'll probably be late tonight. Never know when the sheikh will arrive. I want to make sure he's happy before I head out. I'll take a service from the airport."

"Honey, I don't know why you have to babysit him," she complained with a pout. "He's a grown man, and you're much too important to do this kind of stuff. Doesn't he have people?"

He smiled, gave her a hug, and kissed her forehead, "It's *because* he's an important man that I have to do this." He took a step back and lifted her sad face, up with his hand under her chin so he could look into her eyes. "Don't worry, babe. After tonight you've got me all to yourself for three whole days. Tomorrow is New Year's Eve and I plan on ringing in the New Year inside you."

"Oh!" she squeaked as her body quivered. "Is that a promise?"

"Cross my heart and hope to die," he responded. He pulled her in and kissed her passionately. She reached up and ran her fingers through his hair as she pressed her body into his. She felt his growing hardness. His hands began exploring her supple body as it responded to his touch. She basked in the power and warmth of their love as he caressed her.

Suddenly, he pulled away. "If we keep this up, I might have to fuck you right here on the sheikh's bed."

"Wouldn't want that, now, would we," she responded. "Besides, I really should be going. I've got a lot of grocery shopping to do. We'll be holed up at the cabin for three days. I plan on being naked the whole time. Don't want to have to get dressed because we ran out of food, now, do we?"

"You're killin' me, you temptress." He regained his mental composure and put on his business face. "I'm calling for the driver." He walked over to the phone and placed a call to the concierge.

Zoey occupied herself by giving The Mansion suite one more walk-through. After he made the call he found her sitting outside, relaxing on the private patio. "All set, babe. There's a driver waiting for you out front. They're putting our luggage in the trunk as we speak."

She got up and gathered her things. "Call me just before you leave Reno," she said. "I want to take a long hot bath just before you get home so my body will be warm, moist, and tingly when you get there."

"I love you," he responded. He took her hand and kissed it tenderly. "I'll walk you out."

Chapter 12

When Zoey opened the door of the cabin, it was obvious it had been closed up for quite some time. The last time she was there it was summer, and the green lushness of trees and colorful flowering plants were now long gone. A thin dusting of snow lay on the leafless trees and edged the streets and yards. The air in the house was stale and still, but the feel of the house was warm and comforting. Besides the monthly caretaker visits, Zoey and Mickey were the only people who had been in the private hideaway. Their souls' vibrations permeated every inch of the structure. She could feel the residue of the love and passionate lovemaking sessions they'd shared there through the years.

The caretaker was alerted of their arrival and made sure the heat was turned up and the water heater turned on. Zoey walked over to the gas fireplace and pressed the ignition button off to the side. Almost instantly a roaring fire appeared, giving a warming glow to the room.

After unpacking the car and putting the groceries away, she felt exhausted. It had been a long day. A bath sounded wonderful. She looked at the clock. It was close to eight. With the change in time zones it was actually 10 o'clock for her body. She needed to call Mickey and let him know she'd arrived safely. She picked up the phone and dialed his cell phone number. It went right to voicemail. She hoped that was a sign he was with the sheikh and would soon be on his way home and in her waiting arms. She left a message after the beep, reminded him to call before he left Reno, and hung up.

Even if Mickey called back right now, it would be at least an hour before he was home. Sudden fatigue overtook her. She felt as if her feet weighed a hundred pounds each. She made her way into the bedroom, slipped off her shoes, and collapsed on the bed. Although she only planned to doze for a few minutes, the soothing softness of the bed cover enveloped her very being and put her into a deep slumber.

She found herself back home in her bed in Birmingham, watching the news. A reporter was standing in front of a burning car in a desert. He was talking but she couldn't hear what he was saying. She felt uneasy, and anxious almost to the point of panic. The phone rang next to the bed and she picked it up. All she could hear was static coming from the other end. She heard a man's voice, but it was intermixed with the static. She asked the man to repeat his words. The only words that came through clearly was the word, "Tragedy," lots of static, then "Nothing left". Then the line went dead. She awoke with a start, drenched with perspiration. She looked around to get her bearings and realized she was at the cabin in Incline Village. Glancing at the clock, she saw it was half past nine. She had been sleeping for over an hour and a half.

She nearly jumped out of her skin when the phone next to the bed rang. "Hello. Mickey, is that you?"

It was. "Of course it is," he answered. He detected her anxiety. "Babe, what's wrong? Are you okay?"

Tears filled her eyes as she spoke. "Mickey, I had the most awful dream. I'm sure it was about you. Someone on the phone said there was a tragedy and nothing left." She began to sob.

Mickey felt helpless. As much as he tried to isolate her from the growing danger of his job, he couldn't stop her intuitive feelings. She watched the news, and wasn't oblivious to the changing world and his role in it. "Hon, it was just a dream. I'm fine. In fact, I'm at the Reno airport right now. I'll be home in an hour. Didn't you get my message?"

She was puzzled. "What message?" She looked down at the phone and noticed that the message light was blinking. "When did you call?"

"About an hour ago, just before I left Vegas?"

"Wow," she said. "I must have been more tired than I thought. I kind of passed out for the last hour and a half. I didn't even hear the phone ring."

"Poor girl, you must really be exhausted. I shouldn't have let you go to the cabin alone."

His words calmed her. "Mickey, I'm fine. I just need you."

"I know, babe. I need you, too. I'll be home soon. You gonna be okay?"

She felt better now. "I'll be fine. Just hurry."

"As fast as I can," he said comfortingly. "Why don't you go take that long hot bath you told me about earlier? Take out that fancy oil we bought last summer in Denver and I'll give you a nice massage when I get home."

She took a couple of deep breaths and shook the

dream from her head. The sound of his voice soothed her. "That sounds like a good idea."

"That's my girl," he said with relief. "See you soon. Love you," he said, and hung up the phone.

But try as she might, she couldn't shake the dream and the horrible feeling it gave her. She wouldn't be able to completely relax until he was home. She poured a glass of wine and decided to take that hot bath. She needed to unwind and relax.

It felt good to submerge her body into the deep whirlpool tub. The jets of hot water seemed to ease her tension and help her loosen up. She closed her eyes and did a few deep-breathing relaxation techniques she'd learned in her meditation class. It helped. She felt her muscles loosen, and forced herself to concentrate only on pleasant thoughts. It was working and she felt much better. The butterflies had left her stomach. She glanced up at the clock and saw that forty-five minutes had passed since Mickey's call. He would be home in less than fifteen. She got out of the tub and wrapped a silk robe around her hot body.

She searched the medicine cabinet for the massage oil Mickey had spoken of and placed it next to their bed. She closed her eyes and imagined how wonderful it was going to feel getting that massage. His soft but powerful hands smoothing the oil onto her hungry body, exploring and searching for the sensitive places as she responded to his touch.

She turned on the TV and found a music channel with New Age music. It was soft and soothing, the kind of music you could meditate to. It filled the house with peace. For a moment she stood there with her eyes closed and let the melodic tones wash away her apprehension and fear.

Then she went into the bedroom to make herself

ready for her husband. Her hair cascaded over her shoulders as she pulled out the pins that had held up it up while she'd bathed. She let the robe drop to the floor and looked at her reflection in the mirror. She didn't look like a twenty-year-old anymore, but she sure didn't look her age. She had always taken care of her skin. Her face still had a youthful glow, soft and clear. She admired her still-curvaceous 40-ish body and was glad that she had stuck to her rigorous fitness routine. She ran her hand over her flat stomach. Childbearing had taken the figures of her friends, Carol and Joanne. They worked hard to keep in shape but they both had the unmistakable belly bulge associated with pregnancy. Zoey's belly was still taut and tight. Even at her age she could wear a bikini without embarrassment.

At that moment she heard the sound of the front door opening. "Babe, I'm home." Mickey was calling out from the living room. She threw the silk robe back on and rushed to his waiting arms, bursting into tears.

"Hey, hey," he consoled. "What's all this about? We've only been apart for a few hours. What's going on?" He could feel her tremble in his embrace.

"Oh, Mickey," she said through the sobs. "It's that dream. It seemed so real and so horrible. I felt like my world was falling apart."

He stroked her hair and pulled her close. "Zoey, it was only a dream. Look, I'm here and I'm fine. We're both fine here in Zoey's Place." But his mind was replaying the conversation he'd had with the sheikh just hours ago about the growing danger and unrest in the Arab countries. Extra precautions were being put in place and more security was being hired for his next visit, which would take place in just seven days. Could she feel it? Was the danger so great that she'd had a premonition of some future disaster? Mickey didn't want to think about that now. He forced it out of his head.

For a few minutes they just stood there, holding each other tightly. Zoey stopped crying, loosened her grip on him, and wiped away her tears. "I don't know what I would do if something happened to you, Mickey. You're my life, my love, my very reason for existing."

"I feel the same way, babe."

She looked up and saw his smiling face. The fear subsided and she smiled back.

"That's better," he said as he stepped back and admired his beautiful wife in the dim light. He breathed in her heavenly scent. "You smell good," he said as he reached out and pulled the sash of her robe, letting it fall open and exposing her naked body underneath. "Why don't you pour us some drinks and wait for me in the bedroom. I want to take a quick shower and then I'm going to give you that massage I promised."

She smiled and rushed off to the kitchen, feeling at peace once again and grateful for her life.

For the next two days the outside world ceased to exist and they didn't leave their home. They could have been on a different planet. Their sexual feast celebrated their love and desire, their oneness and commitment to each other. They rang in the New Year in each other's arms and with Mickey inside her.

Chapter 13

In the blink of an eye their holiday was over. Mickey traveled back to the Mideast and Zoey went back to their Michigan home. Weeks and months were filled with a blur of activity, but Zoey didn't mind. It kept her mind off of the nagging fear for Mickey's safety that was always in the back of her mind.

It was the third week of May, and Jonathan's divorce case would be heard by the court in two days. Her office was a beehive of activities. As usual, Annette controlled the chaos so Zoey could focus on the important things. She'd spoken to all of her witnesses and made sure they knew why they were being called to testify. Annette helped her go over the exhibits that would be presented in court: phone records, pictures, and videos. Joanne had called several times. Each time Zoey had to calm her fears and assure her that they had a strong case and, although you could never guarantee how a judge will rule, she was cautiously optimistic that Jonathan would get full custody of his son.

Two weeks before the hearing, Jonathan and Rhonda were able to reach an agreeable property settlement. They really didn't have much to split up, just their cars, clothes, and some household items. The bulk of the furniture from the tiny apartment and a lot of communal possessions, mostly wedding gifts, had been sold at a garage sale and the profits held in escrow. They agreed to use the profits towards their credit card debt, which was split 50/50. They had no real estate or any significant savings. This case was all about child custody.

Zoey had enough witnesses lined up to prove that Rhonda was not only unfaithful to Jonathan, more than once, a fact which might come as a surprise to her current lover, but also the fact that she had made it no secret she had never wanted to be a wife or mother and was really only in it for the money. She foolishly thought that Jonathan came from money, and was looking for alimony and child support. It also didn't help that during the holidays she had been caught and arrested for driving drunk, and in March she was arrested for drunken disorder at a local bar after getting hammered and starting a fight with one of Jonathan's friends who called her a whore. She spent that night in jail.

Zoey had done a background check on Rhonda and found three previous arrest records from Pasco County, two aggravated assaults, and one shoplifting. She had been fined for the shoplifting and had to attend Anger Management class for the first assault charge, but she actually did six months in the county jail for the second one. All of this was before she met Jonathan, who was unaware of her past.

CASA and the GAL had already submitted their reports, all favorable to Jonathan, and they were ready to testify to that effect. This, Zoey felt, was her ace in the hole. She knew how important this was to the judge.

The night before court she lay in her bed, full of

anxiety and unable to sleep. She looked at the bedside clock. It was already 11 o'clock. It would be 6 AM in Riyadh, Saudi Arabia where Mickey was. He told her he always got up at 5:00 AM when he was on the road. She decided to call him.

The phone rang only once before he answered. "Hey, babe," he answered. "Everything all right?" Somehow he sensed her nervousness.

Just hearing his voice calmed her. "Yeah," she said. "Jonathan's case is tomorrow and I can't sleep. I just needed to hear your voice. Are you okay, Mickey?"

"I'm fine," he reassured. "Listen, you're going to do great in court. You've got this woman dead to rights. She's a horrible mother and a horrible person. No judge in their right mind would give that boy to a nut case like her."

She felt better but she knew anything could happen. She missed him, and the sound of his voice, while comforting, only made it worse. "When are you coming home?" she asked desperately.

There was a pause. "Not for a while, babe." His words were edged with sadness. "I was going to call you later. This deal is tougher than we anticipated and Allen and I have to stay here and make it right. Might be another two weeks."

She felt crushed. "It's not fair," she said, pouting into the phone. "You've already been gone for two weeks. You need to come home. I need you. I can't wait another two weeks."

He felt her pain. "I know, hon. Hey, why don't you come out here for a few days?"

She thought about it for a moment. She hated it there, but she missed him more. "Do I have to wear a hijab?"

"Only if we have dinner with the sheikh. Things

have changed since the last time you were here. American women get away with a lot more."

She still didn't like it. Women were treated so badly there. It made her furious. "I don't know," she said with trepidation. "Why can't you come home for a few days?"

"Babe," he said matter-of-factly, "we both know the answer to that. Just come for a few days. I promise you won't have to see anyone. I've got a morning meeting on Saturday that Allen can handle by himself." There was no response from the other end. He continued, "I'm gonna fuck you so hard you won't be able to walk." He heard her giggle on the other end.

"I'll send the car to pick you up from the airport. You can come right to the hotel and we'll have all our meals delivered. We don't even have to have dinner with the sheikh if you don't want to. What do you say? I know you need it and, frankly, so do I. I didn't realize how much I missed you until I heard your voice. In fact, my dick is hard as a rock right now. I'm going to have to jerk off before I leave for work."

She laughed and gave in. "Oh, I can never say no to you," she conceded. "I'll try to get the first flight out on Friday and stay for the weekend."

"Great," he exclaimed. "I'll take care of things on this end. Now, what am I going to do about this hard-on? What are you wearing?"

The next day Zoey presented her case for Jonathan's divorce to the court. She was pleased with the way it went down. The barrage of witnesses and reports showing how unfit Rhonda was as a mother was more than Rhonda and her attorney could handle. They were left fumbling and speechless throughout the day. Their evidence to the contrary was flimsy at best, and most of what was presented was thrown out as hearsay. In fact, even though they had reserved the entire day in court, because Zoey's case was presented so solidly and Rhonda's case presented so weakly, they were out of the courthouse by 2 PM. Zoey felt pleased. Joanne and Jonathan were all smiles.

The only unpleasantness came afterwards in the courthouse parking complex. Zoey and Annette had come together in Zoey's car. Joanne and Jonathan had parked next to them. They entered the complex together and headed towards their cars.

Suddenly Rhonda's car raced around the corner of the lot and came to a screeching halt in front of them. Her eyes were blazing and her face was contorted in an evil scowl. Zoey looked inside and noticed that her boyfriend, Jacob, aka Spider, was sitting next to her, looking just as sheepish as he had looked all day in court. His ill-fitting sport coat and dress shirt had been replaced with a tight camo t-shirt with the sleeves rolled up. For the first time Zoey noticed a tattoo of a spider on his right upper arm. It sent a shiver up her spine.

"You think you're so smart!" Rhonda yelled at her, snapping her back to attention. "You think you won. But you didn't."

Zoey tried to defuse the situation. "Rhonda, you need to go home," she said calmly, but Rhonda would have no part of calm.

"You haven't heard the last from me!" she screamed out. "You'll be sorry you ever crossed me. I'll get you, Lawyer Lady. I'm not done with you yet!"

Her words were still echoing off the parking lot walls as she sped away, squealing the tires and leaving marks on the pavement, the smell of burnt rubber in the air.

Joanne and Jonathan looked at Zoey with fear in their eyes. "Zoey," Joanne spoke, "do you want me to call the police?"

Zoey thought about it for a moment. "I'll be fine. It's not the first time I've been threatened. They usually don't go any farther than that." She wasn't sure if she was trying to reassure her friends or herself. Rhonda was particularly vengeful. Zoey had found that out during the background work preparing for the hearing.

"You need to call the police, Zoey." Jonathan was speaking now. "She's really pissed. I wouldn't put it past her to try something."

"He's right, Zoey," Joanne said. "At least call the Birmingham cops and let them know what happened, and ask them to do a few extra patrols around your house."

"You guys," Zoey tried to sound confident, "I'll be fine. I've got a killer alarm system in the house. No one is going to break in without a million alarms going off and an automatic 911 call. Now go home and relax." She hugged her friends. "The hard part is over. Now we wait. The judge won't make a decision for at least a week. Go home and love up that little boy who needs you both more now than ever. Give him a kiss from Aunt Zoey."

Reluctantly, Joanne and Jonathan left. Jonathan gave Zoey a tight bear hug. "Thanks, Zoey. I really mean it. You were great in there. I'm glad you were on my side."

"Thanks," she whispered back. "You're a good guy." She kissed him on the cheek and stood back.

Joanne pushed in and grabbed Zoey around so hard she couldn't breathe. "I can't thank you enough for what you've done for our family." She barely got the words out before breaking into tears and sobs of gratitude.

Zoey pushed back and grabbed Joanne's hands. She looked her friend in the eye. "We *are* family, sweetie," she said with a smile. "I'd do it a hundred times again if I had to." Joanne's sobs became louder as Jonathan directed her towards the car.

Annette and Zoey got into her car and headed back to the office. "Boss," Annette said, "Rhonda is a crazy bitch. Maybe you should call the police and put them on alert, just to be safe."

'Oh, Annette," Zoey replied. "You know how these people are. They get all upset after a bad day in court and make all kinds of threats that, in the end, don't materialize. She's not stupid enough to do anything now."

"I hope you're right," Annette said. "She just gives me the creeps."

"You and me both," Zoey said, trying to put little emphasis on the incident. "But I'll be fine."

That night Zoey couldn't shake the uneasy feeling she had ever since Rhonda threatened her. The words reverberated in her head over and over again. *"I'll get you, Lawyer Lady. I'm not done with you yet!"*

As a precaution Zoey, did put the Birmingham Police on alert and requested the extra drive-by. That night she noticed a patrol car cruising the block at least once every hour, hesitating in front of her house for a moment or two every time.

It usually took over a week for the judge's decision to come down. But in this case, it didn't take that long to decide. Two days later, as she was packing for her weekend rendezvous with Mickey, Annette called with the news.

"Hey, boss lady. Are you ready for some good news?"

"Annette, what is it? Did I win the lottery?" Zoey

kidded, not having the slightest idea what it could be.

"The court ruled in your favor on Jonathan's case. You got everything you asked for. She even has to pay Jonathan child support. Congratulations."

This last bit of information was even more than Zoey had asked for. "No kidding?" Zoey sat down on the edge of her bed, trying to take it all in. "What about the visitations?" she asked.

"Just what you asked for—once a month for four hours, supervised by CASA, for the first three years, subject to annual review by the GAL after that," Annette answered with excitement. "Hot damn, girl. You did good!"

"Thanks," Zoey said modestly. "I couldn't have done it without you. You know that."

"I know," Annette answered, "but you're the brains. I just follow your lead. You want to call Jonathan, or should I? I know you're getting ready for your trip."

"I'll call," Zoey said. "I don't have to leave for the airport for another two hours." She was anxious to tell Jonathan and Joanne the good news. She felt relieved. This would take a lot of stress off of her and allow her to concentrate on Mickey during their short time together.

"I'll start the paperwork and have everything ready for your review when you get back, "Annette said. "Now, you go and have a good time with Mickey. Don't worry about the office. I'll take care of it."

"Like you always do, Annette. Thanks," she said. "See you next Wednesday."

It was early in the day and Zoey knew Jonathan would be at work, so she decided to call Joanne and let her tell Jonathan. She would have a formal meeting with him after she returned. Joanne answered the phone on the first ring. "We won," Zoey said without any introduction.

It took Joanne a moment or two for the news to sink in. "Oh, my God!" she shrieked, then she realized the impact of Zoey's statement. "Hold on, Zoey. Jonathan is here; he took the day off." There was a pause before she continued. "Jonathan, pick up the phone. It's Zoey!" she shouted out. "Zoey, I want you to tell Jonathan."

She waited patiently, smiling.

There was a click as he picked up a phone. "Okay, Zoey. I'm here," he said.

"Jonathan, the worst part is over. You were awarded full custody of your son. Congratulations," Zoey announced.

"Oh, man," he said, his voice cracking. "Thank you, Zoey. Thank you so much."

"It was my pleasure," she replied. "We got the visitation schedule we suggested. Your ex even has to pay you child support."

Joanne was overcome and couldn't speak. She just kept muttering the words 'thank you' softly into the phone as Zoey explained the details and the next steps of the process.

Chapter 14

The trip to Saudi Arabia was long and boring. As promised, Mickey sent a car to bring Zoey to the hotel where he was staying. The man holding the placard with her name on the front looked American and greeted her in perfect Texan English as she approached him. *Thank goodness for that,* she thought. *No language barrier.* The car was a sleek black stretch limo like the limos she used in the States. The driver didn't say much, which was just as well. Zoey always felt so out of place here. As they drove the flat, hot, white streets of Riyadh she noticed the bearded men walking freely as the covered women sheepishly made their way through the streets, usually with a child or two in tow. It was midafternoon and the heat was unbearable. The few palm trees she saw gave little shade for the women, who she figured must be roasting under all those clothes. She hated this place. Thankfully, she would only be here a couple of days. Days filled with sexual ecstasy, she hoped.

It had been two full weeks since she was with her husband. This assignment had been particularly hard, and their communications had not been regular. When they did talk, the conversations were usually short. She could feel the tension and tremendous stress he was under.

A deal he and Allen had been working on for two years was supposed to close a week ago, but at the last minute other options opened up for the client, most likely a competitor's bid, and the Saudis wanted to renegotiate. She didn't know the details, but knew this was a big deal for corporate.

She had no idea what state of mind Mickey would be in when she saw him, but she knew he would be feeling better by the time she left. She leaned back into the head rest, closed her eyes, and conjured up an image of him naked before her. She pictured his muscular arms glistening with sweat. Hot as molten steel and just as strong. She could almost feel the ripples of his chest and his well-toned body. What would she do with him tonight? Would she let him take charge, or should she? She read somewhere that men who have to make heavy decisions for a living often like to be submissive in sex and turn control over to their partner. It served as a psychological release for them to not have to make choices. That was the course she chose to take. This was going to be fun. She smiled to herself and thought of all the possibilities.

The car pulled in to the driveway of the Four Seasons Hotel at Kingdom Centre. She had been watching the famous 992-foot-high Sky Bridge get closer as they drove from the airport. Its distinctive, immense silhouette was hard to ignore as it imposed on the mostly flat landscape of the desert city, a very impressive and magnificent architectural accomplishment. Mickey had told her about the hotel, but seeing it now was mind-blowing. Although some parts of the huge complex were still under construction, there were parts of the hotel that were open to select guests. Mickey was just such a guest.

The driver brought the car to a stop at the front door and got out. He handed the keys to the attendant and spoke something in Arabic. He opened Zoey's door and offered a hand to help her out. Another young man appeared and spoke to the driver before he brought her bags to the sidewalk and placed them on a hotel cart. The driver handed the young man some money and spoke more Arabic, probably her room number. Then he turned to Zoey.

"Mrs. DeLucca," he intoned.

She looked up and answered, "Yes?"

"Mrs. DeLucca," he repeated. "Please allow me to accompany you to your room. I'm afraid Mr. DeLucca will be delayed and asked if I would see to your comfort upon your arrival. He is expected to arrive within the hour."

"Thank you," she said casually. "Lead the way." She knew women always followed the men here.

Mickey's room was high in the tower. Her bags were already there when she arrived.

The driver, whose name she really wished she knew, walked in first and did what she would consider a security scan before he invited her in.

"The refrigerator is stocked, as is the bar. The room service menu is on the counter in the kitchen. Please feel free to call the front desk should you require anything else. The staff speaks English," he said flatly.

She thanked him and, without hesitating, he took his leave. She closed the door and looked around. The suite was spacious and the view from the tall windows was breathtaking. All of Riyadh lay at her feet. Business papers and files were piled up on the desk in the office area. She knew that Mickey often had meetings there. The kitchen was modern and clean. Inside the full size refrigerator, she found a fruit plate and veggie tray. She grabbed a couple of pieces of fruit and a bottle of water. She began nibbling on a pineapple spear as she explored the rest of the suite. She walked into the bedroom. Off to the left was a bathroom with marble everything, a huge tub, an immense shower with multiple shower heads, a double sink vanity with spacious counters, and even a bidet. She never quite got the hang of those things.

A king-size bed dominated the bedroom. There was another large window looking down onto the city below and beyond. She sat by the window, eating her fruit and taking in all the wonder that lay before her feet. She was a half a world away from home, yet what made it home was right here. At least, he would be soon. Glancing at the clock she figured Mickey wouldn't be there for at least another half hour. On a nearby chair she saw one of his shirts. She walked over to it and picked it up. She buried her face in it and inhaled deeply. It smelled of him, a fresh, clean, musky scent that was his alone. The same aroma she smelled on his pillows at home. Its calming effect was immediate, washing away any built-up stress her body still held. Her knees weakened and she fell back onto the bed. She lay there for a while, savoring his manly bouquet, and imagining how the night would go. She could feel her body aching for his touch. She slid her hand into her slacks and touched herself. She was getting wet. Her body was tingling. She closed her eyes and enjoyed the sensation.

"Sorry I'm late, babe. I see you started without me."

Mickey's words jolted her back to real time. She jumped off of the bed and ran into his outstretched arms. "Mickey, I've missed you so much," she whispered into his ear as she pressed her body into his. She reached down and felt his manhood. It was already hard.

Their lips met and their tongues intertwined as they raced to remove their clothes. He pulled back the sheets and grabbed her tightly as their naked bodies fell onto the bed, bodies entwined, hands hungrily exploring. She felt the hard muscles of his back and the tightness of his ass. She cupped his behind and pushed herself against him. He cradled one of her breasts, velvety smooth and full in his hand, and gently squeezed the nipple as it hardened between his fingers.

"You're so soft," he muttered in between moans of delight. "I can't believe you're really here."

She found herself caught up in the heat of their passion as all of her planned sexual scenarios faded away. She gave in to her basic instinct and melted into his embrace. Reaching down, she guided his rock-hard cock into her body. He let out a groan as he thrust himself into her. The sound of his pleasure sent chills of excitement up her spine. It felt good to have him inside her special place once again. Their bodies moved in synchronized rhythm as their pleasure built to a peak. He was the first to come, with her right behind.

Both lay depleted of strength on the bed, glistening with love sweat, looking into each other's eyes. "Hey, babe," he said, catching his breath. "Welcome to Riyadh."

"Oh, Mickey, I can't believe I'm actually here with you," she said in a voice that was both grateful and tinged with sadness. "I hate being separated from you more and more these days."

"I know, babe," he said with excitement. She looked at him with puzzlement.

"Why are you smiling?" she asked. "What's going on?"

He turned to face her and grabbed her hand. He brought it up to his mouth and kissed it gently. "I was waiting for the right time to tell you this, but I guess there's no better time than the present."

He had her full attention now. She pulled herself up and was sitting cross-legged on the bed, facing him.

"I've been talking to corporate and have decided that I'm quitting at the end of the year."

She couldn't believe her ears. "Seriously?" she asked. "Like, full retirement?"

He nodded. "After the first of the year, the only one I'll have to answer to is you. What do you think?"

She was so ecstatic that she flung her naked body onto his and hugged him with an iron grip. "I think it will be heaven," she said, laying her head on his chest as he embraced her.

"Do you think you would be willing to give up your practice, too?" he asked.

She thought for a long moment, a thousand thoughts rushing through her mind. Then she smiled and said, "I think I can."

He kissed her on the top of her head. "Good. I met with our accountant last month and we've got enough money on hand and in our investments to keep us going for the rest of our lives."

"Will we have to sell Zoey's Place?" she asked.

"We won't have to change a thing," he confirmed.

"Mickey, this is the best news ever," she said, squeezing him tightly.

The most Zoey saw of Riyadh that weekend was what she could see from the hotel suite's windows. Mickey had turned off his phone so they wouldn't be disturbed. Allen had volunteered to handle any business issues that came up. The world outside ceased to exist for two days. With the exception of the occasional waiter who brought them room service, it was as if they were only humans on earth. And that was just fine with the lovers.

Love-filled minutes turned to hours. The blissful hours quickly turned to days. Too soon, their time together was over and it was time to come back to reality. This was the part Zoey hated. It was the uncertainty that made her anxious. He would always tell her everything would be fine. But, considering the current political atmosphere these days, his words did little to console her. Her disturbing dreams had become more frequent. And her fear for his safety grew by the day.

Mickey went with her to the airport. He walked her to the gate and kissed her goodbye. She suddenly became overcome with anxiety and felt lightheaded. He held her tight as he felt her knees buckle.

"Babe," he said with alarm. "What's the matter?"

She was embarrassed. This was the last thing he needed right now. She struggled to pull herself together. After a moment she could feel the fog in her head clear and managed to pull herself up and regain her composure. It was hard, but she put a smile on her face for him.

"I'm fine. Really." She tried to sound reassuring. "I just hate this part." She could see the concern leave his eyes. Those eyes. Those dark, coffee-colored, dreamy eyes framed by his thick, expressive brows. To this day she could get lost in them, never wanting to be found.

"I hate this part, too," he said in a soothing voice. "We should have this deal wrapped up in a few weeks. I'll be home as soon as I can." He could tell that his words were of little consolation. "I'll call you tomorrow night," he added.

The final boarding call for the flight was announced and she knew it was time to go. Although she couldn't shake the feeling of foreboding, she forced a smile and kissed him one more time before she pulled away. "I love you," she whispered. She turned towards the gate and walked away. Before entering the jetway, she turned back and looked at him one more time.

Their eyes met. "I love you," he mouthed. She smiled and walked on as tears filled her eyes.

PART TWO - SORROW

Chapter 15

The flight home went smoothly and Zoey was able to sleep, albeit uneasily. Annette had arranged for a car service to pick her up at the airport to take her home. It was late evening by the time she got there. She was exhausted. Her body begged for sleep. Good thing she hadn't planned on going to the office until the next afternoon. She quickly showered and slipped into bed. Reaching over to Mickey's side she grabbed his pillow, held it to her face, and breathed in deeply. There it was, that tang, or spice, or essence. Whatever it was, it was him. "Mickey," she sighed as she relived their last few glorious days together and his promise to retire at the end of the year.

Stella had a standing order never to wash Mickey's pillowcase while he was away. It was a small thing, but it was a great comfort to Zoey on nights such as this. Seeing first-hand the security team that protected him helped make her feel more confident that Mickey was in no danger, but the uneasy feeling hadn't totally gone away. And the physical emptiness she felt was even more overpowering than before. He would be home in a few weeks. She kept that thought in her head as exhaustion overcame her and she drifted off to sleep.

The next morning, the sound of distant ringing grew louder as it pulled her out of slumber and abruptly threw her into reality. She glanced at the clock. It was nine o'clock. She grabbed the phone, cleared her gravely throat and said, "Hello?"

"Hello, Mrs. DeLucca?" an unfamiliar masculine voice asked.

"Yes," Zoey answered. Without warning her stomach began to churn. She began to perspire and felt lightheaded for some unknown reason.

"I'm sorry, Mrs. DeLucca," the voice continued. "My name is Jake Johnson. I work for Taylor Resource Development with your husband."

There was a short pause.

"I'm sorry, Mrs. DeLucca. I'm calling from Riyadh. There's been an accident. It's Mickey. I'm so sorry, Mrs. DeLucca. He's been killed."

Everything went black for a moment and Zoey dropped the phone. She reached down and grabbed it from the floor. "No, that can't be!" she screamed. "I just saw Mickey yesterday. He was fine. There must be some mistake."

"Mrs. DeLucca," the man began to talk again. "This morning your husband was killed by a construction crane. It fell from a building site onto the limo your husband and his party were sitting in. It's a tragedy. . ." The line went to static. "...nothing left. They're all dead." More static.

Was this really happening? It was the cabin dream. Without grasping the reality of the moment, her mind went into overdrive. "Are you sure it was Mickey? Did he suffer? Who was he with?" She was hungry for details. "Was Allen with him?" Nothing but static, the line had gone dead. "Hello? Hello?" she screamed into the phone.

She hung up the phone and sat in disbelief. She did a quick calculation in her head. It was 4 PM in Riyadh. A million thoughts rushed through her head. Where were the bodyguards? Was it an accident or did someone do this on purpose? Then it hit her. It didn't matter. Mickey had been killed. He was dead, gone. The light of her life had been extinguished by a senseless accident in a country half a world away. How could this be? She must be dreaming. It couldn't be happening. Not like this. She had always been worried about terrorists but this, a construction crane, it just didn't seem possible. Mickey couldn't be dead. "No, no, no!" she cried out loud, her head pounding.

Tears filled her eyes and she fell back onto the pillow on her bed. "Mickey. You can't leave me now. I need you. What I am going to do without you? This can't be real," she tried to reassure herself. "It's just a dream. Wake up! Wake up!" she commanded herself. But nothing changed. She was already wide awake and realized it wasn't a dream. The strength drained from her body as if it was sucked up in a tornado's vortex. She felt her heart shatter like a broken mirror. Sorrow engulfed her very being in a heavy shroud. The searing agony hurt worse than anything she could have ever imagined. Tears flowed uncontrollably in an endless current of grief and pain.

Within the next hour she had been contacted by no less than three representatives of Taylor Resource Development. One person called to tell her that the corporation would take care of all the arrangements to bring Mickey's body home.

Another called with the details of the accident. From what she was told, it all happened very quickly and without warning. It was most definitely an accident and they did not suspect terrorism. At approximately 11 AM, Mickey and Allen successfully closed the deal they were working on and had just entered their limo to return to their hotel. The top of the construction crane snapped a bolt and it fell 40 stories directly onto their vehicle, crushing and killing all inside: the driver, the body guards, and Allen and Mickey. They were killed instantly, never knowing what hit them.

A third corporate man called to assured her that Mickey didn't suffer and to offer counseling services for her and her family. He also assured her they were going to sue the construction company for negligence and that she would be given a percentage of the monetary judgment. He would be sending out some paperwork that she needed to review and sign on that matter and for the redemption of Mickey's corporate life insurance policy.

Zoey listened with numb attention. For the first time, she knew what her clients went through when thrown into the harsh, life-changing reality of divorce. She pictured them sitting in her office as she explained the cold, hard facts of divorce court and child custody. She could see the numbness, the emptiness, the hopelessness in their eyes as she spoke. Now it was her turn. It was all like a horrible movie playing out in her head. She couldn't fully grasp all that was happening and didn't want to believe it was true. After the last phone call she sat on her bed for a full fifteen minutes, trying to wrap her brain around how her life had just changed and its ramifications for her future.

Gradually she regained her senses. Her analytical mind began to function. It was real, it had happened. She had to deal with it. First things first, she called Annette and told her about Mickey.

Before Zoey could discuss her plans for the office, Annette took control. "Zoey, I'm so sorry. Don't worry about the office, boss," she had reassured. "I'll reschedule all of your appointments. I'll push everything out a month. If you need more time, I'll push them out further. There's nothing here that can't be put on hold."

"Thank you, Annette," Zoey replied, her monotone voice barely above a weak whisper. "I knew I could count on you."

"Call me if you need anything," Annette said. "Anything at all. I'll call you in a few days with an update." She hesitated a moment and added, "I'm so sorry." Zoey could hear the emotion welling up in Annette's voice before she hung up.

As if on automatic she called her friends, Carol and Joanne, to tell them the horrible news.

Her next thought was of her friend Fen, Allen's wife. She wondered if she had been told yet. What was she thinking? Of course Fen would have gotten the same calls she had. She grabbed the phone book from the nightstand drawer and looked for her phone number.

"Webber, ah, here it is," she said out loud as she cradled the phone against her shoulder and dialed the number with her free hand. The line was busy. She wasn't surprised. They had a large family, and Zoey was sure that they were all rushing to her side in this time of need. Zoey didn't have family per se but she had Carol and Joanne. Blood couldn't bind them closer.

By noon, both friends had arrived to console their 'sister' and help her deal with her worst nightmare.

For the next three days, Zoey didn't leave her room. She couldn't even get out of bed. She couldn't eat or sleep. She sobbed uncontrollably and endlessly. Her friends did everything they could to help, but it didn't matter. She refused to take the prescribed tranquilizers her doctor had offered, saying she wanted to face this without being in a drug-induced fog.

The week it took for Mickey's body to be returned to the U.S. was the worst. Zoey was in a haze. Her friends made all of the funeral arrangements and Zoey allowed herself to be led around and told when to eat, what to wear, and where to go. With the help of her friends, she picked out the urn that would be Mickey's resting place after cremation.

They had always intended to talk about where they wanted their ashes spread, but never got around to it. Mickey wanted the Grand Canyon, but whenever he brought up the subject she had come up with some reason to not talk about such morbid things. Besides, they had plenty of time. Now her life was a horror show, punctuated with a canyon full of sorrow and a river of tears.

A small service was held at one of the local restaurants three weeks to the day of his death. The owner closed the eatery to the public and provided all of the food free, out of respect for Mickey. The memorial was private, just friends and a handful of acquaintances. Taylor Resource Development sent a representative who actually knew and worked with Mickey. There were no more than 20 people in attendance. Annette closed the office so all of the staff could attend. Lenny and Dave shared touching memories of Mickey through the years. A few others got up to say a few words as well. Zoey was glad it didn't go on for long. It was all she could do to sit there while others spoke. Joanne and Carol were ever at her side.

That evening she wanted to be alone. Her friends

drove her home and helped her place Mickey's urn on her bedroom dresser. She said she thought that's where Mickey would want to be. She took a great deal of time trying to convince her friends that she would be all right. They stayed for coffee, but when the evening turned to night she insisted they go home to their own families. Her devoted friends were still concerned for Zoey's state of mind and didn't think she should be alone, not just yet. They wouldn't leave her alone. They continued to take turns keeping her company for two more weeks after the service.

Joanne was sitting in the living room with Zoey one afternoon, looking through old photo albums and remembering the good times they had all shared, hoping to lift Zoey's spirit.

"You know, sweetie," she said, "it's hard to see good at a time like this, but when you think about how much fun we had in the last twenty years, we've been very fortunate."

Zoey looked up in disbelief. "What about the next twenty? Who am I supposed to make memories with now?"

Joanne hugged her. "That's not what I meant and you know it. You've seen enough of life to know that not everyone, heck, not most people get a chance to do the things we've done, to go to the places we've been, and you and Mickey even more. We've all worked hard and we deserve the pleasures we have, but we've all been at a place where the opportunity presented itself. I wouldn't trade my memories with the six of us for anything in the world. No matter what happens, we'll always have that friendship and love that few people will ever know."

Zoey was listening quietly. Joanne could tell she was contemplating her words but wasn't convinced. "I know what you say is true, and I *do* treasure our times together. That's all I have left of Mickey now, memories. It's just that I wasn't prepared for it to end so cruelly and so soon."

"Hon," Joanne comforted, "this isn't the end of your life. You're still here, and so are we. And as for the next twenty years, both of us know firsthand that life can change in the blink of an eye. You don't know what or who is waiting for you out there."

"Joanne," Zoey interrupted abruptly, "I'll never fall in love again. I don't want to. I can't even think about it."

Zoey burst into tears and Joanne cradled her as if she was a child, murmuring comforting sounds to soothe her.

"I'm sorry, Joanne," Zoey apologized, pulling away and making an attempt at straightening her appearance. "I'm just so confused right now."

"I know, hon," Joanne said to her friend. "It's okay." The women sat quietly in the comfort of their friendship.

It was Joanne who broke the silence. "Zoey, are you regretting not having children with Mickey?"

Zoey closed her eyes and shook her head. "No, not at all. I can't imagine the extra horror of having to tell my children that their father was killed. I'd have to raise them alone, with all the hardships and sacrifice that it brings. Talk about not having a life! And I still wouldn't have Mickey." She grabbed for a tissue from the nearby end table and blew her nose before continuing.

"No, it was the right decision. I can't imagine having a child that resembled Mickey so much that every time I looked at him or her all I would see was Mickey, making the hurt fresh every day. I'm not that strong. The only way I'll get over this is if I keep my life with

Mickey in a secret box hidden away in my heart, or I'll never learn to live with my new reality."

A few days later Zoey explained to her friends that they had been 'babysitting' her for three weeks, and she really could handle being alone now. Reluctantly, they left.

That night the house seemed quieter than it ever had before. Zoey had never felt more alone. As she walked through the empty living room, her eyes drifted to the pictures on the top of the bookcase. One was their wedding picture. They were still in college. They looked so hopeful. The love in their eyes was true and strong. Next to that was a picture from the Caribbean cruise they took to celebrate their fifteenth anniversary. They still had that same look of love in their eyes. It was just a few years ago, but seemed like a lifetime now. The love was still there, but Mickey wasn't there to share it. She felt like she was trapped in a dream, a bad dream. She wanted to wake herself up but knew she couldn't. She was awake and her life had turned nightmarish.

She found herself in her bedroom but she didn't remember climbing the stairs. She undressed and got into the bed, leaving her clothes in a heap on the floor, something she'd admonished Mickey for doing more than once. She reached over and grabbed his pillow, now streaked with a trail of her tears from the last three weeks. Mickey's smell was still there, very faint, but there nonetheless. She looked up at the urn that held his ashes. She breathed in his scent on the pillow. The pain was overpowering and she began to cry. Her tears flowed in an endless tide. Her sobs shook the walls and filled the hallways. Why did this happen? How could she go on without the love of her life? What was to happen to her now? She had no answers, only deep sorrow. She clung to his pillow and wept until she had no strength to stay awake.

By the end of the fourth week, she had forced herself to adapt to her new reality. Frequent walks though the Robert Kidd Gallery helped her organize her thoughts. Mickey was gone. At least he hadn't suffered. It was up to her now. She had to do something to keep her mind off her grief. Zoey didn't know what she was going to do with the rest of her life, but knew she had to do something. Mickey wouldn't want her to waste away and live a meaningless life. For starters, she felt it was time to go back to work. She picked up the phone and dialed the office.

"DeLucca Law Office," Annette answered. Her voice was warm and soothing, like a cup of hot cocoa. She knew she had made the right decision.

"Annette," Zoey said with confidence, "I'm coming back to work. I'll see you tomorrow."

Annette was thrilled but cautious. "Are you sure?" she asked hesitantly.

"Yes," she replied. "I have to."

"I understand," she consoled. "It will be good to have you back, boss,"

Thoughts of her friend, Fen, came to mind. Zoey hadn't thought of Fen since her unsuccessful attempt to call her on the day of the tragedy. Until now the accident had been too fresh, too raw, to even think about talking to the one person who knew her suffering intimately. But now she knew she had to talk to her, if not out of respect then out of friendship and a shared sorrow. Once more she reached for her phone book and looked up Fen's number.

The phone rang three times before someone

answered.

"Hello?" said an unfamiliar young voice.

"Hello," Zoey answered, unsure if she had dialed correctly. "I'm trying to reach Fenella Webber. Did I reach the right house?"

"Yes," the voice said coldly. "Mrs. Webber is very busy. Do you have a phone appointment?" the voice said impersonally, without emotion.

"This is Zoey DeLucca. My husband was killed with Allen and—" Zoey didn't get to finish her sentence.

"Mrs. DeLucca, I'm so sorry," the voice interrupted, the tone and tenor changing drastically. "My name is Jenna. Fen is my aunt. I've been staying here with her to, you know, help out and stuff."

"I understand," Zoey replied.

"I didn't mean to sound like a bitch to you," the girl interjected apologetically, without giving Zoey a chance to speak. "You know Aunt Fen is really social and the newspapers and about a zillion clubs have been calling to get interviews or whatever. It's exhausting. Some of those guys are such jerks. Aunt Fen needed an assistant, and since I'm not working right now I said what the heck."

Doesn't this girl ever take a breath? Zoey thought. She listened while Jenna talked about the who's and what's of all the phone calls she'd been fielding for her aunt.

"Listen to me, talking your ear off," the girl apologized. "I've been insensitive. Mrs. DeLucca, I'm so sorry for your loss. Aunt Fen has told me what a good person you are. She really respects you for the work you do."

"Thank you," Zoey replied. "Jenna, is it?"

"Yes, ma'am."

"I was wondering if Fen is available right now. We haven't spoken since the accident. I tried calling once but the line was busy."

"Of course, Mrs. DeLucca." Jenna sounded much cheerier now, and much more polite. "Aunt Fen tried to call you a couple of times, too. One time the line was busy and the other time you weren't home and she didn't want to leave a message. She'll be really glad that you're calling. Just a sec while I get her."

Zoey could hear the phone being set down and the clickity-clack of Jenna's shoes on a hardwood floor as she called out, "Aunt Fen, guess who's on the phone?"

In less than a minute she heard a familiar, friendly voice. "Zoey, honey, how are you?"

Fen's voice was as comforting as a warm blanket. "I'm doing about as best as I think I can do. How about you, Fen?"

"Oh, about the same, I guess." Zoey could hear and feel the still-fresh pain in her voice.

"I've tried calling you," Zoey continued. "I've wanted to talk to you."

"Me, too," Fen broke in. "But I want to see you, too. Why don't we meet for lunch next week? Are you free on Tuesday? I'm meeting some friends in Chicago on Monday. I can stop in Detroit on my way back to New York."

"Yes," Zoey replied without thinking about her work schedule. "I know a place we can go. It's quiet and private. I need to see you, too."

"Sounds good. I'll call you Monday and you can tell me where it is." There was a pause. "It's been hell, hasn't it?"

"Yes," Zoey answered softly, feeling the tears well up in her eyes. "See you next week."

She hung up the phone and broke into a million pieces.

Chapter 16

Fen would be in Detroit only long enough to meet with Zoey. Then she would continue on to New York. Zoey had reached her at her home in the Hamptons. But Fen and Allen also kept an apartment in Manhattan, and most of their extended family lived in the New York boroughs. Both women felt a strong need to see each other, so the travel detour seemed the right thing to do.

Zoey selected an exclusive, member's only downtown Detroit café called Maxwell's. The food was gourmet, as were the prices, but the ambiance was second to none. Each booth in the small establishment was a three-sided, recessed alcove, very private, and all were open to the kitchen, which was transparent to the eating public via a wall of glass that served as the only separation between the two.

Monday through Friday, lunch customers were serviced by all-male waiters and kitchen staff. Except for the chef, they were between the ages of 18 and 40. And from the looks of it, employment there required a gym membership. Maxwell's was notorious for its good- looking help. It was a private club, and management had decided that it would cater to upper-class ladies during the lunch shift. In the evenings and on weekends, women shared duties with the men. It was a decision that had proved very profitable for management. Mickey had bought her a membership for her birthday last year.

Although Zoey had been to Maxwell's for lunch before to enjoy the view, it was the privacy the booths afforded that had been the deciding factor today. No doubt there would be tears and conversation that the new widows wouldn't want to share with outsiders.

Zoey had just situated herself in the booth when she saw Fen approaching. She was wearing a long, black wool coat with a plain black shift underneath. Zoey stood as she approached and the two fell into each other's arms, sobbing and clinging to one another for strength. Unspoken words expressed the shared pain and torment of the last month. The restaurant was surprisingly empty, and no one really paid much attention to them as they cried in each other's embrace.

After a few moments of consoling each other the women seated themselves and held hands across the table. "What do we do now?" Fen asked. She reached into her bag, pulled out a lace handkerchief, and dabbed her eyes.

"We go on living," Zoey said with little conviction. She cursed herself for not thinking to bring a hankie. She used the cloth napkin to blot the tears from her face.

"How?" Fen asked, with a look of utter desperation and hopelessness.

"I don't know," Zoey confessed.

And for the next two hours the women talked about the life they had once had and their uncertain future. Crying, laughing, remembering, and generally reassuring each other, giving and getting strength from the common horror they shared.

Zoey told Fen about her plans to go back to work. Fen said that she had found it helpful to immerse herself in her charity work with the help of her niece. She also received great support from Allen's and her extended family.

It felt good to speak freely about Mickey's death with someone who shared the experience, someone who knew exactly what she was going through and didn't treat her with pity. Both women were realists and knew that life goes on, even after a tragedy such as this, and that their respective husbands wouldn't want them to waste away in mourning for them. She felt a great release when she kissed Fen goodbye. As the women parted, they promised to keep in touch. Zoey went back to her empty house. Everywhere she looked she saw something that reminded her of Mickey. It had been over a month now, but it still seemed like one never-ending nightmare.

The holidays were especially hard, and painful. At the insistence of her friends Zoey made appearances at their holiday parties, but only stayed for a short time so as not to put a damper on the festivities. Other than that, Zoey spent the holiday season in seclusion. On New Year's Eve she watched the ball drop alone for the first time in over twenty years and cried herself to sleep, hugging the pillow that still faintly held Mickey's essence.

For the next few months she tried to throw her entire being into work and find meaning and purpose in service to others. Being busy helped delay real thoughts about her future. But each day became harder and it was becoming a laborious task to achieve the motivation to get out of bed. The bright flame of joy she had once gotten from helping her clients had diminished to a dim glow, and the effort she had to put out became a chore. Before Mickey's death, when he talked about retiring she thought about giving up her business as well. By summer her drive to succeed at her career vanished, so it seemed like the logical thing to do. What she would do after that, she didn't know. Right now she didn't want to do anything, at least for a while.

It took three more months to finish the cases that were already near completion with court dates, and to find suitable attorneys for her remaining clients. She owed them that. They all understood, considering the circumstances. She even found another job for Annette. Through the years the two women had become very close, and Zoey knew that they would always remain friends.

For a while after her 'retirement' she wandered around in a daze. The emptiness of the house seemed to engulf her. Trips to her favorite places lost their charm. She felt as if she was just filling time, and there was no meaning in her life anymore. It was early fall now and the leaves had begun to change. There was a chill in the air and Zoey became restless. This wasn't how Mickey would want her live. Mostly because she wasn't living, only existing. She had no direction, no worth anymore.

She decided she needed to change her life completely. Her life with Mickey was over. It was time to quit living with a ghost. At that moment she decided she should sell the house. It was far too big for one woman to live in alone, and every room held memories of the love and sexual exploits she and Mickey had experienced over the years. The blissful recollections were now a painful reminder of what was lost. It was almost unbearable to think she would never again be so sexually free and satisfied. The sooner she was out of that house the better.

She called a former client of hers whom she'd represented in a nasty divorce. The client was a real estate agent and Zoey won the case, granting the client full custody of his children and a healthy child support judgment.

The house was in a good neighborhood, had been well maintained, and had a great floor plan. In less than a month offers poured in and the house sold. During the 90-day escrow period Zoey went room by room, separating out her life memories and deciding which ones to keep and which ones to sell at a garage sale. She had called upon Annette with her organizational skills to assist her. She was more than willing to help out.

Zoey saved the special hidden playroom for last. This was a job she would do alone. She hadn't been in there since Mickey's death. It took great force of will to make the decision to enter the little room. Taking a firm grasp of the doorknob she took a deep breath, blinked a few times, opened the door, flipped on the light, and walked in.

She looked around. Sex toys of all shapes and sizes, floggers, feather ticklers, hand cuffs, and more, costumes and suggestive underwear for both sexes, DVDs, they were all there. To a stranger it would look like the inside of a sex shop. The haunting memories of games and encounters with these items created myriad images in her mind's eye that spun a beautiful web, expressing the love between two people devoted to the sexual happiness of one another.

Tears of delight tinged with loss welled up in her eyes and she reached for the tissue box she knew to be by the light switch. As she pulled on the box it moved and revealed two 8" x 10" photos of Mickey in her favorite sex fantasy outfit—the cowboy.

She took the pictures herself, experimenting with lighting. The first one was a profile body shot using back-lighting. He was looking straight ahead and his cowboy hat was pushed back to expose the beautiful line of his face, a vision of strength and masculinity. You could just barely make out the fuzz of stubble on his face. A few black curls of hair escaped from the hat and hung down on his forehead. A red bandana was tied around his neck. He was bare-chested and the hair on it looked electric. The only thing he was wearing below the waist was a pair of chaps and cowboy boots. In the crotch opening of the chaps, his penis was hard and at attention in all its glory. His hand was cupping his balls. The outline of his tight ass was sharp and solid. His back foot was propped up on a small stump of wood. You could see the outline of the boot on it.

In the other picture he was standing straight on forward. His hat was tipped over his eyes but you could still see his full sensuous lips. She had used side-lighting for this one so that half of his body was in shadow and half was in full brightness. His hands were on his hips and his penis stood at center focus. She clutched the pictures to her breast and, overcome with emotion, fell to the floor and cried. A surge of tears flowed for the memories, for the pleasures, for the loss. Finally gaining her composure, she decided that it was not yet time to say goodbye to this. She put the entire contents of the room in a plastic tub and closed the lid. *Too soon,* she thought to herself. *I just can't. There will be time later.*

Zoey had spent many sleepless nights making the decision to leave Michigan. Leaving her home and all her friends would be bittersweet. She would be leaving life-long friends who treated her like family, familiar places and the comfort of home, but trying to create a new life here wouldn't be possible. She could no longer take the looks of pity she got every time she ran into someone she knew. Her friends walked on eggshells around her, treating her as if she was a fragile doll. Life had changed. She couldn't press the reset button like it was some video game. It was time for a complete transformation of lifestyle.

Her house had been sold; time to start fresh. She decided to make the permanent move to Incline Village. They never had company in that house. They had no friends there. It had always been their place. Zoey's Place. The home inherited the name after the sale of the lake house. In fact, it was the proceeds from that sale that helped buy the Incline Village house. She wondered if she would be able to live there with so many memories of Mickey or if she would have to sell that place, too. Although they spent time there, it was always more of a getaway. They never really set up house or lived there. She thought about it long and hard. It felt right. For the time being she had no choice. She decided to just go with the flow. What did she have to lose? So, it was goodbye Michigan and the life she had known before. Hello Nevada and whatever it brought.

Chapter 17

The Incline Village home in Nevada had always been a safe haven. Zoey wasn't ready to part with that part of Mickey just yet; maybe never. She couldn't pretend that he'd never existed. He had, and he always would in her heart and her memories. Even though the heavy sadness within pulled her down constantly, there was abundant loving and treasured memories she couldn't erase because they were a part of her. They were the fabric of her life. They were what made her what she was, Zoey DeLucca, a woman who once loved and was loved. Now alone in the world, she was a woman who faced an uncertain future without her beloved. She was thankful in her heart that she'd had a love like Mickey's. That love had been a precious gift to be cherished, and Zoey didn't want to erase it from her life.

Although this house held memories of Mickey, they were different than the Michigan house. It was where they went to get away from it all. And now that was exactly what she wanted to do. It would be quiet and peaceful, and just the right place to put her life back on track. She looked forward to having no responsibilities and no one to answer to.

What she didn't foresee was the life full of lonely hours that she would have to endure without her husband. She had to live with the fact that she would always be coming home to an empty house. She would never feel Mickey's strong, loving arms around her, his warm body next to hers, his hardness against her thigh, his mouth tasting her, his cock taking her, his familiar hands touching every part of her body. A touch that reached into her very soul. The endless wanting, this was the hardest to bear. Until recently the shock of Mickey's death blotted out all thoughts of sexual pleasure. But now in her solitary life, those feelings had resurfaced. It took great effort to force the thoughts from her mind. She tried to move on; she thought it's what Mickey would want her to do.

She had felt his spirit the moment she entered the house. He was everywhere, but she learned to handle it. In fact, it became a sort of comfort. As the fog of his loss began to clear and she accepted her fate, a new life began to take form. She was able to take pleasure in simple things. Sorrow no longer gripped her when she went to restaurants and other social places she had frequented with Mickey. She was beginning to feel happy and safe in Zoey's Place once again.

But along with her feelings of safety and happiness, she was still missing the frequent sexual escapades she and Mickey had shared. It was such a huge part of their relationship and their love. Still, she couldn't even think about having sex with another man. It just seemed wrong. But the cravings became so intense that it hurt.

She had shipped out the few personal belongings she didn't sell after the sale of the Michigan house, including the storage bin full of the sex paraphernalia. It took many tearful days to go through the bin and decide what should stay and what should go. She kept Mickey's chaps and cowboy hat, a few feather ticklers, her favorite dildo and one or two other sex toys, but disposed of the rest of the collection. The thought of having sex with someone else was hard to fathom, let alone to be free enough to engage in the type of sexual fantasies she and Mickey had thrived on.

Slowly her sexual urges coaxed her back and once again she found pleasure in masturbation. Jondalar was her lover now. He never got jealous when she looked at her naked Mickey pictures while he serviced her.

About this same time, short little snippets of dreams began to occur almost nightly. In them she was being ravaged by Mickey. At least she thought it was him. She could never really see his face. It was more the familiarity of technique that she felt. In some dreams he spoke. He would whisper her name and she knew it was her cherished husband. But in some dreams her lover didn't speak. Sometimes she was so absorbed in the passion of her own personal pleasure and the bodily sensations she was feeling that she gave no thought as to who it was that was obliging her, nor did it seem to matter. It did not diminish the orgasmic pleasure level.

She had never been unfaithful to Mickey; the thought had never occurred to her. But now, as she reflected on the dreams, she had the feeling of enjoying sex for sex's sake without the love factor. That wasn't entirely true. There was love; it was for herself. She was enjoying the sex for herself. It was a one-sided, selfish love. Not the complete, whole love of marital bliss that she shared with Mickey. Their lovemaking bonded them, as they loved themselves and each other, taking pleasure in each other's orgasms. But now, in some of her dreams, the gratification was hers alone, and it was okay for it to be that way. It was a strange, warm, comfortable feeling.

As part of her self-healing she forced herself to get out of the house and explore the community, to keep her sanity more than anything. She even started taking Zumba classes at the local rec center. She found the women there very friendly and welcoming. They lovingly called their instructor Zumba Mama. Zoey thought that was cute.

One day she discovered a small, quaint restaurant just off Lakeshore Drive that had recently opened just a few months before, called Keith's Kitchen, and began to frequent the establishment often. It catered to varied culinary tastes with an ever- changing menu. The seafood special was flown in daily and the chief always created a tasty and unique masterpiece that never left her unsatisfied.

On this particular night the hostess seated Zoey at her usual table, a corner table in the back with a clear view of Lake Tahoe. It had been a beautiful cloudless day and the sun shone bright on the surface of the water. She was in a good mood, life was manageable.

As she looked into the still, quiet blue of the lake she was interrupted by the waiter. "Good evening, ma'am. My name is James. Would you like to hear about our specials?"

Eyes as deep and blue as the lake met hers and sent a spark of electricity down her spine. She could feel the hairs on the back of her neck rise and she was sure she was blushing. She blinked and focused.

He was new. She'd never seen him before. He was tall, handsome, and well- built. His physique was not unlike that of Mickey's. But he was also everything that Mickey wasn't. Mickey was dark-haired and brown-eyed. His skin was olive-toned, with soft dark hairs covering most of his body. His face was strong and angular with a beard so thick, even after he shaved he looked like he had a five o'clock shadow. He had a molten sexuality.

The man before her was dirty-blond and blue-eyed. This guy looked like a tanned California surfer. His shiny long hair was wavy and thick, and touched his shoulders. With the sun at his back the golden hairs on his arms were aura-like around him as he held up the order pad, waiting for her answer. The face before her was soft and smooth, and he was young. So young. But still, there was something about him.

For a moment she felt a pang of sexual arousal. Her mouth went dry and she couldn't catch her breath. Her nipples rose and hardened and her legs closed involuntarily. The sensation frightened and thrilled her, but in an instant it was gone. Thoughts of Mickey flashed in her mind and she was beset with sadness, the sudden emotional change showing on her face. She reached for her glass of water and drank.

"I'm sorry," the young man said, perceiving her grief. "Did I offend you in some way?" He looked distressed, but somehow sympathetic.

She looked down and regained control of her emotions. Once again, she looked up into eyes the color of a wild Wyoming sky. "No. No, you didn't. I'm sorry if I made you uncomfortable. It's just that..." How do you explain to a stranger that you're in mourning for your husband? That you hadn't had real, hard physical sex in almost a year, and that for just a moment the stranger made you feel like a sensuous woman again? "Well, it's a long story." She paused. "It doesn't matter. Yes, please tell me about the specials, James."

After he took her order, Zoey's sudden infatuation with young James returned. She found it quite unsettling, but she couldn't stop herself. During her meal she searched him out and found comfort as she watched him go about his work. Once, he looked up from where he was as if he could hear her siren call to him. Their eyes met. She looked away shyly, but he didn't. She could feel him looking directly at her, piercing her very soul.

At the end of the meal James brought her check and lay it down on the table. "Hold on," she said as she reached into her purse for her credit card. She lay it down on the black leather folder. He reached down and put his hand on top of hers. She looked up into a blue abyss.

"I'm sorry for your loss, ma'am," he said compassionately. He glanced over at the hostess, then back at Zoey. "She told me you lost your husband last year. My deepest sympathies."

She nodded in thanks, but couldn't speak.

"I was wondering," he said, then hesitated. "That is, if you ever need a sympathetic shoulder to cry on." He stopped. "I mean, it's just that you look so lonely, and I've been told that I'm a good listener."

His kindness kindled a flame in her heart. She smiled back. "Thank you. I might take you up on that." And she meant it. It would be comforting to speak to someone about her feelings, someone who didn't know her before the loss of Mickey and wasn't as wrapped up in the sorrow as she was.

He smiled back. "Please, any time." He took her credit card and left. When he brought the receipt for her signature, he slid another small piece of paper toward her. "Here's my number. Call when you need me."

She looked down at the paper, but couldn't look up

as tears began to fill her eyes. When she did, he was gone. She signed the credit card slip, folded the smaller paper, put it into her pocket, and left.

That night she slept restlessly. In the brief moments that she managed to drift off flashes of Mickey came before her eyes, but as she reached out to touch him, the face before her turned into young James. She awoke in the morning drenched in a cold sweat, feeling troubled and confused.

She couldn't explain the strange feelings she had about the young man. Was it sexual? No. Wait, maybe yes, but not the hot passion that she felt for Mickey. But yes, sex with James would be somehow satisfying, different, yet exciting, and perhaps calming. She wondered if he felt the same way. Did that make sense? She shook her head. "I'm delusional," she thought out loud. He had offered his shoulder to cry on and a sympathetic ear, not a cock to fuck her with. Christ, she was old enough to be his mother. Not really, but she was older. Much older; she figured almost 20 years. Holy fuck, she *was* old enough to be his mother, she thought again. She was giving herself too much credit.

As time went on Zoey fell into a routine. A quick simple breakfast followed by a meditative walk at the lakeshore. She spent her afternoons reading or visiting the few acquaintances she had in town. They were ladies she met at the Zumba class which she tried to go to once a week. She couldn't really call them friends, not like Carol or Joanne. They didn't know her inner self, but they were nice and generally seemed to like her and care about her.

She found herself going to Keith's Kitchen more and more frequently, and was surprised at the disappointment she felt if James wasn't working and the joy when he was. One night as James came by to take her order, she decided to take their casual but friendly relationship to the next level.

"Good evening, Zoey." They were already on a first-name basis. "Do you know what you want tonight?"

She looked up into his smiling young face. "Yes," she said casually. "I'll have the halibut, and a sympathetic ear."

He looked up from his pad, confusion on his face. "Excuse me?"

"If you're still willing, I'd like to take you up on the offer you made the day we met. Maybe we could meet for coffee tomorrow? That is, if you're still willing."

His face beamed with a welcoming smile. "Of course; I'd like that very much."

It wasn't long before the two had a standing 'date' every Tuesday morning, rain or shine, to walk the beach. It was the only day during the week James didn't have classes at the local Sierra Nevada College, where he was pursuing a four-year degree in business administration. He worked five nights a week at Keith's Kitchen and Zoey didn't think it was fair to steal him away on his nights off. He was young and handsome and, although he never spoke of it, surely he had a social life.

Soon after the walks began their friendship grew closer, and before long they became the highlight of her week. It was refreshing to get James' take on her life and what she had done with it up to this point. She also found it easy to speak to him about the healthy sexuality she had shared with Mickey without feeling as though she was being judged a pervert or weird. James seemed genuinely interested and seemed to enjoy their talks as much as she did. He was considerate and she valued his opinion. And, yes, he was a good listener.

She found him very mature for his age. He had a realistic look on life and didn't sugarcoat his thoughts. He was always honest with her, and she respected that.

It was therapeutic to talk about her life with Mickey. Talking to James was almost like talking to Mickey. She could talk about anything. It had been a long time since she'd spoken her mind to a man, heck, to anyone. The intimate thoughts she had for him had subsided. He never showed any interest in taking their relationship to a sexual level, so she forced herself to suppress the amorous feelings she'd felt for him. She felt very comfortable with him now, as a friend.

"You know," she said one day during their walk, "I could never figure out the thing about getting hookers for his clients. How could those men enjoy sex knowing that the women were having sex with them only because they were being paid?"

James was silent for a moment. She could see that he was trying to find the words. Finally, he answered, "It's different for them. The kind of sex they have with their wives is a different kind of sex. They have to be respectful. After all, these are the mothers of their children. They share a house, a family, a religion. Sex with a stranger is like a forbidden pleasure, an escape from the ordinary. It's just the act of sexual gratification, not love."

She laughed. "That's what Mickey used to say. I guess that's why he and I never strayed. I wasn't the mother of his children. Our sex was open, it was crazy and, in some people's minds, maybe depraved. But it had plenty of love."

"Did you enjoy it on a physical level?" he asked

with sincerity. "Was it fulfilling?

"Of course we did. And yes, it was," she replied proudly.

"Did you or Mickey ever hesitate to ask each other to do anything sexual, no matter what?"

"No, of course not," she replied.

"Did you or Mickey ever refuse a request?"

"No, never."

"Well, then you didn't need to go outside the marriage for sexual satisfaction. You just happened to be lucky enough to have love in the mix. It's a different culture in the Mideast. It would be disrespectful for a man to ask his wife to cater to his sexual desires if they're outside the respectful norm, at least what they consider normal."

"Thanks a lot," she said. "Are you calling me a pervert?"

"Not at all," he said seriously. "I consider it a healthy way to keep the marriage alive and well." He leaned over and grabbed her hand without thinking and gave it a squeeze. She looked down, and just as quickly he let it go.

They walked for a while in silence.

"What about now?" he asked.

"What do you mean?" she replied.

"How do you get sexual release now, without Mickey?"

"Well," she thought, "at first I didn't even think about sex. I couldn't. I was so wrapped up in my grief that I couldn't think about anything except Mickey being gone forever."

"And now?" he asked sincerely.

She stopped abruptly. He had struck a nerve. She could feel her face flush deep red. Truth be told, just these past months she had been thinking of sex just for sex's sake. She had been relieving herself with masturbation and pornography, but it just didn't satisfy like real sex. She missed the physical touch, the raw smell, and warmth of a man's body next to hers. But the thought of having sex with anyone but Mickey made her stomach churn.

She looked up at him. Should she be honest with him? They had been honest with each other so far, so why quit now? "I'm not sure," she said truthfully as she began walking again. "I've been getting horny again for the first time since Mickey died. I don't really know what to do about it. I'm certain I'm not ready to have a physical relationship with another man right now."

James turned his head to look at her face. She was looking straight ahead but he could still see the slight blush. "So," he said, "how have you acted on your horniness?"

Zoey chuckled. "Who's the pervert now?" she said, trying to get out of answering the question.

He looked serious, and it was obvious he wasn't going to let it go.

"Well, if you must know, I've been masturbating," she said honestly. "I told you, I don't think I'm ready to be with another man yet."

For a quick moment she thought she saw a twinkle of amusement in his eyes. It was quickly replaced with one of disappointment. Then it was gone. He cleared his throat. "Well," he said, "that's a start."

Summer came and went and turned into fall. Fall was quickly turning to winter. Zoey lived her routine life. But sometime around the beginning of December she realized that her life had become stagnant. It wasn't that she was bored, but she began to feel that life had become too predictable. She longed for a new adventure.

"So, you must be getting anxious for school to be over," she said to James during their regular walk on a bright but chilly morning. James was set to graduate at the end of the winter term.

"I'll say," he said with enthusiasm. "Just one more week of classes, then finals."

"Then graduation," she said just as excited. "Don't forget about that. It's been what you've been working for all these years."

He looked perplexed. "It's almost anti-climactic," he said with little emotion. "I've been so involved in school and working for the past four years that I really don't have much of a life outside of that. I won't know what to do with all my free time."

"Well, have you thought about where you want to work, what kind of company you want to work for?" she asked.

"Yes, I've thought about it, but nothing excites me. I'm pretty sure I could work for a big corporation, maybe find something in Vegas, but I don't want it to be ordinary. I want to work for a company that doesn't do regular things."

She was confused. "What do you mean by regular?" she asked.

"Well, for one," he said, "I don't want to have to wear a suit every day."

She smiled. "That doesn't seem like too big of a hurdle."

"For another," he continued, "I don't want to work for a meaningless bullshit company. I want to work for a company that does exciting things, but at the same time helps people."

"Well, that is a tall order, isn't it?" she said.

"Yes," he answered. "It is. I want the company product to be stimulating and different. You know, unique."

"Any ideas?" she replied.

"None whatsoever," he laughed. "But I'll know it when I see it."

She looked at his handsome face and felt a familiar stirring between her legs. She felt slightly out of breath and weak-kneed. There was no denying that he was an attractive man. Any woman would think so. And she *was* a woman, a woman in need of a man's touch. She held back, not yet.

But she couldn't shake the sexual energy that she felt that morning. It plagued her throughout the day, stirring up feelings deeply hidden since Mickey's death. That night she found it hard to sleep until she masturbated.

Chapter 18

James received his diploma on December 12th with honors, but little fanfare. There was no family in attendance to praise his achievement, only Zoey and a few fellow employees from Keith's Kitchen, including Keith.

She felt bad for him. This was quite an achievement. It was something to celebrate. Where was his family? His friends? She decided to ask him as they walked together towards the parking lot after the ceremony.

She put her hand on his arm and he turned toward her. He could see the concern on her face. "I'm a little surprised your family isn't here to celebrate," she noted. "You know, I just realized that on our walks all we do is talk about me. Well, Mickey and me. You've never spoken of your family. Aren't you close to them?"

"I'm an only child of only-children parents, just like you, and both my parents are dead," he said matter-of-factly. He had no extended family to share his holidays, birthdays, or other special occasions with. He was alone, just like her. He told her his story and her heart wept for him.

His father had moved the little family to Incline Village for business reasons just before James started high school. Until this time they'd lived in Chicago, where James was born. His father felt Incline Village would also be a safer environment for his family. He didn't say what his father's business was, and Zoey didn't ask. His father was diagnosed with liver cancer a year after the move and died six months after that. His mother passed of pancreatic cancer two years after, when he was a senior. It took her in ten months. He felt fortunate that he had received enough inheritance money to supplement the grants and scholarships he received to pay most of his college expenses.

"I learned early in life that I had no one to depend on but myself. I had a good financial start, a lot more than most students had. And my parents always taught me to be self-sufficient. They also taught me about morality and mankind.

"I believe everything happens for a reason. We may not understand it when it happens. Sometimes the reason reveals itself later, sometimes it never does. Anyway, I knew my ticket to a good life was a good education, and that no one was going to hand me a free ride.

"I always felt like an outsider in high school, and never really stayed close to any of my classmates after we graduated. Most of the kids didn't really take life seriously and couldn't wait to get out of here anyway."

Zoey chuckled. "But surely you have an old girlfriend or two hanging around. You're not a virgin, are you?"

He smiled and looked into her eyes. "No, there are

no girlfriends hanging around and, no, I'm not a virgin. It's just that I've had no serious romantic relationships." He stood up straight and smoothed his hair back, cleared his throat, and continued. "So, here I am. Now you know who I am and what I've been doing for the last four years."

She hugged him tightly and closed her eyes. "I had no idea. I feel so selfish." She could feel her eyes fill with tears.

He pushed away from her, turning her to face him, and tenderly held her chin. He looked into her tearful eyes. "Don't feel sorry for me. I don't, and neither should you. Life threw me a curve ball and I did what I thought I had to do to make the best of it."

She shook her head. "You're wise beyond your years, and I'm proud to be your friend."

"And I yours," he responded, and hugged her.

"Well, friend," she said when they parted, "what you did was amazing and we need to celebrate. I've got some leftover chicken and broccoli casserole and a garden salad at my place and lots of wine. Would you care to join me?"

"Got any Scotch?" he asked. That's what Mickey drank. It made her think of him for a moment. She knew there was still an unopened bottle of Glenlivet in the cabinet.

"As a matter of fact, I do. It was Mickey's," she said. "He was saving it for a special occasion."

He looked at her with a sideways glance. "I knew he was a man of good taste. You don't mind?"

"No, I don't," she answered with authority. "He's not coming back, and I know he wouldn't mind. This is a special occasion, isn't it? So, are you coming?"

"You mean I finally get to see the inside of Zoey's Place?"

It was true. James had never been inside her

home. Although he'd picked her up for their beach walks, she was always waiting on the porch when he arrived. He dropped her off at the same spot. She never invited him in. In fact, no man had ever been inside since she moved in permanently, except for the stray delivery men who never made it past the front door. James knew this for fact.

"Yes," she said, rather shyly. "It seems we have a lot in common. To use your logic, fate has thrown us together for some reason. Let's go with it."

He grabbed her hand and held it. "Since you put it like that, I accept," he said as he kissed the back of it in gallant fashion. "I'll follow you home, milady."

Zoey opened the front door to her house and walked in. She turned to see James standing at the threshold. "Are you sure about this?" he asked with trepidation.

She looked back and around the room behind her, then at him. "I'm very sure," she said confidently. "Welcome to Zoey's Place," she said with a curtsy, stretching out her hand towards the inside as he walked in.

In short time they had consumed most of the casserole and salad. James had put a dent in the Scotch, and Zoey drank almost a bottle of wine by herself. She was feeling bold and asked a question that had been burning in her mind for hours. "James, friend," she said, feeling a little light-headed.

"Yes," he answered, looking up from his just emptied glass of Scotch, "Zoey, friend?"

"Can I ask you something really personal?"

"Anything," he answered. "You should know that by now."

"Well..." She was actually blushing. "You said you're not a virgin and that you hadn't had any serious relationships."

"Yes," he replied in confirmation.

"Well, may I ask how you lost your..." she hesitated. "Do you..." She grappled for the right words. "What I mean is," she paused, "who do you have sex with?"

He smiled, picking up her train of thought. "I lost my virginity to Mandy Collins in the 10th grade, at the Autumn Cotillion. She was two years older than me and definitely not a virgin."

She smiled. "Oh, my! An experienced older woman."

"To say the least," he said. "She opened up a whole new world to me that night, if you catch my drift." He gave her a wink and she laughed. "Her mother was a hooker at a brothel. It's a respectable job around here, you know."

"So I've heard," she replied, rolling her eyes.

"Anyway, she moved right after that and, well, to tell the truth," he confessed, "since that time I've only had sex with hookers; fast, easy, no ties."

Zoey was blown away. "You mean to say that you've never had sex for love?" she asked.

"Nope," he said, shaking his head. "Never felt the need. Didn't really have time for that."

She was speechless. Their earlier talk about Mickey's clients and the hookers he used to get for them came to mind. It all began to make sense.

"So," she wondered, "you can just go and have sex with a woman who you know doesn't love you, and is only doing what she's doing because you're paying her to do it?"

"Yes," he said calmly. Seeing her look of concern, he added, "It's no different than me serving you a dinner at Keith's."

"Excuse me?" she interrupted, feeling both a little

insulted and a little turned on. "I hardly see the connection."

"Look," he said. "It's simple. I'm being paid to be nice to customers who come into the restaurant no matter who they are. The chef is being paid to cook without becoming emotionally involved with the people who will eat his food. Everyone gets what they want. Everyone walks out happy, same as in a whorehouse."

It was a quite a stretch, but, damn his logic. She was starting to see it his way, against her better judgment. "You sound as if you could be a gigilo just as easily as a waiter."

"Maybe I could be," he retorted without thinking.

"So, if I put a hundred dollars on the table right now and told you to fuck me, you could do it without any hesitation or feelings of love?"

"That's a bit cheap for a fuck but, damn straight," he said, feeling confident albeit a little tipsy. "Why don't you put your money where your mouth is and see what happens?"

"Well, maybe I will," she said, and without a second thought she reached into her nearby purse, fished out two $50 bills, and slammed them down on the table. She could feel her body heat rise. What was she doing? What if he picked up the money? She finally admitted to herself that she did want him in a sexual way and to her dismay it was pure lustful want and not love. Did he feel the same?

James glanced down at the cash on the table then up at her. "Are you sure you want to do this and it's not the alcohol talking?" he asked.

"Very sure," she groaned as she started to unbutton her blouse. Her head was a bit fuzzy from the wine but she knew what she was doing. No turning back now, morality be damned.

He pulled his shirt over his head, exposing his very well developed chest frosted with curly blond hairs that formed a directional line leading right down to his crotch. He stood up and moved close to her. He lifted her up by her ass and pulled her in close. She wrapped her legs around him tightly as they headed towards what he assumed was a bedroom. He planted a wet, full mouth kiss on her hungry lips and explored the edge of her mouth with his tongue as they entered the room. She kissed him back, hard and willing. He lay her down on the bed and began to undress her until she was naked. Kicking off his shoes, he dropped his pants to the floor. Lying down naked next to her, he began to fondle her breasts. His tongue gently flicked the soft mounds, then he licked each tip before blowing on them softly. The shock of the cold breeze on her sensitive, moist nipples made them stand up straight and hard. He took one between his finger and thumb and massaged it softly before kissing her again on the mouth.

She reached down and grabbed the manly hardness she had been longing for. He thrust his hips toward her. Feelings of guilt tried to edge their way into her head. But human nature and erotic yearning won over. It had been too long since she had been fucked. Yes, fucked, that's what it was. She and Mickey had fucked thousands of times. This was no different. Although there was love with Mickey, there was none now, and it didn't matter.

Experienced hands manipulated her body. He touched, kissed, and licked her from head to toe, pausing at just the right spots to heighten her sensations. Every contact point tingled with erotic electricity as he brought her body back to life from its long hibernation.

Sorrow, worry, responsibility, and reality faded into

a weightless vapor. Her only awareness was his touch on her body. He was kissing the back of her neck now and she felt helpless to move. She allowed herself to be controlled by him as he twisted and turned her to reach her sensitive parts. His hands moved to open her legs. She didn't resist as he began to lick and kiss the soft inner flesh of her thighs and explore her secret garden. He positioned himself on top of her but didn't enter her. He teased her with his penis, letting it touch her nether region and gently rub against her. He humped between her legs until she could stand it no longer.

"Fuck me, damn you!" she yelled. "Fuck me. Fuck me. Fuck me." She dug her nails into his back.

He thrust himself deep inside her. She groaned in delight and abandoned herself to their shared desire, joining him in an unholy orgy of lust and debauchery.

She came first, releasing the pent-up sexual frustration, desire, grief, and longing she had been holding in since Mickey's death. It came pouring forth in an explosive orgasm that contorted her body and made her moan like a cat in heat. His orgasm came after a few more deep thrusts and he collapsed on the bed next to her.

They both lay motionless, sweaty, and breathing heavily for several minutes before Zoey broke the silence. "I need some water," she said as she got up and went into the adjoining bathroom. He was still lying naked on the bed when she returned a minute later. She was wearing a light robe to cover her nakedness and offered him a sip from the glass she was holding.

He sat up and brushed his blond surfer hair back. "Did I make my point?" He took the glass from her.

She closed her eyes. "Yes, damn you," she reluctantly admitted. "I don't love you, but I sure as hell enjoyed it."

"Same here," he said, putting the glass down. He stood up and began to get dressed. "I rest my case, Counselor," he added teasingly.

"You're an ass," she laughed, "but I concede."

Chapter 19

After James left Zoey lay on the bed, reflecting on what she just experienced. She performed sex just for the pure ecstasy of it. The intensity of her orgasm had been strong, almost like what she'd had with Mickey. She had to admit it felt damn good. Did it really matter that love wasn't involved? She thought for a moment. Yes. Yes, it did. Love was the one elemental ingredient in making love. That's what she'd had with Mickey. No matter how different, unique, or strange the sex was that they shared, it was always with love—making love and giving love. But logically she couldn't dismiss the fact that her climax with James had strength and intensity; even minus the love factor, she had enjoyed it. She and James fucked, hard.

Could she live with it? She reviewed the facts in her head. Mickey was gone forever. She had no intention of trying to find a new love interest, but she sure as hell wasn't ready to give up sex. This was a different kind of sex, a new perspective, yet it was totally satisfying in a strange sort of way. Isn't that what she moved to Nevada for, a new life? Hell, yes. She could get into it. No emotional bond. She could never love another man like she'd loved Mickey. There could never be another man like him and now there didn't have to be. She didn't need anyone but herself. It was a new beginning and she was starting to like it.

And it wasn't like James was a stranger. They were friends. She had to admit that he was extremely good-looking. She liked him a lot. She was comfortable with him. But did she love him? No. It wasn't love. She was positive she didn't love him. But she strongly liked him in a sexual way, especially now. "Friends, as it were, with benefits," she thought out loud, laughing.

After her logical analysis of the morality as it relates to non-emotional sex, she decided to delve into the mechanics of the evening's activity. James was definitely proficient on the female body. She would have to rank him right up there at expert level. He knew where and how to touch every sensitive spot on her. Waves of excited sensation rippled down her spine at the thought of the explosive orgasm she'd had that night. Did he learn that from the prostitutes he'd been sleeping with? She'd have to ask. Too bad all men didn't fuck like that. It was a pity that more women couldn't experience that kind of sex. If James wanted to be a male prostitute, the women would be lined up for miles for a piece of his action.

Her mind flashed to Mickey and the hookers that he procured for his clients. Then she thought of all the stories of horny old women that Fen told her about. Could this be the same thing? Kinda, sorta? Maybe? All this moralizing was making her brain hurt. Then an idea hit her like a bolt of lightning. Why not open up a male brothel? She knew that Heidi Fleiss had tried it and failed, but she'd had it wrong. She came from the wrong angle. It had to be a classy place, clean and crisp. Make it look like a spa; sex would be only one of the services offered. And she knew the team she needed to assemble to help her to turn this dream into a reality.

She wanted to cater to rich clientele, so she would need Fen's vast social network to solicit potential clients. That lady knew every rich old woman from coast to coast and which ones were in need of a good fucking.

Hire only young, handsome men. She would have James teach them everything he knows about how to please a woman. He could also help out with his business management knowledge. She'd give him a unique business to run, all right. All those educational dollars would be put to good use.

Her brothel would be upscale. She would offer massages, hot wraps, yoga, health foods, and all the things the expensive spas offer. But there would be a menu of sexual delights the ladies could choose from as well. And the kicker? Each sex room would be themed, just like the scenarios she and Mickey used.

But who could she get to run the day to day office paperwork? She didn't know if she wanted to handle all of that. James would be far too busy managing the prostitutes to take reservations and office bookkeeping. She needed an office manager. It had to be someone she trusted completely, someone who was competent. The answer came quickly. Who better suited for this position but Annette? It would be good to work with her again.

What a great idea! Now she just had to sell all three of her friends on the plan. She was excited, but she was also exhausted; better to start fresh in the morning. An involuntary twinge brought her legs together. She felt soreness in her lady parts that she hadn't felt in a very long time. Her hand instinctively reached down to her crotch. She was still moist, and smiled as she relived some of the pleasurable moments of the evening. She closed her eyes and fell into a deep, restful, satisfying sleep.

The next day she put together a business plan, intending to run it past James as soon as she could. If she could sell him on the idea, she was sure she could get the ladies on board. Now that James was finished with school, he had more free time. He agreed to meet at her house for a drink the following afternoon.

James settled down in the large overstuffed recliner with a glass of Scotch on the rocks. Zoey sat across from him with a glass of wine.

"So," he said after pleasantries, "to what do I owe the pleasure of your company and this fine Scotch?"

"We'll get to that soon enough," she replied. "First, I've got to know. Where did you learn to fuck like that?"

He laughed as he took a sip from his glass. "Well, Mandy was a wealth of information."

"I gathered that," she said, "but you were too young, and she couldn't possibly have enough time to teach you everything. I was extremely impressed with your performance last night, in case you hadn't noticed."

He blushed. "Much obliged, ma'am," he said in a mock western tone as he tipped an invisible hat. "Did you forget that I said I've only had sex with hookers?

"I spent a lot of time in one particular house; was a regular for a while, got to know the girls personally. Wasn't long before they were showing me what felt good to them and what they were looking for in sex. They were more than willing to let me practice on them. They said it was a nice change to be on the other end and have someone servicing them. It was kind of a quid pro quo."

"I'll bet," she said, feeling slightly jealous. "Well, they taught you well, sir."

He bowed his head in acknowledgement. "Is that what you called me over her for, or were you looking to book another session?"

She smiled. "Definitely, but not right now." She hesitated for a moment then sat upright in her chair, gave him a serious look, and said, "Did you find a job yet?"

He frowned. "Of course not," he said with a puzzled look. "You know that."

"How would you like to be partner, staff manager, and trainer at an exclusive, high-priced brothel/spa for rich old women?"

He laughed out loud. "Sounds exciting." He relaxed into his chair. "Do you know where such an establishment exists?"

"It doesn't yet," she replied with excitement. "I'm going to start it. You want in?"

His facial expression went from humorous to dead serious as he mulled the idea over in his head. "Could work, I suppose. Where would the clientele come from?"

Her face glowed with excitement. "I know a lady who knows every horny rich woman in the country, hell, probably in the world. She hasn't agreed yet. She doesn't even know about it. You're the first person I've told. But I know she'll do it.

"And I've got an office manager in mind, too." She was bouncing in her seat. "Oh, James, I really think it would be a success. And no one knows more than I that there's a need. Tell me you're in. We could do it. I know we could."

She could see the wheels turning in his head as he

slowly sipped the Scotch. "Would I have to come up with any of the money? You know I'm dirt poor."

"No," she answered. "Your skill is your gold. We'll work out the details later." She put on her best how-can-you-say-no-to-me face in hopes it would have the same effect on James that it had always had on Mickey.

It did. James looked at her and smiled as he put his drink down. "I may be crazy," he said, "but damn it, I think it might work. I'm in."

She jumped up and into his lap, hugging him tightly. "Thank you. You won't be sorry. I really believe in this."

He emptied his glass and looked at her. "Should we fuck to seal the deal?"

It took her by surprise but in a good way. Without hesitation she said, "Why the hell not?" She grabbed his hand and they headed to the bedroom for another satisfying romp; two in less than one week. Zoey was feeling almost normal again.

The next morning as she sipped her herbal tea, she was contemplating the incredible sex sessions she and James had and the fantastic future she pictured for both of them. One down and two to go. She was excited for the first time in a very long while.

Who should she call next, Annette or Fen? She really didn't think she'd have trouble convincing Annette to get on board. She'd better call Fen. Face it, without clientele you had nothing no matter how efficient your office was or how skilled the men were.

Would Fen go for it? Had she had enough time to mourn Allen? It had been almost three years. The deep, searing pain of separation would never go away, she knew that. But she had come to realize that Mickey was NEVER coming back. He wouldn't want her life to stop just because his did. Regular phone calls with Fen *had* brought the two women closer.

After their lunch in Detroit they committed to stay in touch. At first the calls were infrequent. Back when the pain was so raw that just thinking about talking to Fen brought up visions of Mickey dying and she would be enveloped in such distress that she couldn't go through with the call. She could tell that Fen felt the same way. In the beginning their conversations were polite but short. They usually ended with both women in tears. But as time went on, they became comfortable in the sorrow that they shared. It was like a weird kind of sisterhood. They had always been kindred spirits, but now the bond had become tighter with the great grief that they both felt but seldom talked about anymore.

Eventually their conversations had become longer and the range of things they talked about grew. She felt confident that Fen shared most of her philosophical if not political views. She knew that Fen was no prude, but would she go so far as to be a part of prostitution? Yes, that's what it was when you come right down to it. Some people thought it was wrong, a sin against God.

The thought toyed with her conscience for a moment. God. Who is God? What is God? Does anyone even know for sure? If we are all God's children, doesn't God, our Father, want us, his children, to be happy? Happiness has a different definition for different people. Her logical and educated mind deduced that there was at least a 50/50 chance that her interpretation of what God is was correct.

Now, could she get Fen to see the logic of it? There was only one way to find out. She took a healthy swig of the red wine she had poured for herself and dialed Fen's number.

"Hello?" a familiar voice answered. She sounded relaxed. This was good.

"Fen, its Zoey. How are you?"

"Oh, Zoey, I can't believe it's you. I was just thinking about you the other day. Something happened that made me think of you."

"Really?" Zoey was intrigued. "What was it?"

"I was at a fundraiser and had a rather unpleasant experience with Dorothy Lucas. Remember her? Old, wrinkled, rich widow with a big hairy wart on the side of her chin?"

Zoey thought a moment and laughed. "I remember her. Has the worst taste in clothes; always clashing in style and color. And not the sharpest pencil in the box as I recall. Crotchety old bag, too, isn't she?"

"That's her," Fen broke in. "We always said she had to have been good in bed to have landed a rich husband because she couldn't have done it with her looks, brains, or charm."

"Do tell, girl. Whatever did you do?" Zoey asked with anticipation.

"Well," Fen explained. "I was trying to explain why it was important to protect the animals in Africa from poachers to her and a group of other women and she kept asking the most asinine questions, just to annoy me I think. At least it felt like that. I really wasn't having such a good day. I had a headache brewing and was in no mood for her kind of ignorance. I can't even remember what it was that made me snap but it ended with me telling her she needed to lighten up, find a man, and get laid. I told her it would do wonders for her."

Zoey was shocked. "You didn't!"

"I did," she said proudly. "And you know what? It

made me think of you. I felt like I was channeling you; speaking my mind, being free, and it felt good."

Zoey felt proud. "Thanks, I think."

"Oh, it's all good," Fen replied. "I was going to call you today and tell you about it. That's why it's so weird that you called me. So, what's up?"

"Funny you should mention old women getting laid," she said. "That's kind of what this is about."

Zoey told her about her experience with James and her idea for the brothel. At first Fen didn't sound interested. But the more Zoey told her about how it felt to have James touch all the private pleasure places that had been neglected since Mickey died, and how liberating it felt to enjoy sex for the sake of sex itself, free of guilt, she began to come around. Zoey told her that with her list of women who probably would benefit greatly from a good bedding by a professional skilled in the art of pleasuring a woman, they would be doing womankind a favor. Not to mention make a few dollars on the side, not that either of them needed money. Each widow had received a $5,000,000 settlement from Taylor Resource Development six months after the construction crane accident that killed their husbands. It meant financial independence for Zoey, but Fen came from money and the settlement really had no financial impact for her.

"I've got more money than I could ever spend," Fen had proclaimed.

"Me, too," said Zoey. "But what good is the money if we don't do something with it? We owe it to the women of the world, at least the ones who can afford us."

Fen laughed. "Oh, what the hell. What have I got to lose? I'm in."

"Wonderful!" Zoey exclaimed. "Welcome, partner."

Two down, one to go.

She thought the call to Annette would be a piece of cake. Zoey hadn't called or heard from her former office manager for several months. They had tried to keep in touch after Zoey moved to Incline Village, but Annette had met someone shortly after and gradually the calls became less frequent. She had met her lover on the job at the plumbing supply business she was now working for. Connie was a plumber. Annette seemed smitten for the first time since Zoey had known her. She hoped that it would all work out for her. If anyone deserved a little happiness, it was Annette. She was about the best office manager around; competent, alert, always on top of what going on and how to fix it if it wasn't. She was kind-hearted and sensitive, even though a little too naïve. She had been a good friend and employee, and Zoey felt a little guilty that she had allowed the closeness between them to widen.

A sense of guilt swept over her. She remembered the last conversation she had with Annette. She and Connie had hit a rough patch, but Annette said that they were going to see a couples counselor. She was hopeful the relationship could be saved. Zoey hadn't spoken to her since. She should have called just to see if the therapy was successful. Inwardly she hoped it hadn't.

She looked up Annette's phone number in her contact list and made the call.

"Hello?" the woman who answered didn't sound like the optimistic, self-confident person Zoey had once known. She also sounded tired and congested, like she had a cold.

"Annette, is that you?" Zoey asked.

"Yeah, who is this?"

"It's Zoey," she replied with concern. "Are you all right? Are you sick?"

There was a pause. "Zoey," she cleared her throat. "I'm fine. You caught me napping," she explained.

"Annette, it's me. I know you," Zoey said with even more concern. "You don't take naps. What's going on? You don't sound right. You sound all stuffed up. Have you been crying?"

It took a few minutes to get it out of her, but finally Annette broke down and told her about the break-up. Connie had left her for a younger woman just a few days before. Annette was devastated.

"I thought I had finally met my soul mate, Zoey," Annette cried into the phone. "We did everything together. The sex was phenomenal and she cooked! I was in heaven. I thought she was just as happy as I was. She even told me she loved me." At this point she started sobbing uncontrollably. "And now she's telling me that she just wanted me for my money." Zoey had given her a very generous severance package. "And now that my money is gone, she, she, she left me." Annette broke down again.

"Annette, sweetie," Zoey consoled. "If she just wanted you for what you could buy her, she wasn't worth it. How dare she break your heart. You are a beautiful, caring woman. Your soul mate is still out there somewhere."

After a while Zoey was able to get Annette to see that her life wasn't over. She was just going through a bad time.

"Zoey," Annette said. "I miss you. You can always make me see the other side of the situation. That's why you were such a good lawyer."

"Thanks," Zoey said meekly. "So, you say your money ran out?" Zoey was thinking this could work to her advantage.

"Yes," Annette said apologetically. "I'm sorry, Zoey. You were very generous and I was foolish to spend it on Connie. It's just that, well, let's just say she was very needy and I—" She paused. "She said she loved me. No one had ever said that to me before."

"Annette," Zoey broke in, "you don't owe me any explanations. That money was yours to do with as you wished. I'm not judging. And even if I did, there's no blame on your part. That Connie is a bitch and doesn't deserve you."

Annette laughed. "I miss you, boss."

"Good." Zoey pounced. "How'd you like to come and work for me again?"

This interested and surprised Annette. "Are you practicing law again?"

"No," she said carefully, and with some hesitation. "Something better and completely different this time, but I think you'll fit in just fine. Interested?"

After she gave Annette her fifteen-minute sales pitch Annette was hooked. The timing couldn't be more perfect. Annette was ready and willing to put as many miles as she could between her and Connie the Freeloader.

Three down. The plan was coming together.

Chapter 20

The date was April 1, 2005. Zoey looked around her living room at her crew. She cleared her throat and called the meeting to order.

"Okay, everyone," she said with authority. "We've made a lot of progress in the last couple of months and, although I've meet with everyone individually, we've pretty much been working solo. I thought I'd call an official meeting so we can get a good picture of where we are." Nods of agreement and excited faces filled the room.

"Let's start with our new place of business. Annette and I have been looking all over Storey County since that's the closest legal county to here. The damn county has so many restrictions on where we can locate it almost cuts out half the town. And where it is permitted, all we've seen is a lot of shit." Annette chortled, and shook her head. "But I think we finally might have hit pay dirt."

Fen and James looked up with enthusiasm. "There's an old estate with easy access from I-80. It's north of the Virginia City limit line so it's away from the town. It was converted to a bed and breakfast years ago and has everything we need: a large main home with about a dozen guest rooms, all suites, a fully equipped kitchen and good sized dining room, large exercise room, a couple of common areas, and a full size pool and hot tub. There are three little cabana-type buildings on the property, too. It's on a large piece of land and not visible from the road, but that will work in our favor; no nosey neighbors. By law we'll have to fence the entire lot. That will be expensive. Add to that the fact that it's worn down and needs some cosmetic repairs but nothing we can't handle or afford. I think we can still make our target opening date of October 1."

"Fen," Zoey said, getting everyone's attention. "How's the client list coming along?"

Fen had come a long way since the first phone call from Zoey inviting her to be a partner in her brothel. Right away she had agreed in principle that the need was genuine, but she wanted to keep at arm's length from the activities. After a few more heart to heart talks, Zoey discovered that Fen and Allen had had a very satisfying sex life. And although she wasn't interested in getting married again, she did miss not having the physical contact of sex. Fen confessed that she recently had been fanaticizing about a tall dark stranger who would satisfy her sexual needs without the emotional bond. Zoey had told her that her dream could become a reality and that every woman deserved to be sexually satisfied. Reluctantly Fen had accepted an invitation to visit Zoey at the Incline Village house and have a 'session' with James, who was wearing a brunette wig. He was more than happy to show off his sexual prowess. His expert skill and knowledge of a woman's body was all it took. From that point on, Fen was on board and couldn't wait to share her experience with her wealthy acquaintances.

Fen shuffled the papers she was holding. She glanced down and then up at her cohorts. "Well, I must say that October 1st is perfect for our opening. That's opening day for hunting in a lot of places, and a lot of my lady friends will be alone. I've got three confirmed for October 1st to the 3rd. I've got two for the next three days. There are some others who want to book around the holidays, you know, widows who have a hard time with Christmas and New Year's Eve. I got some others who will probably come around but are still grappling with the idea of sleeping with a prostitute." She looked at James. "No offense."

"None taken," James said without concern. "I won't be fuckin' 'em. My guys will."

Fen smiled at James and continued, "They see the benefit of no-strings-attached sex, but it goes against the moral code they were raised with."

"Most of those women have unfaithful husbands, if I recall," Zoey chimed in.

"Yes," Fen explained, "But they always held themselves on higher ground."

"Fuck that shit!" Zoey exclaimed.

"Don't worry," Fen broke in, "I know they'll get on board once they see what kind of operation we run. I mean, even without the sex, it's going to be a high-class spa. Who could refuse that? I'm getting calls every day from interested parties."

"Good," Zoey said. She looked at Annette. "You want to tell them what we found out on the legal end?"

Annette didn't look thrilled, but opened the folder she had on her lap and pulled out a few papers. She slipped on a pair of readers and said. "Prostitution is only legal in cities where the population is less than 400,000. Since Storey County has less than 5,000 we're in the clear. Each county has unique licensing requirements and licensing fees. In Storey County the annual fee is $100,000." Fen and James' collective gasp was audible.

"Don't worry, we'll make that in a few weeks once we're in operation," Zoey reassured.

"There're tons of laws about medical testing; some are done weekly, others monthly, and must be done on every prostitute who works here. And by the way, we're lucky in that the legal age for a prostitute in Storey County is 18, not 21 like most others."

A collective "Oh!" went through the room.

"The prostitutes must work as independent contractors so, technically, they're not employees, although we'll have a written work agreement with them and are legally responsible for anything that happens in our establishment. There are lots of laws about mandatory condom use, cleaning the sheets, how and where we can advertise, how many signs we can have out. By law our sign out front must have the word 'Brothel' on it. I'm putting together a little handbook for our guys with things that pertain to them." She looked at James. "I'll need to discuss a few things with you, James." He nodded. "As long as we stick to the rules religiously, pay the fees and taxes, and jump through all their hoops we should be fine," Annette concluded.

"James," Zoey looked directly at him. "I'm counting on you to keep your men in line and make sure they know and follow these rules to the letter." She emphasized the last three words with a pointing finger.

"No problem," he said. "I've already contacted a doctor in town who will do the weekly and monthly testing and exams and submit them to the state."

"This is very important, James," Annette said. "If they don't get examined and tested and maintain a current work card, we could lose our license. Oh, and they're responsible for paying the doctor, not us."

"Got it," James replied.

"Annette," Zoey turned to look at her, "what about the other part of our establishment, the spa end? Where do we stand on that?"

"Well," Annette spoke carefully, "I didn't find any laws that say we can't be a spa, too. And believe it or not, a lot of the health rules for spas are similar to those of the brothel. We'll need a license for the spa end, too. Lots of inspections, rules, and regulations here, too. The masseuse will be an independent contractor much like the prostitutes. They're required to keep their licenses up to date.

"Oh, and all of the independent contractors are responsible for their own income tax. We don't have to withhold anything. Just give them a 1099 at the end of the year.

"We'll need to get a liquor license and a permit to serve food and alcohol in the dining room. The Health Department is going to spend a lot of time here inspecting everything and everyone. And on a final note, as soon as we get a location nailed down, we can start the pleasant task of actually getting the all the licenses. That's going to involve interviews, meetings, tons of paperwork, background checks, and money."

"All right," Zoey said, and turned her attention to James. "And now to the meat of our business." Her bad pun was met with a round of groans. "How many man-whores do we have now?" The women laughed.

James smirked, cleared his throat, and took a sip from the glass of Scotch he was holding. "I've interviewed about a half-dozen guys, four of whom seem promising. I've got three more interviews scheduled in the next two weeks. I think we need to have at least six for starters. Eventually I'd like to get nine or ten if the concept goes over."

"Just make sure they know what and who they have to do. The clients will be mature women. They must be treated as welcome guests. Your men will be expected to role-play the character of the clients' choosing," Zoey stated.

"They will know everything and they'll roll with it."

"Have you set up the training program? I want them to know as much about fucking and pleasing a woman as you do. They've got to be the best."

"They'll be ready," he assured her.

Zoey smiled. "You'll be happy to know that Fen and I have decided to audition the men before we turn them loose on the customers. So just let us know when those four have finished their training. We'll let you know if they're ready or not." She looked over at Fen and met her smile. Annette looked at the two of them and rolled her eyes.

"Oh," Annette said, "I think I've found a masseuse for the spa. The only problem is that it's a woman. Is that okay?"

"Depends," Zoey answered. "Does she know that it's also a brothel for mature women?"

"Yes," Annette said hesitantly.

Zoey could tell there was more she wasn't sharing. "What it is, Annette? There's something you're not telling us."

"Well," Annette confessed, "it's just that Michelle, that's her name, she's a lesbian." She could see the concern on Zoey's face. "Don't worry. She's not my type, but she gives a hell of a massage. She can do the body wraps, facials, and hot stone massages, too."

"In that case," Zoey said, "who gives a fuck? As long as she doesn't try to finger the clients I don't see why not."

"Unless they want her to," Fen added.

"Not really," Annette said matter-of-factly. "We can lose our license if an unlicensed employee has sex with a guest."

"Then we'll make sure that doesn't happen," Zoey said. She turned to Annette again. "Why don't you tell them about the kitchen and housekeeping staff?

Annette told them that she and Zoey did some research and most of the kitchen and housekeeping employees could be found locally. The partners agreed to pay $2.00 an hour above the average pay as extra incentive. That would bring in employees as far as Reno, especially since they planned on providing housing for the staff.

"They'll be all male, right?" Fen asked.

"Yes," Annette and Zoey said at the same time.

Zoey turned her attention to Fen. "Why don't you tell everyone about the score *you* made," she requested with excitement.

Fen smiled. "Perhaps you've heard of the famous Chef Marguerite and her lover/sous chef, Malcolm?" Fen explained how she had stolen the gourmet chef from one of the big Reno casinos. Chef Marguerite and sous chef Malcolm specialized in making nutritious food look and taste gourmet, and were quite successful at it.

They were also the most unlikely couple you could ever imagine. Their relationship had spanned over 20 years. They weren't married, but the two couldn't be more in love. They were caring, sensitive, and attentive to each other's feelings and needs. Chef Marguerite was about 10 years older than Malcolm, outweighed him by at least 40 pounds, and towered over him by six inches.

She was boisterous and confident. Her sous chef

was shy and unassuming, but always at her side, anticipating her next request. The perfect assistant. The two worked in tandem like a well-oiled machine, to create and present the most exquisite culinary delights you could imagine. They loved what they did, and worked with a positive attitude and a smile on their faces.

The two were under contract at the Reno casino until September 1st. Since the plan was to open the brothel on October 1st, the timing was perfect. Fen had assured the chef that the kitchen would be stocked to her specifications. Fen, Zoey, and Chef Marguerite had already worked out an epicurean menu for the guests befitting the high price they were going to be charged. Annette and James were impressed.

"Anyone else have anything to say?" Zoey asked.

"Yes," said Annette. Everyone turned to look at her. "What are we going to call this place anyway?"

Zoey looked surprised. It was then that she realized that she hadn't even given it a thought. "That's a good question. I don't know. Any suggestions?" She looked around the room.

"The Fuck Factory," James blurted out.

The women groaned and looked at him in dismay. "Good thing you fuck so well," Zoey said. "That's about the worst idea for a name I've ever heard." All the women agreed.

After a minute of looking at blank faces she said, "Come on. If we can't even come up with a good name, how are we going to run this high-class joint?"

Annette spoke up. "I think we should keep it low-key and discreet. How about Zoey's Place? That's what it will be, after all. It's all your idea."

Zoey let it sink in and roll around in her brain for a while. "I think it might fly. Any other ideas? Fen?

James?"

"I like it," James said with enthusiasm. "I just had a great marketing slogan." He extended his arms and framed each word with his hands. "Zoey's Place, where the customer always comes first."

After the chuckles died down Zoey spoke. "Actually, that's not a bad catch phrase. Damn, James, looks like that college degree is paying off."

"Sounds good to me," Fen agreed. "I kind of like it."

"Descriptive and seductive," Annette said. "I like it, too."

"Good," Zoey said firmly. "Our brothel will be known as Zoey's Place, where the customer always comes first. Oh, one more thing— I want you all to see the old mansion we want to buy so we can put an offer in on it. I'm planning a field trip for everyone tomorrow, so clear your calendars. It's about a two and a half hour ride." A mixture of moans and laughter filled the room. Zoey smiled at them and said, "And with that, let's order take-out. I'm starving."

The next day they all piled into the new company Suburban Zoey bought and drove to Storey County to check out the estate. It was run-down, but had a good foundation and great possibilities just like Zoey had said. Everyone approved and they put in an offer to purchase at $40,000 less than the asking price. As it turned out, the owner was motivated to sell and accepted her offer. Now the real work could begin.

During the next months every building and room was renovated. The pool and hot tub were resurfaced and a pool maintenance company was hired to keep it looking pristine. The first four suites closest to the entrance were assigned to the partners and redecorated to their own individual tastes. The remaining eight suites were modernized and furnished with high-end décor befitting its high class clients. Chef Marguerite was granted every request for her kitchen. The new dining room design was elegant, regal, and included a giant crystal chandelier as the centerpiece. The old exercise room was converted into two relaxing, personal massage rooms. There was still enough room for a small workout room equipped with weights, a treadmill, and an elliptical bike. Not a lot of time and effort went into this part since it was agreed by all that most of the physical activity would be conducted in the converted cabanas serving as the sex rooms.

The three existing cabanas were constructed in a single file line next to each other. Zoey's team decided to expand on the theme and added three more cabanas across from them. All six looked the same from the outside; like a row of little clapboard homes, whitewashed but trimmed in a different color. It almost looked like a rainbow. There was a unique address posted to the right of the door. Each cabana was furnished so that they could be used for multiple types of sex fantasy scenarios with quick and minor decorating changes.

A large garage/shop was converted into an apartment building for employee housing. It was separate and fenced off from the rest of the operations. This area was off-limits to guests. It would be where Chef Marguerite and Malcolm, the prostitutes, and any other staff members would have the option to live.

Michelle, the masseuse, also opted to live in the employee apartment complex. She'd moved there from California and had no other home. Annette was right. Both Zoey and Fen sampled various types of massages and facials, to their delight. Michelle's magic fingers could find the built-up tension and knead, rub, and massage the knots away. Her hot rock massages were so relaxing Zoey fell asleep during the first one. She had several types of facials that left the customer's face feeling clean and tingly fresh. Michelle's smooth, melodic voice and gentle way of speaking combined with just the right music and scented oil created the perfect atmosphere to help you relax. The ladies were going to love her.

Fen and Zoey had auditioned over a dozen men but eventually had hired only six. They were mostly college guys wanting to make a little extra money on the side. A few were just looking to make a career change. Being that it was Nevada, a career in prostitution was a perfectly normal profession. It still made Zoey shake her head in amazement every once in a while. She was proud of the professional way she and Fen had conducted the evaluations. They put together a checklist of traits and qualities that the men were to be graded on. They always discussed the evaluations at the weekly staff meeting with the four partners.

James had trained them well on the mechanics of making love to a woman, and the session with Zoey or Fen was to assess their skill and personality. They were evaluated to see if they felt comfortable with a more mature woman; more importantly to confirm that they could make the client feel relaxed, beautiful, and special. Fen and Zoey relied on their intuition for this scoring, each trusting the other's instincts to determine whether or not the men were fit to represent Zoey's Place.

At first Zoey thought that a younger man having sex with an older woman for money would seem bizarre, but after thinking about it she compared it to a young woman having sex with an older man for money, as most female prostitutes do. When it came right down to it, it was the same thing.

The prostitutes would work a four-day week and had to be on call and available 24 hours on those days, depending on the whim of the clients. After all, they wouldn't be fucking all day, only when a client requested sex. Most of the sessions were scheduled in advance due to set-up time and scheduling of the men, but Zoey knew that it would be good business if they were flexible and she gave the men the option to work more days than the required four. It would be an opportunity for the guys to earn extra money, kind of like hooker overtime. She also tried to accommodate the college students so that their shift didn't interfere with their class schedules.

The kitchen and housekeeping staff consisted mostly of all local townspeople and most didn't require housing. There were some who came in from out of the area and required company apartments.

A landscaping company, Diego's Desert Landscapes, had been commissioned to revamp and replant all of the current landscaping, making the place look like an oasis. There were two wells on the property that supplied an abundance of water to the newly installed sprinkler system. Diego's was also contracted to provide maintenance for the property greenery.

A remote-controlled gate was installed at the property entrance. The newly paved driveway ended in a circle at the covered lobby entrance, highlighted with a fountain at its center. A Greek Adonis-like statue, naked with an exposed penis, stood central, pouring water from a pitcher suggestively held out in front of himself. The pool maintenance company contracted to keep the pool and hot tub sparkling clear also maintained the fountain.

It was decided that James and Annette would live

on the premises full time. Zoey and Fen had their own rooms, but didn't consider it their home. Zoey wanted to keep her Incline Village home. For the time being, Fen also kept the mansion in The Hamptons and the Manhattan apartment. She flew back east for a few days every other week. It was mostly to see family. She told Zoey she would probably let the Hampton home go if the brothel made good. She liked Nevada, and her suite at the brothel was actually quite comfortable.

Annette concentrated on the day to day office management and paperwork end of the business, including all the licensing rigmarole. She shuttled Zoey to meetings and helped her with the extensive background checks required and the piles of paperwork. Their combined legal backgrounds were a definite asset to the proceedings. This was a concept never before put in action, so they were reluctantly granted some wiggle room by the county authorities.

There were delays, setbacks, frustrations, extra expenses, and many extremely exhausting days. It seemed like Zoey's Place would never become a reality, but eventually the persistent group of now very close friends completed their assigned tasks. Finally, the construction and conversion were concluded.

Chapter 21

October 1st, opening day for Zoey's Place, arrived. The morning was a busy blur of bodies putting the final touches on the guest rooms and common areas. Zoey was busy organizing the fresh flower arrangement by the lobby door when she felt James' arms encircle her waist. He kissed her neck and whispered, "You ready for this, madam?"

Zoey groaned without thought. She was confident that the business would be a success but she was still very anxious about being the 'Madam' of a brothel. "I guess so," she muttered. She turned to face him, put her arms around his waist, and looked up into the deep pools of his azure-blue eyes. She felt a twinge of warmth and weakness but disregarded it. "By the end of the night I'll know whether to thank you or hate you."

He looked surprised. "What does that mean?" he asked as he indignantly stood upright.

"You put the seed in my head that night that you fucked my brains out and proved that it could be done without love. I wanted to spread the feeling with all of womankind," she said with mock superiority. She looked at him and shook her head. "But now I don't know if I'm cut out to be a pimp."

James laughed and pulled her tight to him. "It's a great idea. And we've got the dream team to pull it off," he reassured her. He bent down to whisper in her ear. She could smell his cologne, woodsy and fresh. It didn't smell like the aftershave that Mickey wore but had the same intoxicating effect on her. "Tell you what," he said. "After we get everyone settled in for the night, how about if I join you in your room for a little private celebration?"

She knew what that meant; they would be having sex. The thought sent pleasant shivers up her spine. She had to admit, now that she had sampled many different sexual styles and techniques, next to Mickey James was the best. They fit together like peas in a pod. She could relax and know that he needed no instruction. He knew every inch of her body, especially the extra receptive spots, the places that could get her breathing heavy and give her shuddering orgasms.

In the months since that first encounter, she learned what to do to satisfy him as well. Their sex was sometimes playful, intimate, and always gratifying. Something Zoey thought she would never have again. Because of their beach walks they had formed a sort of emotional bond even before the brothel project was conceived, but working in such close proximity to each other day after day had only strengthened their close personal ties. They knew the connection existed and sometimes acted on it, but only in a playful or sexual way. The subject of love was never brought up. Zoey wasn't ready and James, never having been in love, was able to function without it. Or so it had been until lately.

She noticed that in the last few months he had

become more attentive to her. He would stand just a little bit closer to her than he used to, and it had become his habit to kiss the back of her neck. He knew this really turned her on sexually and she would always moan involuntarily, to her embarrassment and his delight. Whenever he was near her, he would put his arm around her protectively. He began to hold her hand when they crossed the street. The sex was more frequent, too. They had gone from once or twice a month to once or twice a week. The tone of the sex had also changed and had turned almost romantic. Most of the time James spent the night, insisting that they cuddle and spoon together. Not that she minded. She missed that. He was doing all the things that someone would do if they were in love, which of course they weren't. She shook her head. He couldn't be falling in love with her. She wasn't falling in love with him either. She couldn't. She shouldn't.

But James *had* started thinking about her in a different way. It began when she and Fen started having sex with the trainees. Twinges of jealousy tortured his thoughts on the nights the sex took place. He would lie in his bed in anguish, knowing that Zoey was letting a stranger into her most private parts. It bothered him that someone else was touching her velvety skin, kissing her soft lips, smelling her intoxicating fragrance and, worst of all, sticking his dick in her lovely, sweet pussy. James could barely stand to listen to her evaluation of the sexual performance at the staff meeting. He tried to ignore the situation. It was a strange and uncomfortable feeling, one that he didn't particularly like.

This morning as he was walking to the kitchen, he saw Zoey fussing over the flower arrangement. She looked particularly beautiful. Her hair was hanging loose about her bare shoulders. The floral sundress she wore was close-fitting and accentuated the curve of her breasts that rose and fell as she breathed. The sun was shining through the window on her and gave her an angelic glow as it glistened off of her shiny hair. He felt a sense of pride knowing that he could be with her any time he wanted. He wanted her right now in the worst way. Why? What was happening to him?

Until now he had forced himself to believe that his feelings for her were on a professional level. She was his business partner, and yes, someone he really enjoyed having sex with, but there was no love. Or was there? What was love anyway? How would he know if it was? He cared for her, that's true. But they were friends and friends cared for each other, didn't they? But did friends feel so emotionally attached to each other that they wanted to be together twenty-four hours a day? It had only been three years since they met, yet now he couldn't imagine his life without her. She was kind and caring, smart and beautiful. In the morning after her shower she smelled like fresh flowers, and she had the most perfect body, even at her age. He closed his eyes and imagined lying naked with her. His cock began to harden and rub up against his jeans.

"Oh, fuck," he said to himself. "I think I love her." He felt uneasy at the feeling and wondered what she would do if he admitted it to her. She had never even hinted that she wanted a new love situation. They liked each other. That was certain. They knew how to please each other sexually. That was a definite plus. But love? No. It wasn't the right time; not for him, not for Zoey. He had to control his emotions. He had been burned once before. He hadn't thought about it for a long time and he didn't want to think about it now, and he sure as fuck didn't want that to happen again.

That afternoon, around three, James left for the Reno airport to pick up the first three guests. The airport was about an hour away and Zoey was expecting them to arrive back at the brothel around five, just in time for dinner.

The guest list was impressive. First was Mrs. Eileen Douglas from Pennsylvania: age 70, wealthy, widowed for ten years, and horny as hell according to Fen. She had reserved the football player experience. That meant Trent would be servicing her. He was a big hunk of a young man who had actually played football in high school and college. He had a youthful face with dreamy blue eyes and full lips. He was well built and filled out his football jersey perfectly. He looked too big to be gentle but his audition with Fen had gone very well. She said he had all the right plays to score big with the clients.

Next was Mrs. Claire Alexander, age 68, from New York City. She'd been widowed for only one year but hadn't been fucked in ten. That's what she'd told Fen. She, in reality, rejoiced when her husband died of lung cancer. She reserved the Scottish highlander experience. Ian had been assigned to her. He was of Scottish heritage and could speak with a Scottish burr, and even had his own kilt. Zoey had sampled his skills and had found him quite gratifying.

The third and last client was Mrs. Tiffany Tilton of South Hampton, New York. She was only 60 and still married, but in a very unhappy marriage. Her husband was hardly ever home and had been caught in several affairs. Mrs. Tilton didn't mind because she knew that they would never last. She claimed that her husband had a penis the size of a cocktail wiener and didn't know the first thing about how to use it. She requested the weight lifter experience and specifically requested a large penis.

That job had been assigned to Max, or Cly Max as he preferred to be called. Some of the men had given themselves nicknames. Max's former job was as a dancer at a strip club. He was dark-haired and tan, with hazel eyes. He stood about 6' 3" and every muscle on his body was rock-hard and bulging. His dick was so big that both Fen and Zoey had to try him out. They both agreed that bigger was very fullfilling.

The cabanas had been decked out to match the theme of the men. Mrs. Trousdale would be escorted by Trent, dressed in his football uniform, to a cabana decked out in football memorabilia, football trophies, team pennants, pom-poms, and a green bed cover that resembled a football gridiron.

The highlander cabana, where Ian would take Mrs. Alexander, was rustic with a large, dark wooden bed covered with a red plaid quilt, occupying the center of the equally red-plaid-accented room. A large highlander sword and the Scottish flag hung on the walls. Bagpipe music filtered in gently from the sound system. Ian would be dressed in full highlander regalia.

The muscle builder cabana, which also doubled as the S&M room, looked like a gym with a bench and weights. All the other furnishings were leather-upholstered. High intensity motivational music added to the heat of sexual passion waiting to be explored. A red light gave it an erotic glow. Max would be wearing a black tank top, a pair of very tight black gym shorts, and fingerless black leather gloves. His body would be glistening with oil.

All of the cabanas were equipped with an assortment of sex toys laid out in plain sight for quick access. They could be expertly used by any of the men. But with the sexual skills they had acquired from James, the toys would probably be more decorative than functional.

It was almost five now. Zoey was nervous. She stopped in the main house to make sure all was ready. Taste-tempting odors wafted from the dining room into the lobby. When the guests arrived they would be hungry from their travels. She thought the dining room would be a good place to loosen up the ladies before the evening's sexual adventures. Trent, Ian, and Max would serve the ladies dessert before accompanying them to their individually chosen fantasy cabana.

Zoey walked out of the dining room and into the entryway. She was just in time to see the gate open and James make the turn into the driveway by the discrete Zoey's Place, Spa/Brothel sign above the entry gate. She watched as he pulled the champagne-colored Suburban to the front portico and stop.

"It's go-time," Zoey said quietly to herself as she approached the door. Suddenly it opened and three elderly but elegant ladies, bedazzled in silk and jewels, crossed the threshold and stood in the entrance hall, looking around in astonishment at the plush surroundings.

"Welcome to Zoey's Place, ladies," she greeted. All three women brought their attention to Zoey and smiled with approval. "My name is Zoey and I'm honored to be your hostess during your stay.

"My staff will show you to your rooms, where you can unpack and change into something casual. We have a delicious dinner prepared for you. It will be served at 6:00 in the dining room, which is to your right. This will be followed by an even better, made-to-order dessert." She paused for dramatic effect. The ladies looked at each other and smiled knowingly.

She continued her welcome. "Feel free to let the staff know if you desire anything else. If you enjoy your stay, please pass it on. *Bon appétit, mes chéris.*" And with that three handsome young porters appeared, picked up the ladies' luggage, and escorted the guests to their rooms.

Chapter 22

Fen and Zoey were standing at the entrance to the dining room to greet the ladies as they came down for dinner. They engaged in casual conversation with them as the drinks and appetizers were served by shirtless, bow-tied men. The women seemed relaxed by the time the salad was served, and Fen and Zoey saw this as their cue to depart. They left the women alone to enjoy their dinner and the evening's entertainment. After a quick stop in the kitchen they retreated to their own rooms with a plated dinner in hand.

After she ate, Zoey undressed and slipped into a lacy black nightgown in anticipation of James' visit. She knew he would wait until after his men were hard at work. The pun was intentional. This meant she had time for a well-deserved drink to help her relax. It had been a stressful day and she was looking forward to unwinding with her lothario. She poured herself a shot of Crown Royal and downed it fast. A smooth, pleasurable burn coated her throat as she swallowed. She half expected to see fumes when she exhaled.

She poured another, added ice, and sipped.

Soon after, she peeked through her bedroom window as the first three guests of Zoey's Place were escorted to the fantasy cabanas. The men looked magnificent in their role-playing costumes. She knew the ladies would be in for a night to remember.

A knock at her door brought her attention back. James entered and closed the door behind him. He was barefoot and wearing nothing but a pair of well-worn faded jeans. They reminded her of the jeans Mickey used to wear. She was feeling glad and sad at the same time. James could see the mix of emotions on her face.

"What's wrong, Zee?" he asked, a tone of concern in his voice. 'Zee' had become his pet name for her. It was one of the intimacies they shared. Only he called her that, and it endeared him to her when he used it, making her feel special.

"It's nothing," she said unconvincingly. "You just reminded me of something."

"Something about Mickey?" He knew her so well.

"Yeah, he had a pair of faded, ripped jeans like those."

They rarely talked about Mickey anymore. She told James all about her storybook life with him during their lakeshore walks. He knew about the fantastic sexual closeness they had, their role playing, their fantasies, their willingness to try anything, and the trust they had in each other. She'd shed many tears reliving the romance and joy of the life she had lived with her husband. She also shared the feelings of loneliness and separation she felt towards the end when Mickey was away for so long, and the never-ending sorrow she now felt by his eternal absence.

James knew that Mickey brushed it off when Zoey

spoke to him about the dream she had of the tragedy shortly before it happened, and how it felt when she got that life-changing call that took the love of her life away from her forever.

He knew he couldn't replace Mickey, but he tried to ease Zoey's pain. He was attracted to her from the first time he saw her but never thought of a long term romantic relationship with her, or any woman for that matter. It just wasn't part of the plan.

But even before they'd had sex, he knew that their relationship was special. She was different. He felt possessive of her, and that scared him because the last time he felt like this he got his heart ripped out. He never told Zoey how he felt about her. He denied it himself at first. Working with her every day and being close to her only made it worse. This morning he had to admit to himself that he loved her and he wanted to tell her. He just didn't know how or when the right time would be. One thing was for sure, with everything going on it wasn't now.

James walked up to her and held her in his arms. She collapsed in his embrace.

"Sorry," he said softly, apologizing. "I didn't know. I've had these forever but I guess I never wore them in front of you before. We've been so busy getting ready for the opening that I didn't have a chance to do laundry and all my other jeans are dirty."

She smiled. "It's okay. I'm all right. It just took me by surprise."

He tried to lighten the mood. He let her go, took a step back, unbuttoned the jeans, and pulled the zipper down. "I hate to see you so upset. I'll take these sons-a-bitches off right now." He pulled them off and threw them on the floor. He stood before her completely naked and held out his arms in presentation. "Is this better?" he asked.

She couldn't help but laugh and shake her head. "You are such a weirdo. Do you know that? Loveable, but a weirdo nonetheless."

"So I've been told," he agreed. "And you are a beautiful woman. Did you know that?" he said sincerely. He reached for her hand, held it up to his lips, and kissed it gently.

She looked up and saw him staring at her. He looked like he wanted to say something. She waited but he didn't speak. He just stood there, naked, gaping at her.

She smiled. "Do I have spinach between my teeth? Why are you staring at me?"

He smiled, led her to the bed, sat her down, and positioned himself next to her. "I'm staring at you because I like looking at you. In fact, I like everything about you. You're smart, kind, and caring."

She was getting embarrassed and felt a little uncomfortable. "Okay, okay. You can stop buttering me up. We're gonna have sex, you don't have to—"

Before she could finish her sentence, he pulled her in and kissed her strong and hard on the mouth. She kissed him back and surrendered herself to him.

He helped her slip out of her nightie and gently lay her on the bed. She was like putty in his hands as he explored her soft and supple body. It moved in welcome to his touch. Her breasts heaved upward as his hands cupped each one. Her nipples hardened like acorns as he kissed them. She reached down and felt his hardness. He kissed her full mouth as she pressed her hot body close to his. They knew each other intimately. He moved to kiss her gently on the back of her neck. She let out a moan and a deep breath. Reaching down between her legs, he spread them apart as he straddled himself on top of her and entered her private garden. She thrust herself upward to him as they began their dance of desire.

The subject of love was not brought up nor was the word uttered by either. But it was love that was made that night. It was passionate and personal. They were two unwittingly becoming one.

*****

The guests stayed for two more days and tasted all that Zoey's Place had to offer. A program of scheduled activities had been set up with each guest before they arrived, so there would be no surprises and preparations could be made in advance. Massages, meals, sexual encounters, and free periods were all prearranged. The ladies were kept busy. Their smiles grew by the hour. On the morning of the last day they seemed sad to depart, but depart they must because there were more guests arriving that afternoon.

James had loaded their luggage into the Suburban and Zoey and Fen waited for the ladies in the lobby to give them a personal send-off.

"Well, ladies," Zoey addressed the group, "we certainly hope you enjoyed your stay."

She was answered with an enthusiastic chorus of positive feedback and promises to return. "Wonderful," she continued. "Make sure to tell your friends about us and we hope to see you again. Here's a parting gift for you to remember us by." She handed each woman a gold-plated circular key chain with the shape of a Z engraved on one side, the words, "Zoey's Place, where the customer comes first," and the phone number engraved on the other side.

After the car pulled away, Zoey and Fen looked at each other and smiled. "It worked. We did it!" Fen exclaimed, and the two women hugged each other tightly.

That night, after the new guests were in the cabanas, the partners had dinner together to discuss the day's activities, what went right, and what could be improved upon. The feedback was positive and the partners were in good spirits.

For dessert, Chef Marguerite had prepared a cheese cake made with tofu instead of cheese. Zoey took a bite. "Delicious, Chef," she said. "You've done it again. By the way, your Portobello Parmesan got stellar reviews."

Chef took a bow and walked proudly back to the kitchen. Annette cleared her throat and got everyone's attention. She looked perplexed.

"Did you want to say something, Annette?" Zoey asked with concern.

Annette looked flushed. "Yes, actually," she hesitated. "I'm not quite sure how to say it."

"Just blurt it out," James stated. "You're among friends." He had a slight tone of unease in his voice.

"Well, I don't know exactly how it happened, but..."

"For crying out loud, Annette, what is it?" Fen sounded concerned.

"Okay, here goes." All eyes were on Annette. "Michelle and I are dating."

Her three friends sighed with relief. James patted her on the back and said, "Good for you." Fen and Zoey squealed in delight and approval. They ran up to her and hugged her.

Annette looked at ease. "I was afraid it would cause problems. I didn't want to put the business in jeopardy."

Zoey looked at her. "Annette, why would we mind? If you and Michelle have something going, far be it from me to tell you no. I like her. I'm happy for you, girl. You deserve some happiness in your life." Fen and James voiced their agreement.

"Don't worry," Annette added, "I won't let it interfere with our duties. There won't be any PDA in front of the guests."

Everyone laughed. James spoke up, "They're here to have sex with prostitutes. You think seeing two lesbians holding hands or kissing is going to be too much for them?"

For the next fifteen minutes, Annette gushed about her relationship with Michelle and how it started, and how happy they made each other. The other partners were supportive and suggested that Michelle join them for dinner the next day.

As they were departing the dining room, Zoey tapped Annette on the shoulder to get her attention. Annette turned around and Zoey gave her a huge bear hug.

"Annette, I'm so happy for you, truly. Just be careful; I don't want you to get hurt."

"Thanks, boss," she said sincerely. "I think it's the real thing this time. We took it slow and got to know each other before we started dating. I didn't think she was my type but we've got so much in common; we like the same music, the same movies, and we have the same taste in clothes." She paused for a moment and looked up in contemplation. "Let me put it this way— I like what she wears and she likes what I wear. She's been in relationships before, too. She's been hurt just like I was. We just get along so well. It's like it was meant to be." She was beaming from ear to ear.

"Then go for it, sweetie. Don't let love pass you by. Grab it and hold on for dear life." Zoey gave her a peck on the cheek and headed toward her room, thinking of Mickey and love that got cut short.

Within the next few weeks and months Zoey's Place was a hive of activity, with clients coming and going on a steady basis. Staff meetings were held to get feedback. They tweaked things here and there to make the clients' experience more exceptional. Whatever they were doing worked. The reservations came pouring in as word spread about this oasis for rich, lonely, horny, older women. The partners' bank accounts grew as well. All was good in the world.

Chapter 23

In the year that it had been open, Zoey's Place had become a bigger success than any of the four partners had imagined. The constant flow of customers kept the guest rooms full and the cabanas rockin' and rollin' every night and sometimes during the day, depending on the customer. Zoey noticed the list of repeat customers was growing as well.

Annette had reported that in their first year they had recouped all of their investment capital and were now debt-free. This meant raises for the employees and bonuses for the four partners of Zoey's Place, Inc.

The team worked in total sync and the smooth operation of the spa/brothel was a testament to its success. Employees were loyal and trustworthy. Everyone knew what was expected of them, and did it enthusiastically without complaint or hesitation. The male prostitutes were regular in their medical exams and kept their work cards current. Everyone followed the rules. Turnover was very low, and for every employee that quit two prospects were waiting in the wings, regardless of what area it was, be it housekeeping, kitchen help, or prostitution.

Michelle's massages and facials were so popular she had to hire an assistant to keep up. As it turned out it was another woman, but she was straight. This put Annette's mind at ease and actually freed up some of Michelle's time so they could enjoy the fruits of their hard labor together. It made Zoey happy knowing that Annette had someone in her life to love.

A Nevada newspaper had conducted a poll and found that Zoey's Place had the happiest employees in the state. Word got out and it became a very desirable place to be employed.

Besides the football player, the highlander, and the muscle man, they had expanded their sex fantasy choices to include the superhero, the cowboy, the baseball player, the hockey player, the basketball player, the appliance repair man, the delivery man, the auto mechanic, the Native American warrior, the carpenter, the minister, the English professor, who also doubled as the English spy, and the BDSM master or slave. Quan, who was Chinese, gave the ladies the Asian experience. He was popular because of the hereditary trait of not having body hair from the neck down. His hairless, muscular, smooth body, coupled with his sexual skills, was quite popular.

Also, because of frequent requests for the Mandingo experience, they hired Leon, a 6'4" black man, strikingly handsome, dark as coal, arms like steel, and a huge cock that was just as hard. He also was very popular. It took quite a few auditions before Zoey and Fen found the perfect man to befit that name with honor. There was something for everyone at Zoey's Place.

The men had learned to play as many roles as they could, and seemed to have a friendly competition going to see who could come up with the best costume for the character.

Because things were going so smoothly, Zoey surmised that she could get away for a while without causing a problem. She wanted to go back to Michigan and see her friends and their families. It had been at least two years since she had been back, and although she spoke with Carol and Joanne frequently on the phone she longed for the familiarity and personal comfort of being with them and their families. It was the closest thing Zoey had to her own family and she missed them.

She had been invited to Carol and Dave's for Thanksgiving and she accepted. She planned to travel with James and introduce him to her friends. He was in for a treat because he had never been to a family Thanksgiving dinner like the ones her friends hosted, surrounded by laughing children, tipsy adults, and enough food to feed a small nation. Annette and Fen had agreed to mind the store in exchange for a Christmas get- away.

The first thing James noticed after they arrived in Detroit, three days before Thanksgiving, was how cold it was. The temperatures in Nevada were still in the forties and fifties. Winters in Incline Village were cold and snowy at times, but rarely went below freezing, and seemed way warmer than what he was experiencing now. Michigan's cold came with bone-chilling windchill. Just his luck, they were in the middle of an early winter cold snap. The slightest breeze was a frozen assault on any exposed skin. His body wasn't accustomed to this degree of frigid weather. The temperature dipped to the low teens and below at night, and rarely went above freezing in the daytime. He was totally unprepared. Dave let him borrow a jacket to keep him warm. James noted that he didn't even own a jacket that could keep him warm in this freezer of a city.

Although he was introduced as Zoey's friend they shared the guest room, mostly for the exchange of body heat at night. It had been a long time and Zoey had become unaccustomed to the chill as well. She had forgotten how cold it could get, and was as grateful for the warmth James provided at night as he was of hers.

They still hadn't professed their love for each other but had settled into a comfortable place. They cared for each other deeply. They protected each other. They did everything together, everything except admit that they were in love.

The first day in Michigan, Zoey went shopping with Carol and Joanne. She was relieved that the subject of James never came up and that her friends had welcomed him warmly.

James hung out and bonded with the men. There was a little tension at first. This was the first time anyone from Michigan had seen Zoey with anyone besides Mickey, and it took some getting used to. James was nothing like Mickey in looks or manner. He wasn't much older than some of their children. But his openness and friendly personality won them over. At the end of the second day the one thing that was abundantly clear, even to the men, was that James was truly in love with Zoey. It was the affectionate way he looked at her, the way he lit up when she entered the room, the tender way he touched her, and the attention he paid to her every whim.

She was obviously in love with him, too. Her friends noticed the sparkle in her eye when she looked at him, and a peaceful demeanor that her friends hadn't seen in her since Mickey's death. When he smiled at her, she glowed. Even a blind man could see the love.

The third day, Thanksgiving, was a whirlwind of activity. There was food and drink from morning 'till night. Zoey was amazed at how much the children had grown in the few years she had been away. Carol and Dave's kids, Mary and Betty, were both in high school.

Joanne and Lenny's oldest son, Franky, was the first of the kids to be in college. Sam had just received his driver's license. They were children no longer. Jonathan was there with his little one, who was now almost eight. Little Jon, now in third grade, could talk your ear off about his two new video games—The Legend of Zelda and Pokémon. He was a cutie pie and looked like a young clone of his father.

Zoey made it a point to pull Jonathan aside and ask how the custody was going. He said that because Rhonda was always falling behind in her child support, he had gotten Child Services to attach her pay. As far as the visitations, they were still supervised and now down to two hours a month. Because she couldn't keep a civil tongue when speaking to Jonathan at the hand-offs, and because she continued to try to poison Little Jon's mind against his father whenever the restrictions were relaxed, the court had ordered the visitations to be supervised until her son reached the age of 12.

Seeing all of her friends brought back bittersweet memories of past Thanksgivings when she, Mickey, and their friends were all together and the kids were little. She quickly forced it out of her mind. The past was the past. The future was something to look forward to. She had to think like that. It was the only way to survive.

After dinner everyone lent a hand to clear the table. The women then suggested that the men to go into the living room and watch football so they could finish the cleanup. They didn't have to say it twice.

Mary and Betty began to load the dishwasher and put the leftovers away. This was an annual event and they knew the drill. Joanne grabbed three glasses and a bottle of wine from the counter. She and Carol corralled Zoey into the small breakfast nook and Joanne poured wine for the three of them.

Zoey thanked her and took a sip. When she put the glass down, she noticed that her friends were staring at her with mischievous grins. She became self-conscious at being the center of attention.

"What?" she asked as she looked at them.

"Okay, spill," Carol demanded.

"Spill what?" Zoey responded, trying to avoid the question that was on everyone's mind.

Joanne spoke first. "You didn't think you could bring your new boyfriend here and not expect to give us all the juicy details, did you?"

"He's not my boyfriend," Zoey insisted.

"Like hell he isn't," Carol blurted out. "I see the way you two look at each other. You can barely keep your hands to yourself."

"We're just friends," Zoey stated.

"Friends who have sex with each other," Joanne added.

"Well," Zoey said, blushing, "this is true. But remember I run a brothel now. James is my man-whore scout and trainer."

Both her friends laughed. "And that's why you brought him to meet your family?" Joanne asked sarcastically.

"It's complicated," Zoey said. "We like our relationship the way it is." She was unconvincing.

"We know you, Zoey," Carol said. "You're in love with the guy. Have you told him?"

"I'm not in love with him. I like him very much but

it's... I can't... it's just not the right time," she said, trying to sound strong. "I told you, it's complicated." She could tell by the expression on their faces that they weren't buying it.

Joanne asked, "What are you waiting for? If you wait too long, you'll miss out. How would you feel if he found someone else? You and Mickey had one of the best marriages I've ever seen. But he's been gone for a long time and you've got this hunk of a guy who loves you right now. Life has given you another chance at love. Don't blow it. We love you, sweetie. It broke our hearts to see you mourn for Mickey. James isn't Mickey, but he loves you deeply."

Zoey took another sip of her wine and thought about what her friend had just said. Everything Joanne said was true. She had to admit it. She *did* love James, and she was pretty sure the feeling was mutual even though he had never said the words.

"I know what you're saying," Zoey replied. "But I feel like loving James is somehow a betrayal of Mickey's love. Besides, James has never said he loved me. What if he doesn't?"

Both women hugged her. "Honey," Carol said, "if that's not love I see in his eyes when he looks as you then I don't know what is."

"He's young, he's cute and, knowing you, he's got to be good in the sack or you wouldn't be with him," Joanne threw in.

Zoey smiled. "You have no idea. He can..."

"Okay," Carol quickly interrupted, holding up her hand like a stop sign. "We don't need to hear the details. We believe you."

Everyone laughed. "Tell him you love him," Joanne said sternly.

"I will," Zoey agreed. "Soon." The women hugged and got up to help the girls finish cleaning up.

James and Zoey both overdid it with food and drink, and by the end of the day they thought they would explode if they took one more bite of pie.

That night as they snuggled in bed together, James turned to face her and said, "Thanks."

She looked at him strangely and asked, "Thanks for what?"

"For bringing me here and showing me a side of you and a part of your life that I never imagined. I like your friends. They love you very much."

She looked relaxed and a bit embarrassed. "Yeah, they're pretty cool. I've known them for a very long time. We share a lot of memories."

"Memories with Mickey," he stated with a hint of sadness.

She nodded. "Yes, with Mickey. We've been friends since college."

He looked at her intently. "Is it weird being here without him and being with me?"

She thought for a moment. "It was at first. But you know what? Nothing has been the same since Mickey died. I'm not the same. How could I be? I had to change. I had no choice."

"A new Zoey," he said.

"Yes," she confirmed. "A new Zoey."

"Well, I didn't know the old Zoey," he said as he gathered her up in his arms, "but I sure like this version."

She looked into his dark blue eyes coyly. "Do you now," she stated as she slipped her hand down to his crotch. She could feel his cock growing. "I guess you do at that." She thought about what her friends had said to her earlier about love. Should she tell him tonight? An official declaration of love might change their whole relationship. Did she want to throw that into the mix now? No, she would wait until they got back home. It was all too complex. Now she just wanted to have him inside of her.

She squeezed his balls and rubbed her body against him. He read her signal and smiled. "I do," he said firmly. "Now let me show you how much." And with that he kissed her tenderly on the mouth, grabbed her by the ass, and pulled her close. He tasted of the Scotch he had been drinking. It was the one thing he and Mickey had in common. She felt his breath on her neck and it turned her on. She moaned and once again relinquished herself to him and her desire.

Their lovemaking was hard and intense. It was a good thing their bedroom was in the guest quarters above the garage and not connected to the house where everyone could hear them making loud, crazy love. Zoey's climactic groan of pleasure could have woken the dead.

PART THREE - HOPE

Chapter 24

The next day, their last full day in Michigan, was spent reminiscing about old times. Everyone had stories to share when the old photos were brought out of storage. They marveled at how young they were in the pictures and talked about how much they'd changed. James enjoyed seeing the pictures of a younger Zoey. He had seen pictures of Mickey at the Incline Village house, but there were only a few. There was one formal wedding picture and a few pictures of the two of them taken just a few years before Mickey died.

    It made James sad, seeing how happy Zoey and Mickey appeared in the pictures. It wasn't until then that he felt the full impact Mickey's death must have had on her and the heavy sorrow she still carried within. Their life seemed so storybook. He questioned whether or not he could make Zoey that happy again. He felt and sensed the pain in her face as she went from page to page, memories and feelings surging through her. He saw her eyes tear up and he squeezed her hand for comfort, hoping she realized that it was okay. He hoped Zoey would know he was there for her now. He would take care of her. He loved her.

Too soon, their time in Michigan was over and they had to return to Nevada. Joanne and Carol took them to the airport and dropped them off in front of the terminal. James gave the ladies a hug and thanked them for their hospitality. He grabbed the bags as Zoey hugged her friends one last time and said her goodbyes.

The women were all teary-eyed as they parted. Carol leaned in to Zoey and whispered in her ear, "Tell him you love him," before getting back into the car.

Zoey was quiet and subdued on the flight home. When James questioned her about it, she brushed it off as exhaustion. They decided to spend the night at the Incline Village house and head out to Zoey's Place in the morning. For old time's sake they had dinner at Keith's Kitchen. Keith was delighted to see them and had the cook prepare a special dinner for them.

After they finished their meal, they were enjoying a cup of coffee when a pretty young blond woman entered the restaurant and looked around. Recognizing James, she came up to their table.

"James?" she queried. "I thought it was you."

He looked up in recognition and smiled. "Suzie?" he responded with a slight blush on his face. Zoey looked up, too.

Suzie was wearing a body-hugging turtleneck that accentuated her full breasts and skinny jeans that showed off her lean but curvy butt. She had long blond hair hanging halfway down her back. Her skin was clear and perfect, and so were her crystal blue eyes.

The flush of red on James' face signaled to Zoey that the two knew each other very well. He looked uncomfortable, but more from surprise than guilt.

He cleared his throat and stood up. Suzie gave him a quick peck on the cheek, which he politely returned. "Suzie, good to see you." He looked down at Zoey, who looked shell-shocked. "Zoey, this is Suzie. Suzie, Zoey." Introductions made, he sat down.

He could see confusion on both women's faces. He looked at Zoey. "Suzie and I had a few classes together through the years." Zoey nodded in acknowledgement. "Zoey and I are partners in business," he explained to Suzie.

"Oh, I know who she is," Suzie quipped cheerfully. "You two are famous around here. Everyone knows all about Zoey's Place." She looked at Zoey with disapproval but smiled at James.

Zoey couldn't explain her uneasy feeling. Her stomach was in a knot. Was it woman's intuition? She didn't like Suzie, but she didn't know why. Was it because she seemed so familiar with James? Obviously, she didn't think Zoey was his girlfriend. No woman on earth would walk up to a man who was having dinner with another woman and just start talking to him. Then again, she had no claim on James. She couldn't help but notice that he didn't introduce her as his girlfriend. He called her his business partner, and that kind of hurt. Was she jealous? She remembered what her Michigan friends told her about telling him she loved him before it was too late; the warning of what would happen if he fell in love with another woman. Could that happen?

While she was thinking about the possibilities and feeling wounded, Suzie explained that she was meeting a friend there and asked if she could sit with them for a while until he got there. Without waiting for approval, she sat down. Zoey noticed it was a 'he' she was waiting for. She watched as James and Suzie chatted, and her jealousy grew. They seemed way too comfortable with each other. Damn it. She did love him. The thought of him with another woman drove her insane.

Suzie started talking about Zoey's Place. The spa/brothel had become notorious, and everyone in Incline Village knew who Zoey and James were. Suzie had just come to town to visit her parents. It was painfully obvious she knew that Zoey's Place was exclusive and was looking for an invitation. Zoey got the impression that it gave James great pleasure to tell her that he wasn't in charge of making reservations and, besides, he didn't think she could afford it. The look of stunned silence on her face was priceless. Just then Suzie's friend came in and she left abruptly. Inside Zoey did a victory dance.

"So," Zoey queried, "how well do you know Suzie?" She tried to act nonchalant and not let James know that his interaction with Suzie bothered her.

But James knew her all too well. He looked at her coyly. "Why, Zee?" he responded with his own question. "Are your eyes turning green?" He looked pleased.

She became flustered at being caught. "No, well, oh, I, just never mind." Her face reddened. He saw through her ruse.

He looked at her sympathetically, melting her with his piercing blue eyes. He scooted close to her in the booth and put his arm around her. "Hey," he said softly in her ear. "Don't worry. It was a long time ago. We went out a few times. We fucked. It never went farther than that. Actually, it was kind of a strange break-up. That's why I was so surprised she was so friendly at first." He could feel her relax a bit. "Come on," he continued, "I think I need to take you home." He stood up and held out his hand for her in gallant fashion. "Milady."

As they walked out she slipped her arm under his and gave Suzie, who was watching from her table, a farewell glance as they exited. She knew there was more to the story, but she didn't have the energy to find out. The drive home was quiet and uncomfortable.

After they reached the house, Zoey announced she was tired. She wanted to get into her nightgown and get snuggled in bed. James replied he would join her after he got something to drink and asked her if she wanted anything. She declined and headed towards the bedroom.

As she undressed, Zoey evaluated her emotions. Ever since the encounter with Suzie, she was a mess. Why did that woman's name grind on her so? She had to face reality. She was jealous. It was an emotion that she hadn't felt since Mickey. Forgotten feelings resurfaced in flashes.

Mickey's very presence commanded attention by men and women. His magnetic Mediterranean charm was overpowering. She would catch women turning their heads to check him out everywhere; convenience stores, hotels, restaurants, and especially airports. It didn't even matter if they were with another man. After a while she didn't mind. She had always been confident in the bond they shared. It was only natural to be possessive when your husband looked like Mickey. Since they first met, she had always, always been the only one he shared a bed with. It gave her a sense of pride and strengthened their union of body and soul. Closing her eyes, she thought about Mickey. A tear ran down her cheek. She missed him. The emptiness in her heart was almost too much to bear. She wanted to love and to be loved again. Was it too late? Could James be her second chance? Her heart told her 'yes'. She had to tell him, tonight.

James watched Zoey disappear down the hallway towards the bedroom. Seeing Suzie had started him thinking. He told Zoey he'd never had any girlfriends. Well, Suzie was an almost girlfriend. Their break-up was cold and cruel. That's why he was so surprised when she seemed so glad to see him.

James and Suzie were working together on a project for their business management class in college. It was the start of the holiday break. They ran into each other at the campus grocery store. She caught him when he was vulnerable. He was depressed and had no one to celebrate Christmas with, and neither did she. Her family had gone to Europe for the holidays, but she couldn't afford it and decided to stay on campus. She invited him to come back to her apartment so she could make him dinner. She said he looked hungry. She gave him a wink and a coquettish smile. He took the bait. She was the only woman, besides Mandy, that he'd had sex with who wasn't a hooker. After the first couple of days he began to feel like he was making love instead of just fucking. It was a novel feeling and he liked it. They spent days together, holding hands, wandering around the near-empty college town, going to movies, hanging out, watching TV, and sleeping together almost every night. James felt what he thought was love starting. He was happy, more than he had been in a long time.

But as soon as the holidays were over and her friends started to come back to campus, Suzie started making excuses and breaking dates. One day after she stopped returning his calls, he waited for her outside of her apartment building. She looked surprised when he confronted her as she approached the entry doors.

He asked her why she was shutting him out. She replied almost flippantly that he had been a holiday romp. She was never seriously thinking of having a relationship with him. It was just for fun. He did have fun, didn't he? He was so shocked he couldn't think. His pride and self-esteem had been torn away. She walked into the building, leaving him standing there looking dumbfounded and hurt beyond belief.

It was at that moment he reaffirmed he would never fall in love or have a girlfriend. Hookers were fine with him. Fine until he met Zoey, that is. It was because of Suzie's cruel break-up that James was taken off guard by her warm greeting tonight. When he discovered her true purpose, he knew he wasn't wrong about her.

For a long time he'd fought the feelings he had for Zoey but, damn, from the first time he saw her at Keith's she moved his heart. He knew she was something special; she was for him. He wanted to possess her, protect her, and take care of her. He didn't know how. It seemed foolish and illogical, but he couldn't help himself. The more he tried to resist, the more he desired her. He wanted to be with her, be part of her life. Her smile, her eyes, her body, she was just perfect. She was a realist and sincere, too, not fake like Suzie. He loved that she championed the fathers in the divorce cases she fought but was able to retain her femininity and gentleness. She was honest and kind. It was beyond her ability to break a heart. He knew she was still mourning her husband, but the attraction he felt for her was all-consuming.

He always looked forward to their beach walks, and when she came to the restaurant he waited on her even if it wasn't his station. One of the reasons he wasn't looking forward to graduation was that he thought he'd have to move to get a decent job. The thought of moving away from her tormented him. He wanted her sexually, but out of respect he never followed up on it. Not until that drunken night after graduation. That was more of a dare than a romantic quest, but there was no denying the pleasure. That was one gamble that really paid off. Sex with her was the best.

After he bedded her, he lost all desire to be with any other woman ever. Making his inevitable departure that much more foreboding.

When Zoey first told him about the brothel he really didn't feel as confident about its success, but he jumped at the chance to be with her. The fact that her instincts were right and the business became a success was just icing on the cake.

He had to admit he felt jealous of the auditions she had with the prostitutes. He knew he had fallen hopelessly in love with her. He had to tell her. Subconsciously he always feared rejection, but after seeing her in Michigan with her friends and seeing the pictures of her with Mickey, he vowed to make her happy like that again. Tonight he would proclaim his love for her.

He walked into the bedroom and saw her already in bed. The room was illuminated by candlelight. She looked beautiful. She was propped up with pillows and was fumbling with the TV remote. Her hair was loose over her bare shoulders. She was naked and her breasts glowed in the dim, flickering light.

He stripped down and crawled into bed next to her.

"James," she said and put the TV remote down. He turned to face her. How was she going to tell him? She felt like a school girl. "I've been thinking."

"You have?" he replied. "About what?"

"About us." She hesitated. "About our relationship."

He looked intrigued but didn't speak.

Words were failing her. Her mind was a jumble. She decided to just tell him flat out. "I've fallen in love with you."

"That's funny," he returned.

"Not exactly the response I was expecting." She looked hurt.

Suddenly he smiled down at her and pulled her close. It was time. He wanted to tell her know how he felt. "Well," he said, looking deep into her eyes, "it's funny because I was just going to tell you that I've fallen in love with you, too. I tried not to but, damn you, I couldn't help myself."

She could feel her eyes tear up. "You did? You do?" Her heart was bursting with joy.

"Of course," he said confidently. "Couldn't you tell?"

"Well, I knew you liked me."

He shook his head. "Zoey." He was serious now. "I've fucked many women in my time but it never felt like this before. When you and I are together, there's love. I thought I could live without it, but now that I know what it is I don't think I can. I know I can't live without you, Zee. I love you, only you. You're what love is. I think I've loved you from the first time I saw you. I just didn't know how much."

"Oh, James!" She was crying now. But the tears were tears of joy. She pulled his head down to hers and kissed him on the mouth. He embraced her. His hands gently touched her, feeling her tender breasts, her smooth back, and her soft buttocks. He let one hand slide down her round curve until he touched her womanhood with his fingers. She writhed with want and desire and pushed against him.

"I want you in me," she whispered.

With those words, he lost it. Taking the top position, he thrust his hardness into her. She squealed with delight. They moved together as one in the rhythmic dance of shared love.

Chapter 25

Physically, nothing had changed, but because their love was now spoken between them James felt closer to Zoey. He fell asleep spooning her and trying to adjust to being openly in love.

In the morning he woke before her, showered, and made a pot of coffee in the kitchen. He had just poured a cup for himself when she appeared, wearing nothing but an oversized t-shirt. He could tell there was nothing underneath. Her hair was disheveled and her eyes still half shut.

"Good morning, Zee. You look beautiful," James said, drinking in the view and enjoying it as much as his coffee.

She shook her head. "Now I know you love me. Only a man in love would be blind enough to call this beautiful," she said as she swept her hand in front of her herself.

"*Au contraire, mon amour,*" he said as he encircled her in his arms. He gently nibbled her neck, and planted a kiss on her inviting lips. "Your beauty would give sight to the blind."

"Oh, you," she said as she hugged him and

grabbed his buttocks. "I love it when you speak French, so sexy." She broke away and poured herself a cup of coffee. When she turned around, she saw him staring at her.

"What do we do now?" he asked.

She shrugged and said, "I guess we just go on like we have been, except that we acknowledge the love between us. Nothing has changed. I don't love you any more or any less now that it's out in the open. How about you?"

"To tell you the truth," James said with twinkling eyes, "I think I love you more. Because now I can tell the world that I love you. This is a new thing for me, Zee. I didn't think I could ever fall in love. I didn't try. I tried to resist." He looked down into his coffee cup.

"Me, too," she confessed.

He looked up at her in surprise. "You did?"

"Yeah," she replied. "You know, you and your I-only-fuck-hookers and I-don't-need-love attitude. I thought you didn't believe in it. I didn't want to fall for a guy who could never love me back, not after what I had with Mickey."

He kissed the top of her head. "Zee," he said compassionately, "I don't know how you kept going after losing him. Love is so powerful. I never knew."

"I'll never stop loving him, but I know he would have wanted me to go on. I did feel cheated, though," she said. "I thought we would have more time."

"You'll never have to live without love again," he stated. "I'll be here for you always, no matter what. I promise. Hey, why don't we move in together?"

She thought for a moment. "I suppose we could. But the suite at Zoey's Place is already crowded. We could knock down the wall between our suites and remodel the whole thing, I suppose."

"Great idea," he agreed. "Now, what about us?"

She looked at him queerly. "What do you mean?"

"Do we need to get married or something?" he asked.

"Whoa," she said, holding out her arm. "We just admitted our love. Let's let it grow and blossom. Don't forget, I've been there. I don't think I'm ready for that yet. Besides, I want to be courted." She looked at him coyly. "You know, we can do everything married people do until we know for sure."

He got the innuendo. "I thought we already did."

"More than most," she said, smiling, and licked her lips. "You'd better think about this. Now that you're in love do you really want to be married to a whorehouse madam?"

"As long as I'm the only one fucking her, I don't mind at all," he said with a straight face.

She got serious and looked him dead in the eye. "What? Am I hearing you right? You don't want me to fuck anyone else? What about the new recruits?"

He blushed. "Especially new recruits," he admitted. "That was one of the clues that led me to realize I was in love with you. It drives me mad when you audition the new man-whores." He exaggerated the word 'auditioned' and put it in air quotes. "I thought I could handle it, but it gets worse and worse with every guy. I know it sounds selfish, but I don't want to share you with anyone."

He knelt before her lifted up her t-shirt, exposing her nakedness, and buried his face in her honey pot, kissing it. He looked up at her. "I want you all to myself, especially this. I love your pussy. I want to spend my life worshiping it." He put his face back between her legs and pulled her in closer.

She moaned and gave in to the feeling. She pulled him up to his feet and led him across the room. He pushed her back on to the bed and opened her legs.

She gave no resistance. He continued his expert adoration of her womanhood with his tongue and skilled fingers. She writhed in ecstasy as he brought her to a mind-blowing climax.

With that the subject of marriage didn't really matter, and was forgotten for the time being.

Fen and Annette had accepted Zoey and James' declaration of love as matter of fact when they were told that night. The partners and Michelle dined together after the guests had retired to the cabanas for the evening's entertainment.

"It's about time you two quit dickin' around it," Annette had said. "Everyone but you two dummies could see it," she added.

Fen was of much the same opinion and congratulated the two on the obvious. She heroically volunteered to take on the task of single-handedly auditioning the new men.

Life at Zoey's Place fell into a smooth routine. As word spread among the rich elite, reservations were pouring in. Everyone was surprised at just how many horny rich women there were in the world. It would appear that $15,000 for two days of gourmet cooking, meditative massage, and expert fucking was a bargain. The price ensured that a certain class of women formed the client base.

Eventually, Fen and Annette took over most of the day to day operations. Zoey and James stayed involved with administrative decisions and Zoey frequently did the guest arrival greeting. James still did most of the pick-up and the drop-offs, managed the men, and did the training, but their prostitutes were loyal and trustworthy and turnover was practically nonexistent. Medical exams were done routinely and rules followed to the letter. This left Zoey and James more time to get away to the Incline Village home and enjoy their openly proclaimed love.

Zoey couldn't believe that her life had once more become filled with happiness, love, and lust. James' sexual appetite was as insatiable as hers, and he threw himself into the love he had thought he never needed. The two seemed to feed off each other's adoration. Their non-stop fuck fests rivaled those that Zoey had with Mickey. They didn't role-play like she had with Mickey. Sex with James was different. It had to be. James wasn't Mickey, nor did he ever try to be. He had a different technique, his body was different, his cock was different, but it was all good. Great, in fact.

By October the Aspen trees had turned golden and the air was crisp and chilly. Zoey and James decided to take a few days off and head for Incline Village. They had just decided to return to the real world after a two-day sex marathon when the phone rang.

Zoey answered. It was Fen. "What? Are you kidding me? Fen, how could this happen?"

James watched the color drain from her face. "It's okay, Fen. James and I will be back by dinner. We'll deal with it. It will be okay. It's not your fault." She hung up the phone.

"What it is, Zee?" he asked immediately.

She looked like she was in a different dimension. Her face was flushed and her eyes were staring into space. The sound of James' voice brought her back. "We've been closed down. The health inspector caught one of the landscape employees having sex with one of the guests in a cabana. He shut us down."

James went white. "They can't do that," he said. "The landscape employees aren't our whores."

"Technically, yes, he is. He's a contract employee just like the prostitutes. The incident happened on our property," she responded.

"Who the fuck is this guy anyway?" He was visibly getting upset now.

"I don't know," she said. Her mind was racing. "Fen said it was some guy named Jacob. Apparently, he convinced a customer that he was one of our prostitutes. The client is threatening to sue. That's pretty much all I know. Fen is a mess. We gotta get back there."

"I'll start packing the car," he said as he grabbed the keys from the counter.

Chapter 26

When they arrived, Zoey's Place felt more like a funeral home than a brothel. Fen and Annette were at the sheriff's office but returned shortly after. Luckily the arrest was made without incident and the other two guests in residence had no idea was going on. It could have been worse. Just that morning four other guests had checked out. The two in residence were told there was a problem with the plumbing and the establishment would have to be closed. They were sent home with full refunds and a coupon for half-off when the brothel reopened. This seemed to satisfy them.

Mrs. Bertha Boone was going to take a little more than a coupon. She was the client who was having sex when the health inspector walked in. She was a wealthy widow from Pennsylvania. After the bust, she was whisked off to a hotel in town by the deputy sheriff. Arrangements were made for her to fly home the following day after the detective on the case asked her few more questions.

Staff was told what happened. They were also told that the partners were optimistic they would come up with a plan and timeline to get the brothel back in operation. Employees from town had been sent home. Housed staffers had been given two weeks off. They'd have a better picture of the situation in a week. A staff meeting was scheduled to get everyone up to speed at that time. But people were moving around on tiptoes. Despite the positive attitudes of the partners, there was a feeling of defeat in the air.

The partners gathered that night for a Domino's pizza dinner in the empty dining room. Everyone seemed to be in their own world as they passed paper plates around and grabbed at the pizzas in front of them. Once everyone was plated and seated, Zoey spoke.

"Okay, what happened and what do we know?"

Annette looked at Fen then spoke, "It's still a little sketchy. I know we don't have all the facts, but apparently one of Diego's Desert Landscape employees decided to make a few extra bucks on the side by convincing one of our guests that he was a prostitute. And while he was servicing her in one of the cabanas, Jack, the health inspector, walked in on them. He called the sheriff's office."

"Were we scheduled for an inspection today? Did you know Jack was coming out?" Zoey asked.

"Yes," Annette said. "It was his monthly inspection day. He came to my office and we spoke for a while after I gave him our monthly report. He knows his way around. I don't usually shadow him."

"Wait a minute." Zoey was confused. "Did Mrs. Boone order a landscaper experience?"

"No," Fen answered. "No, she didn't. Here's the thing, he told her that he was part of a new program put in place by management, spontaneous sex option he called it. An unscheduled, on-the-spot fuck for the bargain price of $100. It was meant to add a touch of spontaneous adventure to the weekend, he told her. The jerk had the $100 bill in his pants when he was arrested. I saw the guy. He's not bad looking. A bit skinny for my taste, but he does look like he could work here. You can't blame the customer for being taken."

"I guess not," Zoey said, contemplating her next move. Then an awful thought came to her. "Do you think this was the first time he did this? What if he's done this before, and when our customers see this in the paper they come forward and say it happened to them, too? Oh, my God." She looked around the room, terror in her eyes.

"We're pretty sure this is the first time," Annette assured her. "Diego said he was just hired a month ago, and the police did say that the guy claimed it was his first."

"I hope the prick is telling the truth," James interjected. "So, what happens now?"

Annette spoke. "I've been looking at the paperwork we got with our violation." She made air quotes around the last word. "Our license is a revocable privilege, which means they can fuck with us if they want to. We have to pay a fine, to be determined by the court. We'll be shut down for a period of time, to be determined by the court. We'll have to appeal the shut-down on the grounds that the guy didn't even work for us. We'll have to kiss ass, jump through hoops, pay huge fines, and hope they let us open again."

"How long will this all take?" Zoey asked, a hint of defeat in her tone.

"There will be a hearing in three days." Annette shook her head. "Don't really know; if things go our way then maybe just a month. If not, it could drag on for a long time, or—" She hesitated. "—maybe forever."

"Don't say that, Annette," Fen broke in. "This wasn't our fault. We shouldn't be penalized for what another company's employee did on our property."

"It's a touchy situation," Annette said, shrugging her shoulders.

Zoey had been silently listening and observing, all the while thinking of ways to get out of this mess. Suddenly she stood up.

"Annette," she said strongly, taking control, "we need to get back into law mode. I want to look up any related cases in the Nevada law library. Fen and James, you can help. We've got to find a loop hole, and for God's sake get Diego out here. We need to talk to him."

After three days the hearing was held. It proved to be more formality than anything. It appeared that Mrs. Boone had filed a formal written complaint against the brothel, and had hired an attorney to represent her. She wanted to close the brothel permanently.

The road ahead was going to be long and expensive. The partners broke the bad news to the employees at the staff meeting the following Friday. They were all laid off indefinitely. Employees housed on-site were given two weeks to vacate.

Chef Marguerite was optimistic that things would get straightened out and decided that she and Alexander would take a three-month Mediterranean cruise. They would check in when they got back.

Michelle took a job in town and vowed to stick it out with Annette. It warmed Zoey's heart to know that Michelle wasn't going to abandon Annette. She might have found a good one this time.

After the staff meeting, the partners got down to the business of trying to find some way out of their mess.

They were told that they were in violation of Section 5.16.180, which gives the board the power to revoke and/or temporarily suspend the brothel license for cause after a hearing.

The cause being violation of Item D. They were accused of permitting the existence of a health hazard on the premises and employing a prostitute when the person did not have a valid health certificate. This also meant they were in violation of Item G; the brothel was accused of being deleterious to the health, welfare, and safety of the general public.

Because of Mrs. Boone's written complaint, they and the county had to go by the book every step of the way. Mrs. Boone became pivotal. The partners were advised not to approach her, as it could be construed as attempted bribery or tampering with a witness.

Since Zoey wasn't licensed to practice in Nevada, they were compelled to hire an attorney. She remembered that Mickey had often mentioned a Las Vegas attorney named Dirk Findley, a relocated New York attorney he had used on occasion when any of his customers got themselves into a legal predicament. He was discreet, quick, and always successful. She remembered him saying that Dirk could take care of anything.

He took her call immediately. "Mrs. DeLucca, how nice to hear from you." He still maintained his thick New York accent. "I was very sorry to hear about Mickey's death. Please accept my sympathies. Now, to what do I owe the pleasure of your call?"

He sounded sincere and genuine. She explained the situation with Mrs. Boone and the brothel.

"First of all," he said with authority, "congratulations on your success, Mrs. DeLucca. Very ingenious and intuitive of you to see and fill a societal need."

"Thank you," she replied shyly.

"These kinds of things can get tricky. I think I need to meet with you and your partners as soon as possible."

A meeting was set up for the next day. The partners flew to Vegas on the first flight of the day. In his office, Dirk explained that a simple violation could be easily handled with the county commissioners by paying a fine. But Mrs. Boone's written complaint complicated matters. He said he would contact Mrs. Boone's attorney and offer an out of court settlement. He inquired as to how high a settlement he could offer. After consideration they agreed to offer $500,000, but would go as high as $1,000,000. After all, no physical harm was really done. She was going to have sex there anyway, and the arrest documentation did state that a condom was in use. Dirk was confident that his connections with the local newspapers could keep it off of the front page. After all, it was only a violation not a homicide. Mrs. Boone really had no grounds to claim damages.

He took statements from each of the partners, assured them that he would do his best, and told them not to stress about it. The case didn't appear to be a difficult one, provided Mrs. Boone could be reasoned with, and he sent them on their way.

That chance for an easy resolution fell apart the next day. Dirk informed the partners in a conference call that he'd contacted Mrs. Boone's attorney, who informed him that Mrs. Boone was so emotionally damaged by the experience that she was under a doctor's care and seeing a therapist. She wanted the brothel closed, and no amount of money could convince her otherwise.

The call ended with Dirk telling the partners not to

give up hope. This was just the beginning. He did tell them that they should be prepared for it to drag out. The brothel would have to stay closed until they went to court, which was December 5th. He said they had until that time to make their case. He assured them that it was sufficient. If not, they could appeal. Of course, it would be more costly and the brothel would still have to stay closed.

As he spoke, Zoey listened but didn't hear. She tried to feel positive about things but was failing miserably. She saw her dreams falling to pieces. Everything she had worked for since Mickey's death; all the time, the money, all the people who depended on her to keep the business going. Was it all for nothing?

That night she barely ate any dinner. Around seven she told James she was worn out and wanted to go to bed. It pained him to see her in such a state. He knew he needed to be with her. James feigned a confession that the last few days had taken its toll on him, too, and that he would retire early as well. He told her he would close up for the night and join her in bed as soon as he could.

By the time he did she was lying on her side with her back to him. Quietly he undressed and got under the covers with her. He snuggled in close. He breathed in her fragrance, light and sweet. It stirred him. Gently he reached out to her and began to rub the back of her neck. Her skin was smooth and soft but he could feel the knots of tension underneath.

After a moment she turned onto her back and stared at the ceiling. "Did you ever wonder what it's all for? The pain and pleasure? Why does it happen? How come we can't just get to a good place and stay there? Why does there have to be anxiety and disaster?"

He wiped a tear from her cheek. "Sure, I wonder," he answered. "I don't know why either, Zee, but I do know that you can't give up. No matter how hard you get knocked down, you gotta get up. Sometimes you can do it by yourself. Hell, sometimes you have no choice. But if you've got someone to go through it with you, then you got it licked."

She gave him a hug and he could feel the wetness of her tears on his bare chest. She felt so small and fragile. Nothing like the strong-willed, confident woman who pulled herself up from the depths of grief, tragedy, and sorrow. The woman who started a successful business that gave pleasure and filled the needs of hundreds of mature women.

"Zoey, you're not going through this alone. We're in this together. You, me, Fen, and Annette. But mostly I'm here, *for* you and *with* you. Lean on me. Cry on my shoulder, use me, abuse me. I love you, and whoever hurts you hurts me. Whatever it takes, we're in this together." He brushed her hair back from her face, gently tilted her head up, and met her lips with a gentle kiss. Her lips were soft as satin. He sucked her bottom lip lightly as she pulled away.

"Why, James?" she asked. "Why do you love me? I'm getting old and worn out. I can't give you a family. You're young. You deserve something better. You deserve a pretty young wife who can give you kids and a real home." Tears were running down her cheeks. She looked forlorn and defeated.

He quieted her with another kiss. "I don't need kids. I don't want any of that. I want you. You're my family and my home. We're one body, one heart now. You give me everything I'll ever need." He stroked her hair tenderly as he spoke.

His words were coming from his heart and she knew it. "Oh, James," she cried. "I love you." She buried her head in his chest and fell apart like a broken toy.

He blanketed her with his arms as she sobbed and shook with hurt, disappointment, and exhaustion. He wished he could absorb her sorrow and give her his strength in exchange. He hated to see her so down and dispirited. He felt helpless and at a loss. Is this what love did to you? His heart never felt so heavy and he didn't like it. Yet, looking at her in his arms he knew he would endure this pain a million times more for her without hesitation.

The next day they met with Diego. Because of the way the laws were written and due to the circumstance in which the 'violation', that's what it was being called, occurred, Diego had no liability in the matter. Jacob was charged with illegal prostitution, which was only a misdemeanor, and he would have to pay a fine and would most likely be given a two-year probation sentence in addition.

Diego was a handsome man in his fifties who spoke with a soft Hispanic accent. He had leathery skin from his years in the outdoors. Silvery grey hair hung out from under his wide-brimmed straw hat as he sat in Zoey's office. His remorseful brown eyes glanced back and forth between Zoey and James as he told them all he knew about Jacob Anderson. He said that Jacob left town right after the incident. He promised to be back for his court date, but he decided it would be better if he just left town.

"Where did he go?" Zoey had asked at their meeting.

"He didn't say, but one of my guys said Jacob told him he had a job offer in Michigan," Diego said.

"Hmm," Zoey commented. "Why Michigan? Is that were he's from?"

"Don't know," Diego answered. "The guy only worked for me for a month. Didn't really know him that well. Always thought he was kind of strange, though."

Zoey was interested. "What do you mean? What kind of strange?"

"No big deal," Diego explained. "It's just that he insisted on working on the brothel grounds, told me he had read about Zoey's Place in some magazine and wanted to be able to tell his friends that he had worked there. I think he secretly wanted to be a prostitute. Maybe he was trying to impress some girl."

"Is that it?" James asked. He was curious to know more about the man who threatened his livelihood and hurt the woman he loved. "He's a wanna-be hooker? Those guys are a dime a dozen. It's not that weird."

"There was something else that struck me odd," Diego confessed. "He knew all about you, Miss Zoey; almost seemed to have a little crush on you. He knew where you were from, and what you did before you opened the brothel. He knew about your husband dying over in Riyadh, too."

Zoey's curiosity was piqued. "Why would he know all that?"

"Don't know," Diego replied. "That's why I thought it was strange. Seemed like a harmless guy, though. That's why I just let it go. Probably should have said something."

"No," James replied. "Don't blame yourself. You couldn't have known. You and I both know there are a lot of weird people in Nevada."

"Our attorney will probably be in touch with you, Diego," James said. "He's going to want to make contact with Jacob, too. Do you have a phone number for him?"

"Yes, of course," Diego replied. "I'm awful sorry

about this. I want to help out in any way I can. I'll have my office gal call you with Jacob's phone number."

Diego looked at James and Zoey. He hesitated a moment before he spoke. "Miss Zoey?" he asked sheepishly.

"Yes?" Zoey replied quizzically.

"The thing is, if you wanted to fire me as your landscaper I'd understand. I just want you to know that. I'm just so sorry about all of this."

"Don't worry, Diego," she replied. "Your company has our place looking like a heavenly floral sanctuary. I wouldn't let anyone else touch it. Your job is safe."

The relief was visible on his face. "Thank you, Miss Zoey. And you, too, Mr. James."

"You're welcome, Diego," Zoey said as she held out her hand. He shook it, turned to James, and shook his hand before heading out the door.

"Diego," James added, stopping him. "If you think of anything else that struck you weird about this guy, give us a call, will you?"

"Sure thing," he said as he went out the door.

Zoey looked at James questioningly after Diego left. "What are you thinking?" she asked.

"I don't know," he replied. "Something about this whole thing smells funny."

"You think there's more to it than a guy living out his fantasy?"

"Yes, I do," he said slowly. She could see the wheels turning in his head. "Don't know what, but there's something we're missing. Did you ever represent anyone named Jacob Anderson in Michigan?"

She thought for a moment and shook her head. "No, not that I can remember. I've represented a couple of men named Jacob, but not Anderson. And besides, I won their cases. Why would they want to take revenge on me?"

"Can you ask Annette?" he requested. "I want to know more about this Jacob Anderson."

Chapter 27

Endless hours of research resulted in confirmation that Zoey had never represented anyone named Jacob Anderson. A connection between Zoey and the wanna-be-hooker couldn't be found. Putting that to rest, they and Dirk concentrated their efforts on Mrs. Boone.The court date was fast approaching, yet no progress had been made. She was more determined than ever to keep the brothel permanently closed. The future didn't look good for Zoey's Place.

    Two weeks before the court date, Zoey and James invited Annette and Michelle to spend the weekend with them in Incline Village as a kind of diversion to their impending demise. They had dinner at Keith's Kitchen.
    As they sat down at their table, memories of the past came flooding back. Zoey and James looked at each other knowingly and smiled. He took her hand and kissed it gently.
    "Do you think Keith would give you your job back?" Zoey kidded.
    "Without a doubt," he said confidently, adding, "If

he doesn't, I'll buy the place." Zoey chuckled.

They were enjoying their meal and, as it always did, the subject of the brothel closing came up.

"I'm so sorry for all of you," Michelle said as she took a bite from the huge piece of strawberry cheesecake they were sharing.

"It's okay," Zoey replied. "At least it brought the two of you together." She smiled and looked at Annette, who smiled back.

"It's bittersweet," Annette said pensively. "Doesn't seem quite fair to the other partners, though."

"I still don't see why that old bitch of a woman is so determined to shut you down for good. I gave her a massage the day before and she told me how much she loved the place."

"Well, she was put in a very awkward and illegal situation," Zoey replied. "I'd be pissed, too, I guess."

"Yeah," Michelle continued. "But to be so insistent on keeping the brothel closed, that's just a little over the edge if you ask me. It's almost like someone is paying her to do it."

Zoey looked up as if struck by a bolt of lightning. "That's it!" she exclaimed.

James and Annette looked up from their plates. "What?" James asked. "What's it, Zee?"

"She's in on it. Gotta be. What if this wasn't an accident? What if this was a set-up?"

Annette could see a spark of Zoey DeLucca, Attorney at Law, glowing and getting brighter. "What's her motive, boss?" she asked.

"Don't know yet, but I'll bet it's connected to Jacob Anderson."

"What's he got to gain?" James asked. "He's got to pay a fine and will be on probation for a couple of years. He doesn't stand to profit from this."

"No, he doesn't," Zoey said, holding her chin and

tapping her lips in Sherlock Holmes' style. She was lost in thought. "He's in it for another reason."

"You know," Michelle broke in, "he was an inquisitive guy. He once asked me questions about time schedules and how things worked with the men."

"You talked to him?" This time it was Annette's turn to be surprised.

"Just a couple of times," Michelle responded. "Twice to be exact. You know how I like to read books on the patio in the wild flower garden. Both times he was out there working, weeding, I think. The first time he asked me what the names of the partners were and the second time he asked me when the hookers were on duty. Said he wanted to talk to one of them about being a prostitute. I told him he needed to talk to James, but he said he wanted to talk to one of the guys first. I didn't think it was anything. And then when he got busted, I thought it was just because of his hooker fantasy. You think he planned it?"

"Did he ask you about the health inspection schedule?" James inquired.

"No," Michelle confirmed, shaking her auburn curls. "Just the men."

"It wouldn't be that hard to find the inspector's schedule," Annette interjected. "Dates of health inspections are public knowledge, and they usually follow a pattern. You don't have to be too smart to figure it out."

"Maybe," Zoey speculated. "But if he knew the schedule, why would he let himself get caught?"

"Why didn't you say something about this before?" Annette asked Michelle.

"I didn't think it was important. I told the police and they didn't think it was either. Why would anyone plan to get busted on purpose?" she answered. "Does this change things?"

"It might," Zoey said. "It sure is starting to look like he wanted to get busted. Only, what does he get out of it?"

"There's got to be some connection," James chimed in. "Zoey, are you sure you don't know this guy?"

"I don't know. What does he look like anyway? Fen said he was skinny. That's all I know." Zoey was wracking her brain, trying to figure it out. Since the lawsuit filed by Mrs. Boone was against Zoey's Place, Jacob's part was simple. He had already admitted to misrepresenting himself as a prostitute, and produced a statement to that effect.

Although Dirk had left several messages on Jacob's phone, he hadn't returned any of them. Dirk figured the guy was scared to talk to him. After interviewing some of Diego's other employees he determined that Jacob wasn't a very bright person, and suggested that including him in the defense would do more harm than good. So he hadn't even been put on the potential witness list. He was just a dumb kid who fucked up.

"Never saw him," James confessed.

"Me neither," Annette added.

All eyes turned to Michelle. "Well, Fen is right; he is skinny, really skinny. He's got long dark hair, long fingers. He's not strikingly handsome. He looks like a million other guys." She looked at Annette. "I really don't pay much attention to men."

Annette grabbed her hand and tenderly held it up to her cheek. "I know, honey, but think hard. Is there something that made him different?"

Michelle closed her eyes, flinging her long curly locks behind her shoulder with a shake of her head, and thought. "Well, he had a big nose. Brown eyes." She was mentally trying to visualize him. "Oh yeah, I remember now. He had a tattoo of a spider on his right forearm. I asked him what it meant and he told me Spider was his nickname."

Zoey and Annette's jaws dropped to the floor. They looked at each other and at the same time said "Spider".

"Who's Spider?" James asked in bewilderment.

Zoey spoke slowly and succinctly, "Spider is the man my friend Joanne's brother's ex-wife had an affair with seven years ago. He's the reason they got divorced."

"Do you think *she* put him up to it?" Annette asked.

"Who's she?" James asked, even more confused.

"Rhonda," Zoey stated with disdain. "That feckless bitch. She's got to be behind this whole thing. She said she would get me back."

James and Michelle looked at Annette. "The ex-wife," she said in explanation.

"The Jacob we know isn't smart enough to pull this off by himself. He's just a tool," Zoey said. "He's just doing what he was told to do. But Rhonda, she's smart enough to plan this whole thing. She could figure out the health inspector schedule, too. I have no doubt this was her idea."

"Okay, okay," James said. "That makes sense, but what about Mrs. Boone? How is she connected?"

"Hmm," Zoey thought out loud. "That's the piece of the puzzle I still can't figure out."

"I'll look up Spider," Annette chimed in. "I'll get a copy of his police record and start from there."

"He's got to be using fake ID," Zoey said. "Last time I saw him his last name was Johnson. If he used fake ID to get the job with Diego, he's in a shit load of trouble."

"That should be easy enough to find out," Annette said. "But finding the connection with Mrs. Boone is the hard part."

"We'll find out. She's in on it somehow. I can feel it in my bones. It's the only logical answer to this whole fucking mess," Zoey said confidently. She turned to Michelle. "Thank you, Michelle, truly. You may have just saved all our asses."

Annette leaned over, gave Michelle a kiss on the cheek, and said, "You did good, girl."

"I'll call Dirk in the morning and let him know what we think," Zoey declared with excitement. "Maybe he can use his connections to find out what we don't know and fill in the blanks."

That night Zoey was noticeably in a better place. James cuddled close to her in bed and kissed the back of her neck.

"Oh, that feels good," she sighed.

"Good," he replied. "You really think the bust was a set-up?"

"Yes, I'm sure of it. It's the only thing that makes sense," she said confidently.

His kisses were replaced with strong hands, kneading and massaging out the tension from her shoulders. "You're not as tight as you have been."

"For the first time in a long time I think we'll be okay."

"Is that so?" he stated. "In that case, I think my hands can be put to better use on a different part of your body." He moved his hand down her back and cupped her butt-cheeks hard.

"Oh!" she squealed in surprise. His hands traveled from her backside to her front. He tenderly moved them up and down her body, stopping at her breasts to gently cup them in his palms.

Her hands reached back and took a firm hold of his growing hard-on. "Mmm, this feels pretty good, too," she said as she squeezed it.

"Hey, don't distract me," he said in mock annoyance.

She wriggled in delight as hungry hands explored her soft, smooth body, pausing for an extra moment as they prodded her nether region.

She turned to face him and pushed herself close, burying her head in his shoulder. He cradled her in his arms.

He smelled strong and manly, yet fresh. Almost outdoorsy. She loved his unique fragrance. She felt safe and loved lying next to him. What she felt for James was uniquely special. Different than what she felt for Mickey, but just as extraordinary. It suited her.

She wondered, was it hypocritical of her to peddle loveless sex but still desire a bona fide, meaningful relationship? To want true, exclusive love? People are different. We're all variations of the theme, not cookie cutter beings. No two people are alike, not even twins. Who was she to judge nature's creation? She knew what love was. She had it in abundance with Mickey. So, she couldn't deny that she felt love for James. It *was* possible to love two men deeply, yet differently. She felt blessed.

Looking up, she studied his face. She traced the outline of his chin with her finger then let her fingers tangle with his hair. She grabbed a handful and pulled his head down so their lips met in a soft kiss. She pushed herself to him and her hard nipples rubbed against the hairs of his chest. "I want you in me, James," she said softly in his ear as his hard cock pressed against her thigh. "I need you in me, now."

"Then come on, baby," he said seductively as he positioned himself on top of her. "Here I am. Come with me."

She spread her legs invitingly and reached down to

guide him in. She moaned with satisfaction and pleasure as she felt him enter and fill her pleasure spot. He thrust himself in her slowly at first, then faster as the crescendo of their desire and lust soared and peaked.

She came first with pulsating waves of bliss, her body contorting as the pleasure shook her. The contractions of her cunny brought him to his climax. He exploded into her as it drained him of his strength.

They lay spent, side by side, slowly coming back from the deep depths of their orgasms. Zoey reached over to the end table and grabbed the glass of water she'd put there earlier. "Oh my God," she said, still breathing heavily. "That was powerful."

"Wow, woman," he gasped in response. "I thought my heart was going to stop. What was in that cheesecake?"

She laughed, grabbed a small pillow from the bed, and poofed him in the face.

Chapter 28

Zoey, James, Annette, and Fen flew to Vegas to meet with Dirk the next day. As they walked into his office, they were cautiously optimistic. Zoey explained her hunch and Dirk agreed that it was a sound theory. Now they had to prove it.

"First we start with Jacob's arrest record. If I can identify him as Jacob Johnson, and not Anderson, from the mug shot, we stand a better chance of getting the police to help us find him," Zoey said authoritatively, automatically slipping into attorney mode. Dirk looked at her and she caught the look on his face. "Sorry, Counselor," she said. "I sometimes think I'm still in practice."

Dirk smiled, and nodded approval. "By all means," he said. "I'm always grateful for assistance. That's precisely what I would suggest, but if he was charged with a misdemeanor they may not have taken a mug shot."

Zoey looked disappointed.

Dirk pushed a button on his phone and a curt female voice responded. "Yes, Mr. Findley?"

"Sarah, could you call the Storey County Sherriff's

Department and get a copy of the arrest record for Jacob Anderson, please?"

"Yes, sir," she responded in sharp military fashion.

Dirk looked at the partners, who were staring at him, questioning the formality in her voice. "Sarah was in the army for a long time. Old habits die hard," he explained, brushing it off.

"Even if we don't have his picture, we'll get an address and go from there. It's a good start," he said to the group. "He still hasn't returned my calls, but that's not uncommon for transient people. They get a pay-as-you-go phone, and when their money runs out they throw it away or wait until they need it again before they add time to it."

"We have to establish a connection between Spider and Mrs. Boone," Zoey interjected.

"That's going to require cooperation on one or the other's part," Dirk said. "It's not likely that they'll give up that information voluntarily unless they need it to save their skin. I know these types. They talk big, but threaten them with jail time and they usually cave."

"I doubt if Mrs. Boone wants to sit behind bars for any length of time. Not her style," he added. "I think she's the weak link."

"And how do we make her crack?" Fen asked.

"You just leave that to me," Dirk answered in a tone that let everyone know that they really didn't want to know the details. The conversation was over.

James picked up on the cue. "Well, if there's nothing else you need from us," he said as he stood up, "you know where to find us." The ladies followed suit and stood as well.

"I think I can handle it from here," Dirk said with confident conviction. "I'm going to take a trip to Pennsylvania and speak with Mrs. Boone and her lawyer. I'll keep in touch." He shook their hands in turn as they filed past him.

One week later, seven days before the court date, they were called back to Dirk's office. He looked pleased with himself as they were seated around a large conference table, Dirk at the head. In front of each of them was a folder.

Once they were served the beverage of their choice he spoke. "Ladies and gentleman, in front of you is a summary of my findings. Please follow along. Open to page one."

Page one was a picture of Mrs. Boone. "Mrs. Bertha Boone, plaintiff. Mrs. Boone claimed, in a written complaint, that, due to the negligence of the brothel known as Zoey's Place, she was exposed to unsafe and illegal sex, causing her embarrassment and extreme mental stress. She states that the brothel is a public danger and requests that it be closed permanently."

There was a round of grunts and groans from the partners.

"Please turn to page two," Dirk continued. There, in full color, was a mug shot of none other than Jacob 'Spider' Johnson, aka Jacob Anderson. There was also a picture of the infamous spider tattoo. "Zoey, you were correct. Mr. Jacob Johnson used fake ID to get the job with Diego. He never planned on returning to Nevada to appear in court. You'll be happy to know that, thanks to you, Zoey, Mr. Johnson is now behind bars awaiting trial for fraud. That picture there," he pointed to the folders, "is his latest mug shot. By the way, he has a somewhat unimpressive record of petty crimes. This is not his first mug shot, just his latest."

"Very interesting, Dirk, but you're killing me," Zoey insisted.

"Hang on, Zoey," he said with a smile. "I spent a lot of your money getting this information. At least let me drag it out so you think you're getting your money's worth. I'm building up to the big finish here." He cleared his throat.

"Please turn the page," he continued. He waited for everyone to glance at the small family tree-type diagram. "Here's the connection between Spider and Mrs. Boone. You can see here that Jacob's mother has a brother named David. David Boone, now divorced, was once married to none other than Mrs. Bertha Boone." He gave the partners time to let this sink in.

He went on. "Mr. and Mrs. David Boone were blessed with a daughter, Megan, who grew up to be a meth head. Her mug shot is above the pictures of her parents. Pretty, isn't she?" This last comment was made in jest as Megan looked more like a walking zombie than a human being.

"Megan was able to sucker some unlucky guy into marrying her and father a child. Needless to say, when the marriage fell apart the father was granted custody."

James and Fen looked at Zoey. "Don't look at me," she said. "I didn't represent him." She looked at Annette. "Did I?"

Annette shook her head. "No, I'm sure of it. I would have remembered."

Zoey looked relieved. Dirk went on. "Well, Mrs. Boone *does* come from money, and she was able to put up a good fight for her daughter, but it wasn't enough. Megan's drug use and, get this, prostitution to get the money for the drugs, was more than enough to stack the deck against her. But Mrs. Boone had enough money to drag the divorce on for a couple of years. It was long and nasty. In the end Mrs. Boone and her family were shamed publicly."

"Cut and dried," Zoey chimed in.

"Correct, Counselor," Dirk said. "It just so happened that the attorney representing Megan's ex was a woman; a female attorney who specialized in representing men, and usually won them full custody. Sound familiar?"

Zoey looked at Annette and they both nodded in agreement. Dirk continued, "Well, this gave her something in common with Jacob, who she always had a sexual thing for."

A collective "Ewww" came from the table.

"Yea, I know, creepy," Dirk said, shaking his head in disgust. "Anyway, she always had a sympathetic ear for Jacob when you, Zoey, represented your friend's brother. Was it a brother?"

Zoey nodded to confirm.

"As I understand it, Jacob was the other man in the love triangle, and he took a lot of grief from his then girlfriend, now wife, Rhonda."

"Wait a minute," Zoey broke in. "They got married?"

"Yes, they did," Dirk continued, "just last year. Turn to page four and you'll see their wedding picture."

The partners did as they were told. After a few comments from the ladies about Rhonda's dress and negative comments about the couple in general they looked up at Dirk.

He took a drink from the cup in front of him. "Being the dutiful husband, or sap, that he is, when Rhonda realized that Zoey's Place was such a huge success, she saw a way to get her revenge and cooked up this little scheme. She got fake ID and a throw away phone for Jacob and together they planned the bust, using Mrs. Boone as an accessory."

"Wait," Fen said. "I still don't see what Mrs. Boone gets out of this."

"Well, obviously she didn't need the money. She hated Zoey for the misery she put Jacob through, and then when the same thing happened to her daughter she was game for anything to get back at the 'kind of bitches,' as she put it, 'that go around taking kids away from their mothers.' Plus, she got her fantasy wish. She finally got to have sex with Jacob."

Again a collective "Eww" came from the partners.

"And Rhonda was okay with this?" Zoey asked.

"It would appear so," Dirk answered. "Her desire for revenge knew no bounds. She told Bertha she could, and I quote, 'fuck his brains out' if it meant the brothel got closed down and it ruined you, Zoey."

"Okay," Zoey said, "so how did you know Mrs. Boone and Jacob were related?"

"Elementary," Dirk stated. "I faked it."

"What?" they all exclaimed at the same time.

"I went into the meeting pretending that I knew more than I did. I told Mrs. Boone that Jacob had confessed to the conspiracy. I suggested that if she collaborated his account of Rhonda being the mastermind, I could get her charges reduced. Once I pointed out to her that she was also facing jail time for conspiracy and fraud, she was more than willing to rat out Rhonda."

"She believed you?" Annette asked.

"These old rich gals," he stated, "they're not cut out for prison. It scared the shit out of her. She admitted her part in the scheme and told me the whole story, including her family relationship and sexual desire for her nephew."

"So," Annette questioned, "what happens to Rhonda?"

"She's been arrested and charged with conspiracy to commit fraud, as they all are since they were in on it. Rhonda will be charged with something for getting the fake ID, and because she was the mastermind she's facing a lot of jail time."

Zoey stepped in. "So now what? What about us? What happens to Zoey's Place? Can we reopen?"

"Well," he said with hesitation, "I spoke with the DA and the Sheriff's office, and I explained the situation, and in light of the new evidence. . ."

"For fuck's sake, Dirk," Zoey pleaded.

"Yes, you can reopen. Based on Mrs. Boone's confession, the county is prepared to drop all the charges against you. The violations will be voided. It's as if it never happened. Jacob is still in trouble for using a fake ID. He really wasn't pretending to be a prostitute, because they were all in on it. It was all part of the plan, so there's no crime there. For that anyway. He's still being charged with conspiracy to commit fraud since he was a participant. There's enough evidence to prove consciousness of guilt and willfulness to participate to get a guilty verdict on all three. I think they're all willing to take plea deals and not go to court, so the press won't get a hold of the story. Mrs. Boone was very adamant about keeping it quiet. If you want, we could take Rhonda, Jacob, and Mrs. Boone to court, drag them through the mud, and expose them for the pieces of shit that they are. Might bring the wrong kind of attention to the brothel, though. Town fathers might not like it either. I'd recommend against that. Just let Mrs. Boone and Jacob plea it out. Rhonda will still get jail time, even if she confesses; no way out of that. My friends at the DA's office are willing to do what you want."

The partners agreed to accept the plea deal arrangement, erupting in hugs and cheers as they realized that the nightmarish events of the last couple of months were over.

Zoey jumped up and hugged Dirk. "Thank you. I can't tell you how much I appreciate this."

"Hey," Dirk said, blushing. "I was happy to do it.

You're Mickey's widow. I always liked him. He was a good guy, always treated me right. I felt like I owed him this one. Now, go get your brothel opened again. I'll send you my bill."

On the way back to the brothel they all decided that Zoey's Place would have a quiet reopening on January 15th. That way everyone could enjoy the holidays before getting back into the demands of running the brothel.

Michelle greeted them as they walked through the lobby together. Annette hugged her tightly and planted a big kiss on her after telling her the good news. Zoey produced a bottle of Crown Royal Whiskey and they all had a celebratory shot together.

Then it was down to business. Fen started calling customer numbers off of the waiting list.

James called the hookers and told them the good news. The ones he could reach were still available and eager to return. He left messages for the others.

Zoey called Chef Marguerite to let her know about the reopening. She was thrilled and told Zoey she had a few new recipes that would surely be a hit with the ladies.

Annette began calling the maintenance staff, housekeepers, and laundry staff from town.

It felt good to be a team again.

Chapter 29

Around six they were all ready to call it a night. They decided to order Chinese and eat together in the dining room. By the time they wrapped up whatever it was they were working on, the food had arrived and everyone settled in to eat. Michelle joined them. The atmosphere was definitely more relaxed and jovial than it had been in quite a while, even though there was still a lot to do to get ready for the re-opening. They ate, making light conversation and pleasantries, just a group of friends having dinner together. It was comforting to all. After they cleaned up, they said their goodnights and parted.

Zoey was exhausted, changing into her nightie as soon as she and James got to their suite. When she walked out of the bedroom, she saw James pouring some Scotch for himself. He picked up a glass of wine he had poured and held it out to her. "To you, Zoey; a woman who never gives up. A woman who is so beautiful inside and out." He paused as he looked her up and down. "To a woman who is sexy, smart, and loving; the woman I love and cannot live without. I love you, Zee."

They clinked glasses and took a sip.

Then she held out her glass and made a toast in return. "And to you, James, the man who gave me the strength to carry on, who always has my back, who made me believe that you *can* fuck without love. But most importantly, the man who showed me that it was okay to love again. My life has meaning because of you. I love you with all my heart."

She tapped her glass to his and drank. He smiled at her and did likewise.

Then James set down his glass and grabbed Zoey by the hand and said, "You look tired. Why don't you let me give you a back rub to help you unwind?"

"That sounds wonderful," she replied, and let him lead her into the bedroom. James' back rubs were delightful. He knew where her stress points were and firmly massaged the tightness away. After a while he got undressed and slipped into bed with her. As they spooned naked in bed, Zoey contemplated the events of her life. Her thoughts drifted to Mickey and the life they'd had together.

James could sense that she was in a pensive mood. "You were awfully quiet at dinner. Zoey's Place is going to open again. You should be happy, yet I know you're not. What's going on in that pretty head of yours? You thinking about Mickey?" he asked.

She turned to look at him. "Yes," she admitted. "I'm thinking about him and everything in my life." She lifted herself up and sat against the pillows. "When Dirk mentioned Mickey today it made me feel guilty that I have another life. I thought Mickey and I would grow old together. We were so much in love. When he died, I thought my life was over. The pain was horrible." She started to get weepy.

"Hey, hey," he consoled, stroking her hair. "It's okay. I'm here."

"There's so much we didn't do; so much of our lives that we were cheated out of. He was going to quit his job. I was going to retire. We were going to live the rest of our lives skiing and traveling and loving each other." She started to cry and James held her close.

"I'm sorry, James," she said between sobs. "I love you, but I loved Mickey so deeply. He was my life for such a long time. I can't just forget he ever existed. I miss him. I miss his love and the little things he did. It's just not fair. And it's not fair to you. Mickey will always be part of me. Are you sure you want to share me with him?"

James held her as her sorrow overwhelmed her. "Yes," he said with conviction, trying to comfort her. "It's okay. I know you loved him. You still do. I'm okay with that. Living with him made you what you are today. I just hope I can live up to his high standard. I'll take care of you, Zoey, forever. I promise."

"Oh, James," she said, gaining control. She looked deep into his eyes. From the start they reminded her of a trip she and Mickey took to Cody, Wyoming. They had explored the surrounding Beartooth Mountains on horseback with one of his clients and stopped for lunch on a mountain peak. The sky was so clear and deep blue up there it was almost dark. It was the exact color of James' eyes. "I don't deserve you. You know, I didn't want to fall in love again. I didn't want to fall in love with you. I thought we were just going to be fuck buddies."

"Fuck buddies, eh? Well, do I thank you for that?" he asked, trying to lighten the conversation.

"You know what I mean," she retorted. "You admitted it; you didn't want to fall in love with me either, did you?"

"To be honest," he confessed, "I thought you were hot the first time I saw you. I wanted to fuck you silly right there on the table at Keith's Kitchen."

"Oh, that's romantic," she said, laughing through her tears.

"I didn't know what I felt for you was love. How could I? I'd never truly been in love before, didn't really believe in it until I met you."

"Did you get me drunk on purpose that first night we fucked?"

"Not really," he chuckled, "just worked out that way. I wasn't exactly sober myself if you recall."

"But I didn't love you then," she said. "And we fucked. And I liked it. What happened?"

"Oh, you were weak and I took advantage," he boasted.

She smiled. "I guess it was fate," she said. "Neither one of us planned it. It just sort of happened. It was meant to be, kismet."

"Whatever it is or was, I'm glad of it," he said. "I love you, Zoey, more and more each day. I want to be your everything."

"Foolish man," she said as she gently cradled his face in her hands. "You already are. Don't you know that? Don't you know that I couldn't have done all this," she motioned to everything around them, "without you?" She leaned over and kissed him gently on the lips.

"But I'm not Mickey," he reminded her.

"I know," she said. "You're you. I'm not looking for another Mickey. What you and I have is different. We don't live the same. We don't fuck the same. I don't want the same. It could never be like it was with Mickey. I would just be fooling myself if I thought it could be. That part of me is over, gone, just a lovely memory. I love my new life with you. We share a different kind of love. It's just as strong, I think, and just as special. I just sometimes feel like I shouldn't be as happy as I am with you. I shouldn't be as much in love with you as I am. I don't deserve it. Does that make sense?"

"I don't know, should it? You didn't do anything wrong," he replied. "I love you and you love me. Isn't that all that matters?"

"Yes," she said, smiling. "Love is what matters."

"Good," he said, playfully grabbing her by the ass. "Now let's celebrate our victory." He rolled her over to face him, kissed her tenderly on the lips, and made gentle love to her.

Chapter 30

Fen went back east for the holidays. She still had an active life there. She never quit her fundraising and charity work and was still close to her large family.

The brothel experience was new and exciting, and the casual sex fit right into her lifestyle; after all, she wasn't interested in finding a new husband. She was enjoying the freedom of being able to make life decisions that fit her career and desires. She felt empowered and in total control of her life for the first time.

Annette and Michelle went to San Diego so that Annette could be introduced to Michelle's family. Things were going well between the two of them. As it turned out, both women had traced their relatives back to the same small French village in the 1800s. They weren't related, but found a common thread in their heritage. Michelle's family members were history buffs and were anxious to welcome Annette into their fold. Michelle brought out the best in Annette. That was important to Zoey. She was happy for them both.

Zoey and James had decided to spend Christmas at the Incline Village house. It was still pretty quiet at Zoey's Place. They had a pretty good jump on getting things back in operation. Staff was moving in, but regular routines hadn't yet started. It could manage a few days without them. They planned to leave the day after seeing Fen and Annette off. Zoey was packing the few essentials she needed to take with her when James walked up to her, spun her around, hugged her around the waist, and planted a big kiss on her lips.

"Wow," she said with surprise. "What's that for?"

James smiled a toothy grin. "Can't I kiss the woman I love for no reason?"

Zoey looked at him suspiciously. "Of course you can. But I know you, James Harrison. Why do you have such a shit-eating grin on your face? What did you do?"

James looked surprised and hurt. "Why, milady, you cut me to the bone." He began to nibble on her neck.

"Stop trying to distract me with your sexy talk and neck nibbles," Zoey interrupted as she pulled herself free from his embrace. "You're up to something. What is it?"

"Damn," James replied in resignation. "I can't keep secrets from you." He looked rejected.

"James," Zoey continued, "if you don't tell me what's going on right now, I swear I won't have sex with you for a week."

"Whoa," he remarked. "That sounds pretty serious. I guess I'd better tell you."

Zoey looked up at him in anticipation. "Yes," she said anxiously. "I'm waiting."

The smile returned to James' face. "Okay, Zee. What would you say to spending Christmas Eve and

Christmas Day in Vegas, ordering room service from your bed in one of The Mansion Estates at the MGM Grand?"

Zoey's jaw dropped. "Are you kidding me? How did you…? What did you…? Are you serious?" She was speechless. She had seen The Mansions, but only as she and Mickey did the walk-throughs before a client arrived. She never thought she would stay in one. "How did you arrange that?" she asked. "We don't gamble."

"You'd be surprised how news travels in the brothel social ring. Our little adventure has made us famous, or infamous if you prefer. You especially. The MGM Grand people remembered you from Mickey and wanted to comp you the room on your legal victory. And besides, I know a guy there. Went to college with him, helped him pass a few classes. He owes me, and this is their slow time of year. Not many high rollers spend Christmas gambling in Vegas, not even the whales, so the rooms were going to be empty."

Zoey laughed and hugged him tight. "I can't think of any place I'd rather be." She expected James to return her enthusiasm, but his body was tense and she backed away.

"Is there something else you're not telling me? Do I have to give some exec's wife a gift certificate for a weekend at Zoey's Place or something?" She was sure there was more to the story.

James looked shy. "You can read me like a book. Yes, there's something else."

Zoey straightened up and gave him a piercing glare. "Spill," she demanded impatiently.

James ran his fingers through his hair and cleared his throat. Zoey was getting annoyed.

"I've been thinking, Zoey… you know I love you."

"Yes, James." She softened, and replied lovingly,

"And I love you."

"That's what I mean. We love each other. So, I was wondering..." He began to fidget again.

"James, what the fuck?"

He regained his composure and smiled, but still struggled for the words. "I didn't think it would be this hard." He cleared his throat again. "Okay, here goes. Zoey, what if when we're in Vegas we go to one of those cheesy chapels and get married? I mean, will you marry me? Guess I should have opened with that, huh?"

Zoey blinked, freezing in place. "You want to marry me? Like for forever?"

"Oh yes, Zee," he said. He was animated and excited now. He held her hands in his. "I've been thinking a lot about life these days. It's short, and happiness is fleeting. When I finally told you I loved you I asked if we should get married, and you said no. I would have, you know. I would have married you right on the spot. I've loved you for a long time. I know now that I have to make you mine or I'll die. I'm committed to loving you for the rest of our lives. Please say yes. We could be married on Christmas Eve and make our time in Vegas our honeymoon. Please, Zee. I love you and I can't live without you."

Happiness and bliss filled her. She had often thought about marrying James. At first, she felt it was a betrayal of the love she had for Mickey. That was the real reason she turned James down at first. But she was beginning to realize that loving James in no way degraded or lessened what she'd had with Mickey. The love she and James had for each other was true. She wasn't being unfaithful. She deserved to be happy, and James made her happy; more than she thought she would ever be again. After she refused him the first time, the subject had never resurfaced. They had been living as man and wife for quite some time now. It suited them. Perhaps this was the right time to accept. Yes, she was sure it was time.

"Oh, James," she cried as she embraced him. "Yes. Yes, I'll marry you, you silly romantic."

"Zee, *mon amour*, I'm the luckiest man in the world right now."

"You're corny, too," she added as she was enveloped in his arms and passionately kissed. "Oh!" Zoey exclaimed suddenly, taking James by surprise. "I'm going to need a new dress!"

Chapter 31

Soon after Christmas, things began to settle down. Everyone returned from their Christmas adventures. Fen looked rested and was anxious to get the brothel up and running again. Annette and Michelle were anxious get back into the swing of things, too. Zoey could see that the future looked bright for the two women. And after the shock of the elopement and disappointment that they hadn't been able to attend the wedding wore off, the marriage of Zoey and James was accepted with great happiness.

Annette insisted on hosting a wedding dinner at Keith's Kitchen before the hub- bub of the brothel got too out of hand; just a private dinner with the partners and Michelle. Keith was honored and delighted at the news, and even provided a small wedding cake for the occasion.

The rest of the Zoey's Place staff had moved back in, and the vibe at the brothel once again felt like the happy place it was before.

The partners hosted a grand feast for everyone the day before the re-opening, with some of Chef

Marguerite's newest menu entrées for all to enjoy. Before dinner Zoey gave a speech, thanking everyone for their patience during the shutdown. Fen followed with a pep talk and got everyone motivated for the re-opening.

James closed by repeating the thanks for the patience and trust extended to the partners during this unfortunate incident. He ended by holding up his glass and inviting everyone to toast his beautiful new bride, Zoey Harrison. This was followed by cheers and congratulations from the crowd as he planted a long, passionate kiss on his wife.

After the feast and a final check to make sure all was in readiness, Zoey and James retired to their room for the night.

"So, Mrs. Harrison," James purred as he snuggled Zoey in bed, "tomorrow's the big day. Are you ready, Madam?" he exaggerated the last word.

She laughed. "I'll never get used to being called that."

"Mrs. Harrison or Madam?" he asked.

"Madam, silly. I'm getting used to being called Mrs. Harrison. In fact, I love it," she replied happily. She smiled, and snuggled into his shoulder. "To answer your question, I'm as ready as I'll ever be. It feels different this time."

"How so?" he asked.

"Well, easier I guess; less stressful than the first opening. For one, we know what we're doing now. Not that we didn't before, we just didn't know if it would be successful. Now we know it works. In fact, based on how fast the bookings came in and are still coming in, I'd say we aren't the only ones who are anxiously waiting for Zoey's Place to reopen."

"That's a fact," James confirmed. "I feel good about

it, too. Our guys are good and are ready to get back to work. We'll be just fine."

They lay there in silence for a while, basking in the warmth of the love between them. Then James propped himself up on an elbow to face her. "So, how do you feel about us?"

Zoey turned to him and looked puzzled. "You mean about being married?"

"Yeah, that. How do you like being married to me? Do you think we did the right thing? You think we should have waited? You don't regret not having a big wedding with all of your friends here, do you? I want to know you're happy."

The look on his face told her that he was looking for her approval. She called it his puppy dog look. She could read his face like a newspaper. There were subtle quirks and twitches that were telltale signs of his emotional state that only she seemed to be able to pick up on. Her mind wandered to the childlike grin he had before he proposed to her, and she chuckled. She looked at his face lovingly.

His piercing blue eyes reminded her of the deep blue water of the Blue Grotto in Malta and the glacier lakes in Alaska. She thought it funny that, throughout her life, some of her most treasured and enjoyable experiences took place around water. In her travels with Mickey, her favorite spots were near lakes or other large bodies of water. Then there was the lake house in Michigan.

It was Lake Tahoe and the Incline Village home that had brought her and James together. She loved their lakeside walks. They still tried to take at least one walk every time they went there now. It had become a tradition.

She reached out to him and smoothed a few fallen curls over his ear. She loved his long hair. She liked to call it 'sophisticated hippy'. It was always so clean and shiny. James was meticulous about his hair. The shades of browns and blondes changed with the light. Seeing it hang out from under a ball cap gave her shivers. She loved to run her fingers through his tangle of curls when he was between her legs, servicing her. Just the thought made the heat rise between her thighs.

"I feel wonderful, James. I don't regret a thing. What you and I have is amazing. Our wedding was special, and personal to you and me. We're the only ones who count when it comes right down to it. Just us.

"I'm sure my Michigan friends are disappointed, but you know what? I wouldn't change a thing. They'll get over it. I'm sure the next time we visit they'll throw us a huge reception dinner.

"As for us? I love you, James, in a way that's wonderful and exciting to me. Our love is unique. It's *our* love. We don't need tradition or conformity to dictate what we should do or feel or be. We think for ourselves and do what *we* think is right, and the world be damned.

"I think that's why God gave us a brain. He doesn't want us to follow the herd and be one of the sheep. We're supposed to use reason and feeling. We listen to our heart.

"I'm in this for the long haul, James. I have been from the beginning, even if I didn't know it then. I don't know how we found each other, but we did, and I know now that my heart belongs to you.

"So, how do I feel about us?" She licked her lips salaciously and gave him a seductive glance. "I feel like I'm married to the handsomest, hottest man on the planet. Just looking at you makes me wet."

"Oh, Zee," he moaned. "Don't you know how horny

you make me when you say things like that?"

"I know exactly how horny it makes you," she retorted. "What are you gonna do about it?" she challenged.

He gave her a devilish smile. "I'll tell you what I'm gonna do. I'm gonna fuck you until you beg for mercy."

She smiled. "Oh, you think I'm gonna beg? You'll be the one begging for mercy, young man," she retorted.

"Young man? Did you just call me young man?"

She laughed, and he pulled her close as he kissed her hard on the mouth. His hands wandered over her soft, curvaceous body, touching and squeezing. She whimpered in submission as she let him navigate to his pleasure.

He put his hand behind her head and gently guided her down so that she could put her mouth around his hard cock. Closing his eyes, he rode the waves of pleasure each time her lips went up and down over him. He could feel his heat rising, but held back the urge to come and pulled her head up.

Now it was his turn to pleasure her. He kissed her again and let his mouth travel down between her breasts, gradually making it to her navel and beyond. His tongue teased and titillated her as it found all her favorite places. Finally, he straddled atop her and gently spread her thighs. He lowered himself on to her as he entered her. She cried out in pleasure as he did. Sparks of electric energy surged between them as the rhythmic tempo of their love play created a sweet melody of passion and desire, building until the thunder of their orgasms drained them of their strength.

"Mercy, milady," he whispered breathlessly as he lifted himself off and lay beside her. "You win."

That night they fell asleep in each other's arms once again, spent, satisfied, and comforted by their love. Ready for whatever lay ahead.

Meet the Author

E.M. Bannock grew up in the Detroit suburbs in the 1950's and 60's. She attributes her love of storytelling to her father whom she says gave her the gift. She left home after high school and traveled to Los Angeles. It was the 1970's and she had many exciting adventures there. She met her husband in Malibu, California. They have a son, a lovely daughter-in-law, and a grandson. In their 40 plus years of marriage, they have lived in California, Oregon, Alaska, Florida, and Wyoming, where she now lives with her husband, dog, cat, horses, and brood of cantankerous hens.

E.M. Bannock is a member of the Romance Writers of America and Rocky Mountain Fiction Writers..
She is a Goodreads Author, and a BookHub Author

If you enjoyed Zoey's Place, check out E.M. Bannock's other book, Totally Devoted, published by 5 Prince Publishing. It's available in print, e-book, and audio.

Contact E.M. Bannock:
Web Site – www.embannock.com
Email – embannock@yahoo.com
Find her on Facebook – E.M. Bannock – Author
Follow her on Twitter - @EMBannock
Instagram e_m_bannock

Made in the USA
Middletown, DE
29 May 2019